WHO WILL REMAIN

Also by Kasim Ali
Good Intentions

WHO WILL REMAIN

Kasim Ali

4th ESTATE • *London*

4th Estate
An imprint of HarperCollins*Publishers*
1 London Bridge Street
London SE1 9GF

www.4thestate.co.uk

HarperCollins*Publishers*
Macken House, 39/40 Mayor Street Upper,
Dublin 1, D01 C9W8, Ireland

First published in Great Britain in 2025 by 4th Estate

1

Copyright © Kasim Ali 2025

Kasim Ali asserts the moral right to be identified as the author of this work in accordance with the Copyright, Designs and Patents Act 1988

A catalogue record for this book is available from the British Library

ISBN 978-0-00-845059-5

This novel is entirely a work of fiction. The names, characters and incidents portrayed in it are the work of the author's imagination. Any resemblance to actual persons, living or dead, events or localities is entirely coincidental.

All rights reserved. No part of this publication may be reproduced, stored in a retrieval system, or transmitted, in any form or by any means, electronic, mechanical, photocopying, recording or otherwise, without the prior permission of the publishers.

Without limiting the author's and publisher's exclusive rights, any unauthorised use of this publication to train generative artificial intelligence (AI) technologies is expressly prohibited. HarperCollins also exercise their rights under Article 4(3) of the Digital Single Market Directive 2019/790 and expressly reserve this publication from the text and data mining exception.

Set in Bembo Std by HarperCollins*Publishers* India

Printed and bound in the UK using 100% Renewable Electricity at CPI Group (UK) Ltd

This book contains FSC™ certified paper and other controlled sources to ensure responsible forest management.

For more information visit: www.harpercollins.co.uk/green

To the man I could have been if I wasn't such a coward.

'British-Pakistani males (…) hold cultural values totally at odds with British values.'

— Suella Braverman, Sky News 2023

APRIL

One

'Where were you last night?' Amir's mother asked him as he stepped into the kitchen.

Amir, wearing his salwar kameez, threads straining against his body, stopped for a second in front of the mirror that hung on the living-room wall. He looked like an adult dressed in children's clothes.

'Where were you?' his mother asked again, stepping into the living room, and before Amir could speak, she pulled at his clothes, tutting, 'These are too small for you, how have you grown so much?' as if he were to blame. Amir opened his mouth to say that his father had bought these clothes for him when he was fifteen and now he was twenty, and that he hadn't grown, not in height, reaching six foot two when he was fourteen and not growing an inch more, but he had filled out, like someone had put their lips to his fingers and blown air into him, but he decided against it. 'You shouldn't wear this,' she said.

'Dad said—' Amir began.

'I know,' she said, standing back to look at him again, eyes up and then down, 'but this looks stupid on you, take it off, wear something else, something nice.' Then, realising he hadn't answered her earlier question, she asked again, 'Where were you?'

'Out,' Amir said, looking back in the mirror at himself. She was right, he looked ridiculous. But whose fault was that? He couldn't be blamed for having changed.

'Out where?' his mother asked, heading back into the kitchen, where she was finishing the kheer she had said she would make for the day, the smell of it sweet, sticking in Amir's throat.

'Just with some friends from university,' Amir said. He fought the urge to add, *Like always, that's who I always spend my time with, nothing is different about this time.*

'When did you get home?'

'Past midnight.'

'Late.'

'Not that late.'

'I heard you,' she said, looking into the room, 'it was past four.'

Amir didn't meet her eyes. 'It's fine,' he said, an answer to a question she hadn't asked, and he heard her take a breath. He waited but nothing else came, so he reached for the door back to his room. What the fuck was he going to wear?

He rifled through his drawers. *Maybe a shirt*, he thought, taking out a black one that he used to wear to Foot Locker when he worked there over the summers between school and college, then all the way through the first year of university, but not this year, struggling to keep up in his classes, there was no space for a job.

Amir, telling his mother he couldn't work anymore because his studying was hard, she, staring at him, saying, 'I won't tell your dad for you,' Amir, having to go speak to his father by himself, telling him, 'The work is hard, I need the time now to make sure I pass, not just pass, but pass well, and then I can get a good job, just like you want me to, then I can contribute, then I can pay for everything,' and Amir's father, smirking at him, saying, 'Well, don't expect anything from me, I've given you enough.'

He had some trousers here somewhere, Amir thought, he just had to iron them. He dug with his hands, tracksuit after tracksuit coming out, jeans with rips in them, some intentional, others accidental, T-shirts that needed to be thrown away, but who would replace them and with what money?

'You good?' Bilal asked, and Amir tensed at the sound of his brother's voice. Then, 'That does not fit you.' Amir closed his eyes. He had told his mother the outfit wouldn't fit him, that it had been years since he'd last tried it on, and yet she had still forced him to go find it, because his father had said so, to put it on for her to see, because it was her eyes that saw truth and no one else's.

'Just trying to find something for today,' Amir said. He turned around to face his brother, who was wearing his salwar kameez, black and minimal, clean, and through the clothes, Amir saw the shape of his brother's body. What had once been fleshy was now tight, all hard lines. 'There's a gym at work,' Bilal had told Amir when he'd got the job, three years ago now, a start-up that had rooted itself in Birmingham, used its location to attract funding and investment, even though its employees were all made to go to London twice a week. 'But,' Bilal said, 'the money is insane, and it comes with all kinds of benefits,' one being the gym, and a personal trainer, if Bilal paid a little on top, which he did. It was as if they had slowly swapped over the last year, Amir putting on weight, his clothes stretching to fit him, Bilal melting into straight lines.

'Do you want to wear one of mine?' Bilal asked, pointing behind him, 'I've got a white one and a blue one.' He looked at Amir as their mother had done. 'Though,' he said, 'you'll be too tall for it.' That, after all, was the one thing Amir had over Bilal, and always would have. Bilal had topped out at five foot eleven at sixteen, believing maybe he would find a couple more inches as he aged, but now, at twenty-six, he had accepted his height.

'Nah,' Amir said, 'I'll find something,' and he turned back to the dresser, insides twisting with shame. He found a pair of black jeans, tore off his salwar kameez, put the jeans on, shrugged on the shirt and looked at himself in the hallway mirror. He looked like a waiter.

Fuck it, it would do.

Two

'Come on, let's go, let's go,' Amir's father shouted from the car, Amir already sitting behind him. He put his hand down on the horn, the sound violent in the empty air, and then Amir's mother came out of the house, Bilal behind her, holding the kheer in front of him.

'Okay, stop, stop,' she said, raising her hands to Amir's father, who didn't look at her but let go of the horn. She went to the front of the car, sitting carefully in the passenger seat, making sure her scarf wouldn't be trapped in the door when she closed it.

The three of them, Amir's mother, his father, Bilal, were all dressed like they belonged to the same family. Bilal in his black, Amir's father in his white, Amir's mother in her dark blue, the outfit she called her grieving outfit, stylish enough to let people know she had spent money on it, but not so glamorous as to be obscene. Then there was Amir, the servant they had decided to bring along with them.

'Let's go then,' Amir's mother said, as Bilal closed the door, holding the kheer tight on his lap, a towel underneath the pot.

They set off then, even though the janazah wouldn't begin

until midday, but they had promised to get there early, to help.

First, they needed to stop by Saqib's house, the door open, Bilal carefully walking in with the kheer, for later, when people would come by after the janazah to eat. He was greeted by a woman, Saqib's aunty, whom his mother waved at from the car, saying she would see her at the mosque, and then they were off again.

The mosque was already buzzing with people when they got there, Saqib's mother there, his grandparents too. Amir stood back as his family greeted them, Saqib's mother crying, a scarf covering her face, and when Amir went to her, he told her he was sorry, and then left before the rest of the words he wanted to say came out.

Amir and his family walked through into the mosque, his mother disappearing, his father too, leaving behind Bilal and Amir, who took off their shoes and walked into one of the prayer rooms, where the carpet was segmented into prayer mats, some men already there, sitting cross-legged on the floor. A man approached, asked if they were there for the janazah. They said yes, and he guided them to the other prayer room.

Now both brothers were surrounded by men who hugged Amir and Bilal tightly, said they were sorry for Saqib's death, said, 'Inna lillahi wa inna ilayhi raji'un,' and the brothers said it back, until the words felt strange in Amir's mouth, like they no longer meant anything.

Amir was glad, then, that Bilal was there, because Bilal was the one who was good at this, who could talk to anyone, and after Amir had been hugged, after he said the words, Bilal was the one who remembered people, their children, birthdays and weddings, and when they asked him what he was doing, he'd say, 'Still working at the start-up,' as if they were in regular communication, and whoever it was would laugh as if this was some old joke running between the two of them.

Their father found them, placed one hand on Amir's arm, squeezed tight. 'The body is here,' he said, voice low, and he led them out of the prayer room, to the back of the mosque, to another, smaller room, and in the middle of it was a coffin, raised on a table. Amir looked at it, mouth dry, stomach tight.

Saqib's mother was by the coffin, as were her parents and a few others from that side of the family, Amir recognising them all, but no names coming to mind, no memories. All he could see was the coffin, and when Bilal turned to him and asked Amir if he was okay, Amir said nothing, and when Bilal put a gentle hand on his arm, guiding him forward, Amir let himself be walked to the coffin.

Amir's parents went right to Saqib's mother, his father putting a hand on her head, even though they were around the same age, Amir's mother giving her a tight hug and then standing next to her, squeezing her arm.

Bilal joined them too, and then Amir's father looked up at him, tilted his head sharply to say, *Get over here now*, but Amir couldn't. His mother looked too, tilted her head in the same way, a touch softer but with the same message underneath, and then Bilal looked at him, and Amir found himself walking to their side of the coffin, standing in the middle of them, and his eyes were dragged over to the window that had been installed over Saqib's face, so they could look in.

It was like he was just asleep, Amir thought.

Amir's mother and Saqib's mother were first cousins, Amir's mother a couple of years older than Saqib's mother, and they'd become pregnant at the same time, Saqib born a few days before Amir. Saqib was the paler one, skin so white that people asked his mother if she had fucked the milkman to get him, and Amir was dark, even then, only growing darker as he aged. Amir was smarter than Saqib and, when he hit his growth spurt, taller too.

They were close throughout primary school, walking back home together when they were old enough that their parents stopped picking them up, and seeing each other on the weekends. Saqib was the first person Amir ever played pool with, the two of them, just ten years old, at the snooker club down the road, the air hazy because it was also a shisha place and everyone smoked, but this was before either of them did, they were just there to play, rocking balls into corners, cheering loudly when the balls went into the holes, groaning just as loudly when they didn't. Afterwards they would walk to Dixy, sit in one of the red booths, eat the chicken down to the bone.

But then secondary school came and Saqib's mother decided that he wouldn't go to Park View, even though it was down the road from where they lived. No, Saqib would go to Washwood Heath, which everyone knew was a worse school than Park View, violent, dangerous, and even though his mother said she was doing it for him, that the school was a better option, the lie was clear.

Everyone said that Saqib's mother used the death of her husband as a way to get out of going to funerals, birthdays, weddings, out of cooking when she didn't want to, out of working, out of anything she didn't want to do, even though she had never liked him anyway, how she'd fucked her childhood boyfriend when her husband was still alive, how she treated him like shit because he was uneducated and from Pakistan, their parents forcing them to marry when they were too young, and Saqib's father was a nice man, a little too nice, everyone said, he could do well with growing a spine, with standing up to her, so meek, sitting silently in rooms as conversations happened around him, how hard it must have been to have a bitch for a wife at home, screaming and shouting at him, he would never be enough for her, the life he provided would never be enough for her, his wife, content not to work and to spend all his money, to make him sleep in a different room because he smelled like the food he spent all day cooking. Saqib told Amir all of this, about the arguments they'd have, on a loop, over and over again, and Amir didn't know what to say, Saqib calling his mother all sorts of things over the years, a cunt, a raging bitch, a fucking demon, because even if all this was true, Saqib's mother was still his elder, still his aunty, still worthy of his respect.

So Saqib went to Washwood Heath and Amir went to Park View, but their friendship didn't falter. At least, not in the beginning. They still met up on the weekends, telling one another about the friends they had made, about what they were learning, how different secondary school felt from primary school, about the older kids that towered over them, who seemed so much more like adults than children, how they would be like that too one day.

Whatever story Amir had about Park View, about the boys who jumped the gates at lunch, who went to the park after school to smoke weed, who dealt it in the school itself, the odd knife alert here and there, the fights that erupted between groups of boys, Saqib would have something worse. Not just a knife brought in but an actual stabbing, not just weed but cocaine, not just fighting but hospitalisations and police.

As time pressed on, it started to feel as if a wall had appeared between them, small at first but growing steadily.

First, there was the rivalry between their schools. Park View and Washwood Heath hated one another, Amir and Saqib running into each other on school trips, squaring up to one another, then seeing each other at their grandparents' house the day after, laughing about how stupid the whole thing was, never questioning what the point of it was, only agreeing that they needed to play the game. They were part of something now, a group, a living organism, and they weren't about to be cast out because of who they were. Besides, they told themselves, every other boy was doing it, and who were they to go against the grain? This was just what teenage boys did, staying loyal to their school, to the boys, and they weren't some star-crossed lovers, Saqib said one day, nudging Amir, destined to bridge the gap between their rivalling countries.

Then there was the weed. It was everywhere at both schools, all the boys were doing it in Year Nine, Ten, Eleven, spliffs handed to one another in the hallways, smoked behind the bushes, rolled up underneath desks. Saqib got into it before Amir did, not telling Amir at the time but later admitting that he had started when he was twelve, given the end of a spliff by one of the boys he ran with.

Amir started smoking when he was fourteen, his first time with Saqib, who had brought the weed with him, offered it to Amir, said, 'We should at least try it,' and maybe Amir should have known then, when Saqib was able to carry on without coughing, and maybe he should have realised, too, when he noticed that Saqib was always high before they started smoking, high whenever he met him.

Then Amir heard that Saqib was running with a gang. It was just a rumour, Amir's mother in the kitchen, telling him someone had told her because someone had seen him somewhere, and she asked him, 'Do you know about this? Are you doing this too?' and Amir had said no to both questions, but his mother continued to look at him as if he hadn't answered. Amir asked Saqib about it the next time they were together, laughing, because it couldn't be true. There were boys at school in gangs, boys who would disappear during the school day, boys who would proudly show off their bruised knuckles and wounds, scars lining their arms, their black eyes, grinning at the girls, saying, 'You should see the other guy,' the boys that no one fucked with because they weren't just boys who would fight, they were boys who would kill if it felt right, and everyone knew that it wouldn't take much to get them there.

But Amir and Saqib weren't like that. There were boys in their own family who were, the boys who everyone whispered about but never confronted, the shame of their parents, their mothers forced to attend social events with their heads down, pretending that their children weren't there because they were working or at university or whatever other lie they could come up with. No, Amir and Saqib were loud, and they swore, and they got into trouble at school, and they smoked weed, but they got good grades, they were down to hang but studied hard, would get into university, get good jobs afterwards. That was who they were.

When Amir asked Saqib, Saqib told him the truth. There was a gang of boys that he was running with, he told Amir, older than him, he was one of the younger ones. 'It's just like school,' he said to Amir, nudging his shoulder, except it wasn't, Amir knew, because Saqib was fifteen and he was selling drugs and he was carrying a knife, and when Saqib told Amir this, when he showed Amir the knife, the small stack of money he had already made from selling the drugs, Amir's second reaction was to tell him not to. His first was to consider it.

Later, he would tell himself he hadn't, but in the moment, he'd considered that he, too, could have this money, what he could do with that money.

All the things he had to do now because he had nothing. Ordering just a burger on its own after school because he didn't have the money for fries and a drink, saying no to hanging out in the city centre because he had no money for the bus, walking to Star City and getting there earlier than everyone else so they didn't see him walking as they all turned up on their bikes. He just had to say yes.

'It's fine,' Saqib had said, taking Amir's silence as something else, 'I'm not stupid, I'm not going to get caught up in anything, trust me, I'm not like the rest of them, it's just good to have my own money, you know, and it gives me something to do.'

Amir had considered putting on Bilal's voice then. *Why are you doing this? It's dangerous, you need to leave, you need to think about your safety, this is wrong.*

But Amir had grinned, laughed, said, 'Of course,' and the rest of the day had played out as it normally would.

They stopped talking. Not with a fight or an explosion but with distance, the two of them slowly fading away from one another.

Over the years, Amir told himself it was on Saqib, that Saqib had changed when he had joined the gang. That because Saqib had stopped coming over to their grandparents' house, because he had stopped coming to family events, to mosque on Eid Day, to a wedding or a birthday or a funeral, Saqib was the only person to blame.

But Amir had also stopped going to him, had stopped calling him, had stopped replying to his texts. Spending time with Saqib had become hard, even with all the weed in the world. Because Saqib had started to become paranoid and angry, telling Amir that someone was following him, he was sure of it, maybe someone who was sent by his mother, to find out exactly what he was up to, his mother would do something like that, the bitch, of course she would, or maybe someone from a rival gang, wanting to take him out, but it was going to take a lot more than just following him around, Saqib would say, his hand twitching, fingers curling around nothing.

The last time Amir had seen Saqib, on purpose, Year Eleven, just before their exams, Amir had worried about him afterwards, worried about what he might do, who he was talking about, what he might be pulled into. He considered telling Bilal, or maybe Amir's uncle, but did neither.

It was easier just to pull away.

The last time Amir had seen him, by accident, was on the streets, Amir just stepping off the 14, walking home from college, second year, coming back after a day of lessons and studying in the library, and Saqib was walking up his road, two other boys with him. At first, Amir didn't recognise him, wider, bigger, older, but then Saqib lifted his head and their eyes locked, recognition flaring. He nodded at Amir, who nodded back, and they passed one another.

Then, three days ago, Amir's mother had walked into his room without knocking, Amir on his bed, an open book in front of him that he'd been staring at without taking anything in. She'd asked him, 'Have you heard?' and Amir had clenched his jaw, closed his eyes, because his mother did this all the time, ask him if he'd heard, a million possible things in the world that she could mean, and he would ask her, 'What? What haven't I heard?' and she would say, 'You haven't heard,' and he would ask again, 'What haven't I heard?' and she would say, 'I can't believe you haven't heard,' and then, only then, would he get the fucking answer, whatever it was that she had just discovered from her network of gossiping women. So Amir did this dance with her, and this time, she said, 'It's Saqib, he's dead.'

Amir asked her, 'Which Saqib, Saqib who?' because he knew it couldn't be his Saqib, but she said, 'Your cousin, Saqib, he's dead,' and she told Amir that he had been stabbed, not even that far from here, a few roads away, he was with a gang of boys and they had been in some postcode war, she said, and Amir knew she had no idea what a postcode war was, had heard the term on the news or from the lips of someone else and was now parading it around like she had invented it, and they stabbed him, she said, left him there on the side of the road, they all ran away. She moved to Amir then, sitting on the edge of his bed, showing him her phone, a video playing. Someone from a house nearby, from the top floor, the video angled down, had taken it, a dozen or so boys all running into one another, and Amir spotted him immediately, he would know that head, those ears, anywhere, right in the centre, saying something to another boy, hand waving in the air, face screwed up with anger, and then they went still, as one, and then they all ran, in whatever direction they could find, and only Saqib was left, who fell to the floor, a knife stuck in the middle of his chest, handle out. It looked fake, like the time Amir had gone to watch a play in school, Year Four, and a character was stabbed in the chest with a spear that flopped in the air as they had fallen to the ground. Saqib laid himself down, holding a hand to himself, just below the knife, and even though it had already happened, even though Amir was watching a video from the past, he wanted to scream at the person holding the phone to go and help him, call someone, save him.

'He died before they got to him,' Amir's mother said, and her voice wavered then, taking the phone from his hands and looking at it before putting it away. She told him that the funeral would happen once they'd got the body back from the police, but Amir couldn't hear her anymore, and when she said, 'Not that the police are going to do anything, what are they even good at?' Amir said nothing, and when she said that she had known this was going to happen, she had been right the entire time, it was a shame to have lost Saqib to something like this, Amir stayed quiet. Then she'd said, 'I can't imagine what his mum is going through,' and Amir had looked at her, seen the tears in her eyes, and he'd reached out to her, put a hand on her arm.

He couldn't bring himself to talk about it with anyone, not Bilal, who had knocked gently on Amir's door the day they all found out, come in, sat by Amir, saying he had heard what had happened, had read about it actually, online, in the *Birmingham Mail* and other places, and showing Amir the articles on his phone, 'There's a few of them,' he said, 'I've read them all, it's a real shame that they're positioning it as endemic to young men in Birmingham, in the UK, and not what it really is, the loss of a person, someone's son, cousin, friend, but that's just what they'll do, paint this as a broader thing, a South Asian problem, a Muslim problem, turn it on us, when really, it's an issue of funding, there's so little support out there for young men, what are they meant to do with themselves?' he asked, and Amir said nothing, so Bilal continued, budgets had been slashed year after year, there needed to be more work done in communities like theirs to teach young men about their anger and how to manage it, and Amir sat on his bed, listening to Bilal say so much but so little, and when Bilal was done, all his words dried up, he seemed embarrassed, Amir's silence teaching him something, perhaps, and he tapped Amir on the knee, said, 'I'm here if you want to talk about it,' to which Amir nodded, and Bilal left the room.

Everyone wanted to use Saqib's death as a reason to talk about something else. It's a problem with our boys, his mother said, a problem with the government being racist, Bilal said, a problem with white disinterest in problems like this, the internet said. No one wanted to talk about Saqib himself, no one wanted to talk about the fact that his father had died five years earlier, that when his father had died Saqib's mother had started to hate him, his face too much like his father's, had always seemed to hate him, that he was never enough for whatever dreams she had for a son, awful to Saqib when he was at home, so he left home. That there were so many other reasons for his anger, for his disillusionment with the world, as Bilal once put it, that other people were responsible for how he spent his time just as much as he was.

That Amir was responsible for how Saqib spent his time,

for how he died. Because when they stood together at Saqib's father's funeral, Amir shoulder to shoulder with him, both only fifteen, how quickly their pretend adulthood had fallen away, exposing the children they were. Saqib had cried, openly, had told Amir that he was all alone in the world now, what use was there for someone like him? He didn't know what to do with himself. Who was going to protect him? Amir hadn't known what to say, and Saqib had wiped away his tears, looked at Amir, waiting, but Amir had stayed quiet, not meeting his eyes, and Saqib had walked away.

Now, here Amir was, looking at Saqib through that square of glass, eyes closed, face wrinkle-free, his frown gone, the anger and sadness around his mouth disappeared, and he thought, was it any surprise that this was where they'd ended up?

That there had been no one around to help.

That Amir hadn't been around to help.

Maybe, Amir thought, it was already foregone, maybe Saqib was always going to be this person, maybe it didn't matter what his mother was like, that his father had died, that Amir had distanced himself. Maybe it was easier for everyone else to pretend that it was the council cutting services, the government not caring about people like them, teachers not paying enough attention to their students, parents not talking to their children, their culture, which gave boys too much space. Maybe it was easier to place the blame there than to admit that maybe Saqib would always end up here.

Three

There was only space for Saqib's mother, bundled into the front of the hearse, to go with the coffin to the grave. Everyone else needed to make their own way.

Amir's mother, flustered, asked him, 'Do you know where your dad is?' and he shook his head. Words were hard to find after standing there, next to Saqib's unmoving body. It had felt like a play rehearsal, with stoic men and wailing women coming in and out. Like Saqib would jump out of the coffin at the end, tell everyone they had done a good job, and they'd all go get something to eat.

Amir stood by himself outside the mosque, cars around him, people waiting for their turn to get out, other cars trapped by cars whose owners hadn't made it outside yet, impatient, their faces twisted into a grimace, but today was not the day for anger, so they swallowed their desires to shout and press on their horns, and they waited.

'Have you seen Dad?' Bilal asked, coming up to Amir, shielding his eyes from the hot sun. It was warmer than it should be for April, the summer was coming along. Amir shook his head. 'Mum's going mad, she wants to get to the graves before anyone else does, but there's no chance of that happening now,' Bilal said, gesturing to the cars all lined up to leave, people weaving between them, like ants. 'You good?' he asked, looking at Amir.

'Yeah,' Amir said, forcing the word out. He kept his eyes on the cars. 'I don't think I'm going to come.'

'Come?' Bilal asked. 'Come where?'

'To the graves,' Amir said, 'I don't want to.'

Bilal laughed, short, sharp, disbelief.

'I don't want to,' Amir said, pushing himself off the wall he was leaning on. 'I'm just going to go home, let them know, when they ask.'

Amir made to move and Bilal reached for him, hand around his arm. 'Hey,' he said, turning Amir around, 'are you sure you want to do that? They're going to be pissed if you do.'

'I don't want to go,' Amir said, and Bilal looked at him for a moment longer, Amir avoiding his gaze, before letting him go. 'I'll tell them,' he said, 'that you were feeling sick or something.'

'Yeah, whatever,' Amir said, and he turned, walking past the cars, the people, out onto the road, and he kept walking, his feet knowing the way home, and they carried him all the way there.

Four

When he got home, Amir went to his bedroom and tried to study. He'd taken a mock exam the day before, printed off at university, and he was going through it now, marking himself, and with every question that passed, he knew he had fucked it. Small, easy mistakes, all those marks fluttering away. Like his brain didn't work anymore.

He got halfway through and then abandoned it, ripping the exam in two, throwing it to the other side of the room. He hadn't changed his clothes since getting in, the shirt tight around his stomach as he sat on the floor. He pressed his palms into his eyes, pushing them in until it hurt.

He didn't know how long he'd been sitting there when his phone rang. He reached for it, bracing himself for his father's anger, his mother's nagging, Bilal's concern. When he saw Mohsin's name on the screen, relief etched its way through him.

'Yo,' he said, putting the phone on speaker, standing up and undressing.

'You busy?' Mohsin asked.

'Nah, just studying,' Amir said. He hadn't told Mohsin or the rest of the boys about the funeral. It had all happened so quickly. Three days and they were burying him, and what was there for Amir to say? That his cousin had been stabbed, because he was in a gang, because he sold drugs. He could imagine Mohsin smirking at him, saying, *Isn't that what happens to all you Alum Rock boys eventually?*

'Fuck that, come meet me.'

'Where you at?'

'I'm just getting back from the gym, give me, like, an hour and I'll come get you.'

Amir glanced at the time, just past three, which meant that the burial was over, everyone would be heading over to Saqib's house to pray, to offer their consolations, to eat. 'Aight,' Amir said, and then hung up.

He pulled out other clothes, clothes that felt familiar and comfortable, a T-shirt that was maybe a touch too tight, trackies underneath, and then he sat back down and reached over for one of his many revision books to read from, but though his eyes could see, he took nothing in.

Amir let the book go and picked up his phone. There were messages in the group chat with the boys, talking about Mohsin's party that night.

Mohsin lived in an apartment building in the city centre, one of the new buildings that had stood as a construction site for years, marked off, forcing people to walk around the yellow lines and orange cones, the men in bright vests and hard hats, the diggers, vehicles with tyres bigger than people, all of it frozen in time before one day revealing itself as a tower block, all sharp lines and edges, balconies jutting out against the sky, so high that it must feel like being God looking down at the world.

Amir's father complained about the new apartment blocks

at any given opportunity, about how ugly they looked, reaching up into the sky like concrete fingers from the ground, how he remembered when the city centre was different, easier to get around, none of these fucking one-way roads, not to mention the congestion zone, and they kept saying this was good for business, these smart flats, these expensive buildings, they would bring new business to Birmingham, show that money could flow here too, not just in London. But it wasn't good for his business, he'd say, spitting the words out at no one in particular, because there were too many taxi drivers now, he could barely get any work. 'I spend my days driving around in the car,' he said, 'hoping that something will come through, just one person, one hand out,' and Bilal, who had been in the room with him one day, had said, 'What about Uber or Lyft or Bolt or any one of those other apps? Have you tried those?' and their father had bared his teeth at Bilal. 'Those fucking apps,' he said, 'do you know what those fucking apps have done to my livelihood? Do you know how little money I make on them? Barely enough to afford the petrol that goes into driving you little fuckers around, and it's always men like you, men who work at companies that don't even fucking exist, sitting in the back of my car, on their little phones, sending emails, ignoring any questions I ask them, headphones in, they don't even look at me as they sit in my car, don't ask me a single goddamn thing, you are the problem, you're what's wrong with this world, and you sit here, in my house, and you ask me if I've downloaded Uber to my phone, you pathetic fuck.'

This had happened a handful of times, when Uber had come to Birmingham after it had bulldozed its way through London, Bilal telling his father its every move, how it had decimated the black cabs in London, how the people had protested, wanting the Mayor of London, a Pakistani Muslim, he'd said, looking at their father, as if to say, *Aren't you proud that one of us got there?*, to take away Uber's licence, but the moment it arrived in Birmingham, Bilal had downloaded the app, telling everyone he was just happy there was an easier way to get around. 'I don't have to worry about carrying cash with me, it's all through my phone,' he'd said, waving it in the air, and their father had reminded him, again, that taxis had card machines too, telling him, again and again, to just get a car. Bilal ignored his first comment and refused on the second, saying it was bad for the planet to get a car, he wouldn't even get an electric one, all the metals they needed to make them, public transport was better, he'd say, launching into a speech about the failings of the government, 'How long have they been in power?' he'd say. 'Over a decade, how little have they done? We need to support our local infrastructure.' But none of that mattered when the car arrived, Bilal glancing at his phone and then jumping up, out of the house, running into the sleek Mercedes or Audi or Jaguar that had pulled up, the sort of car that their father longed for, the kind of car that he had spent his entire life dreaming of owning, because Bilal didn't just order Ubers, he ordered Uber Luxe, said that he could afford it and it was worth the price, for the air conditioning and the seat warmers and the built-in massagers, 'And it's better for the drivers,' he'd say, 'they earn more like this.' What other choice did their father have but to rip into him, teeth bloody with Bilal's morals, Amir watching with muted glee, their mother eventually placing a hand on their father's shoulders, saying, 'That's enough now,' and Bilal saying nothing, his face both pale and red.

In his first year, Mohsin had done what every other university student did, he moved into halls. The university halls were on the edge of the city centre, next to Birmingham Metropolitan College, though to Amir it would always be Matthew Boulton, the college for dropouts, the sort of students who fucked in the hallways between classes. Amir didn't go there, he spent his two years at Joseph Chamberlain, and he often wondered what kind of person he might have become if he'd gone to Boulton instead, taking one bus instead of two, but his mother hadn't let him. 'Under no circumstances are you going there,' she'd said, pulling the form out of his hands to fill out, 'I'll send you out of Birmingham before I let you do that.'

Mohsin had paid for the more expensive room, the kind that came with its own bathroom, which, Amir learned the first time he'd walked into Mohsin's room, was called an en-suite, this circular module that protruded from one of the walls, housing a toilet and a sink and a small shower. 'All mine,' Mohsin had said with pride. But the kitchen and the lounge were shared with four other students, all from China, who spoke English but never when Mohsin was there, so Mohsin was surrounded by the unintelligible squawks of Mandarin, he began dreaming in Mandarin, he told Amir, reciting the words to him, Amir never knowing if what he was saying was actually Mandarin or if Mohsin was just taking the piss. Mohsin hated their food too, couldn't look at any of it, all that nasty fucking shit they bring into the kitchen, he said, feet and brains and livers and all sorts of body parts that should stay inside the fucking body, he told Amir, opening the fridge to show him what was there.

Wasn't it crazy, he'd asked Amir once, that they were all

Asian, the Chinese students and the two of them, they were all Asian, from Asia, but how completely different they were? How weird, he said, that Indians and Pakistanis were basically the same, not that Amir could ever repeat that in front of his father, he'd beat Amir blind before another word could be said, and yet, Mohsin said, these Asians, they were so different, like aliens.

When it came to second year, Mohsin told his parents that he was going to rent a studio flat for himself, in one of the expensive new buildings, not in a dodgy student place.

'How the fuck can you afford this?' Amir had asked, the first day he'd walked in, unimaginable to him, a glimpse of a glittering life that wasn't his.

When Mohsin had told Amir he was renting a studio flat, Amir had imagined something small, where everything lived in one room, like his room in halls. But this was huge. The living room was also the kitchen, neatly segmented into two by a breakfast counter, an island in the middle of the kitchen, Amir running his hands over it, fingers on the smooth marble. He could hear his mother's voice in his head, *Wouldn't it be nice to have an island, marble counters, deep sink, detachable hose tap?*, her fingers tapping on the laminate countertops they had now. The living room was bigger than Amir's parents' bedroom, which was the biggest room in their house, and had floor-to-ceiling windows. 'You can open one of them,' Mohsin said, walking over to the windows, unlatching something and then pushing it out, so it swung open onto a balcony on the other side. When Amir stepped outside, the height made his stomach turn.

The bathroom was all black, glossy tiles, bright lights, 'A rainfall shower,' Mohsin said, turning it on and grinning, 'imagine fucking in that.' The bedroom was just as big as the living room. 'King-size bed,' Mohsin said, leaping into it, right in the middle, spreading his arms out, his hands just about hanging over each side. 'Enough space for a few people,' Mohsin said, laughing, 'and look at this,' he'd said, standing up, walking over to the closet, which was another room in itself, Mohsin already filling it with his clothes, rows and rows of shirts and jumpers and jackets and trousers, shoes on their own shelves. 'The girls are going to go mad for this.'

Amir had felt, that first day, that he shouldn't be there. That he and Mohsin had broken into someone else's flat. He'd glanced behind him as he'd walked through to see whether he'd left a trail of dark behind him, his poor fucking up the carpet.

'My dad,' Mohsin said, answering Amir's question. 'He's a lawyer, partner at his firm, he's got money, so why wouldn't he spend it on me? I am his only son after all.

'Though,' Mohsin added a second later, 'I'm pretty sure he has another family, there's no way that he doesn't, I know he's fucking some other woman, maybe two or three, you know, he's not ugly and he has all his hair and he goes to the gym and, years ago, he got himself lasered, all over his body, he's hairless as fuck now, like a fish, here, look.'

Mohsin had passed his phone to Amir, a photo of Mohsin's father on the screen, he looked young, could pass for just a few years older than Amir, perhaps his older brother. Hair thick, slicked back, no bags under his eyes, skin smooth, eyes bright, and Amir saw what Mohsin meant about working out, because the shirt Mohsin's father was wearing in the photo was tight around his chest, which pushed against the material, his waist, which seemed half the size of his shoulders, the upside-down triangle that other men chased, the curves of his arms, they were clear for all to see. This was Mohsin's future, Amir realised, looking at the photo, seeing bits of Mohsin's face in his father, the shape of his eyes, the length of his nose, the line of his jaw. This was what Mohsin was going to look like in ten, fifteen, twenty years, and Amir, who people often said looked like his father, would turn into that, bald, dark eyes like a raccoon, puffy face, chin melting into his neck, stomach bulbous.

'He loves himself,' Mohsin said, reaching over and taking the phone back, 'more than anything else in the world, once, they got into this big fight, and my mum, she was so angry, and the only thing she could think to do was throw away all his protein powder, poured it down the sink, and when he came home to make himself a shake after the gym, he looked in the cupboards and there was nothing there, and she was watching him, waiting for him to get angry, to say something, but all he did was laugh, told her she was a child, and went to go shower.

'But he pays for me,' Mohsin said, 'gives me whatever I want, probably because he feels guilty for having another family hidden somewhere, another little Mohsin running around, and you know, it's not like it's that expensive here, I keep telling him, it's not like I moved to London, it's only Birmingham, there's nothing good here to spend my money on.'

Since he'd moved in, Mohsin had thrown a party pretty much every week in this new flat, sometimes twice a week, inviting Amir and the boys around, others too, so that he could show off his views, the big windows, the great heights, the sleek countertops. Now that they were reaching the end of the year, with exams coming up, Mohsin wanted to have as good a time in the place as he could, before he had to go back home for the summer.

Amir stepped out of his bedroom, looked at himself in the hallway mirror, in his old T-shirt, the colour worn away from all the times he had washed it, a hole by his neck, which he could pass off as being part of the style, or at least he told himself he could. He thought of Mohsin's closet. 'You can take whatever you want,' Mohsin had once told him, and though he hadn't said anything about what Amir was wearing, the implication was enough. *Take some of my clothes, because you look like shit.* But Amir couldn't even do that, several inches taller than Mohsin, and several inches wider too. Once, when Mohsin had showered, leaving Amir alone for a few minutes, Amir had gone into his closet, pulling out a pair of jeans, and he'd placed them against his waist, the way his mother would have when he was a child, buying him uniforms for school. Even slightly stretched, the jeans didn't cover the width of his body.

'Fuck,' Amir had said, turning away from himself.

Five

Mohsin sent a text to say he was ten minutes away. Amir sat in his room, waiting to get the call from Mohsin, when the front door opened.

He heard his mother first, saying she needed to get changed and then go back, then Bilal, who said he would come with her if she needed, their mother saying, 'No, no, don't worry, it'll be fine, rest,' and then his father, who said, 'Amir, come down.' His father didn't shout the words, just said them, and Amir froze on his bed. But it was better to go down now than to be asked again.

His father was in the living room when Amir walked in, his mother and Bilal in the kitchen, neither moving. Here was a sight Amir had seen before. The angry father, the watchful mother, the cautious brother, and him, the son who had fucked up again.

'Where did you go?' his father asked, not looking at him, taking his shoes off slowly as he sat on the sofa.

'Home,' Amir said. He looked at Bilal, who nodded once. 'I felt sick.'

'You felt sick,' his father said, taking off one shoe and then working on the other. 'Do you feel sick now?'

'No,' Amir said, 'I feel okay now.'

'You feel okay now,' his father said, taking off his second shoe and then standing up. Amir was taller than his father, 'Where your height has come from, I don't know,' his mother often telling Amir, reaching up to tap the top of his head, but whenever he was standing in front of his father like this, though Amir was the one looking down, it was as if he was looking up.

'You feel okay now,' his father repeated, 'but you couldn't come to the graves, and you couldn't come to the house after, and now,' he said, looking at the clothes Amir was wearing, 'you're going out somewhere, with your friends, sitting here, day after day, staring at those fucking papers, and for what?' his father said, and Amir's blood rushed now, but he said nothing, and his father slapped Amir, his hand moving too quick for Amir to see until it struck. It barely stung Amir's cheek, but it was the slap itself that mattered. 'You should have stayed today, that was your duty, to Saqib, to this family,' his father said, 'you have no respect, no shame, I don't know what is wrong with you, this is not how I raised you,' and then he moved to the kitchen and went out into the garden, door open, air coming through. Amir's mother went after him, and he heard them talking, or he heard his father say, 'I don't know what's wrong with him, leaving the janazah like that, does he have any respect for any of us, for Saqib? He's good for nothing, that boy of mine, nothing,' and if Amir's mother said something, Amir didn't hear it, and his father continued on, 'I have two boys, two boys, and one of them loves his job too much to remember he's not a child anymore, not married, still living at home with us, and the other one has no job, always out, what have you given me? Are these your fucking children? They must be because they're not mine, they didn't come from me, my sons wouldn't act this way,' and his mother must have said something else, because then his father said, 'Don't you fucking talk to me like that, who do you think you're talking to? You and these boys, none of you should have come today, none of you, that boy is dead, and you're worried about what people are saying, a boy is dead, and you're talking about whose son got married,' and Amir's mother said, 'I did care,' her voice tight, but Amir's father came back into the house, walked through the kitchen and living room without looking at either son, reached for his shoes and then walked out with them in his hand, barefoot.

When the door slammed closed, Amir looked at Bilal. His brother's lips quivered, as if he was about to say something, and then Amir's phone buzzed in his pocket.

Six

Mohsin drove an Audi TT, black, shiny, the kind of car that Amir had spent hours driving in games when he was younger, on his uncle's Xbox, nicked, his uncle told Amir and Bilal, putting a finger to his lips before plugging it in and handing them controllers. He had one for them too, but their mother had said no once she had figured out where it was from, so Amir and Bilal went to their grandparents' house often, on the weekends, to sit in their uncle's weed-soaked room, racing cars against one another, shoving each other on his bed, careful to sit on the duvet and not under it.

Mohsin's uncle, Amir knew, ran a car showroom, though Mohsin had said when he'd told Amir, 'It's just a front,' and Amir hadn't asked anything else. When Mohsin had come back to university after the summer of first year, he'd arrived in this car, 'a gift from my uncle', he'd said, though he would have to pay for everything else himself.

'What's the plan?' Amir asked as he sat in the car, Mohsin taking off before Amir had the chance to secure the seatbelt around him, his family already at the back of his mind. Here, he wasn't Amir who had just been smacked by his father. He was just Amir, just Mohsin's friend.

'Head back to mine, some of the boys are already there, party later on, you down, yeah?'

Amir thought back to the previous night, also spent at Mohsin's, knowing that it was Saqib's funeral the following day. Amir and Zain had been the last ones to leave, the three of them no longer talking, Mohsin and Zain drunk and high, Amir only high, and there, in his hazy mind, he had thought maybe he should just stay there for the night, fall asleep on the sofa, and not wake up until midday. He hadn't told the others about the funeral, after all, they couldn't make him go to something they didn't know was happening. But then he'd glanced at the time, just after three, and he'd forced himself up, Mohsin asleep in his bed, Zain asleep on the sofa, and he'd got home at four in the morning.

'Yeah, I'm down,' Amir said, 'what else am I doing?'

'That's what I want to hear,' Mohsin said, reaching into his pocket, taking out a spliff and handing it to Amir, who took it and lit up, hands gathered in front of his mouth, taking a deep drag from it before handing it back to Mohsin, who let it hang in his mouth while he reached for his own lighter. Amir moved, took the lighter, his hands underneath Mohsin's face, lighter sparked, flame waving, and Mohsin breathed in, nodding once. 'Here,' he said, speaking around the spliff, handing Amir the aux cord, 'play something.' Within moments, grime pulsed from the speakers, loud.

'I fucking hate coming to you,' Mohsin said as he slammed on the brakes, a car emerging from a side road without a glance at Mohsin, 'you mans are feral down here.'

'Fuck off,' Amir said.

'One of these days, I swear one of you Alum Rockies is

going to try and steal my car,' Mohsin said as the car in front ran through red lights, Mohsin slowing down to a stop.

Amir laughed, 'Have you seen what we drive around here?' he asked, gesturing to the car next to them, sleek, grey, the kind that should only exist in car commercials, not actually out on the road. When he looked through the window, he saw that the man in the driver's seat might have been his age, beard meticulously trimmed, sunglasses on, rings on his fingers, and, as if he could feel Amir's eyes on him, the man looked straight at him, eyes hidden behind the reflected glass, but then the lights turned green and he was gone.

'I forgot,' Mohsin said, following the car, 'drug capital of Birmz.'

'No one wants your shitty Audi, trust me.'

'Big talk for a man who ain't got a car of his own.'

'Fuck off,' Amir said again, hand against Mohsin's arm, pushing, not heavy, not light, and Mohsin laughed.

'I'm getting a new one, don't watch.'

'A new car?' Amir asked.

'My uncle's got a Merc he wants to give me.'

Amir's stomach tightened. 'What are you doing with this one?' he asked.

'I don't know, might just sell it.'

'Your uncle doesn't want it back?'

'Nah,' Mohsin said, 'he said I can do whatever I want with it, sell it, I don't know, invest the cash somewhere or something.'

'You're going to sell it to invest it?'

'Why?' Mohsin asked, looking at Amir, grinning. 'Do you want it?'

Amir's stomach tightened again. 'Nah,' he said, 'I'm good.'

'You can have it, you know,' Mohsin said, 'if you want, I don't mind, and my uncle doesn't want it back.' Amir said nothing, skin itching. 'I mean, you'd have to pay for the insurance and the road tax and all that shit yourself, I ain't paying for everything, but I won't need it, and it's here.'

'Nah,' Amir said, 'I ain't doing that.'

'Too proud, huh?' Mohsin said. 'Big Alum Rockie boy can't take a handout.'

'Fuck off,' Amir said, and this time he meant it, wanting nothing more than for this conversation to be done.

'Well, I don't need to sell it for a while, you've got time to make your mind up,' Mohsin said, 'and if you don't want it, then I'll just sell it, invest that shit into stocks. You're doing it, yeah?'

Months ago, at the start of the year, Mohsin had been vibrating, eager to get Amir back to his flat so he could show him something. 'Trust me,' he said, 'it's good,' and when Amir got there, Mohsin gave him his phone.

'What is this?' Amir had asked, taking it. It took him a second to realise he was looking at a stocks app, and that Mohsin had over sixty grand in there.

'I invested everything,' Mohsin said, 'emptied out all my bank accounts, the student loans, all the shit I've been saving up, and I've put it right in there.'

'Why?' Amir had asked, unable to look away from the app. Sixty grand, that was what Mohsin had, in his savings account. That wasn't all of his money, no, that was just what he had been able to put away. 'Because,' Mohsin had said, taking the phone from Amir, 'it's what we should be doing.'

He'd spun his great theory then, telling Amir about investing in funds and stocks and ETFs and other acronyms, speaking quickly, showing Amir his phone, a video playing, a man staring right at the camera, eyeballs big, pupils circled with white, cap to hide his bald head, the shine peeking through the mesh at the top. He was on mute, graphs and bar charts swirling around his head, the background sometimes disappearing to display a news article from the *New York Times*, *Wired*, *The Atlantic*. Mohsin scrolled, video after video. 'This guy,' he said, 'this guy knows what he's talking about, he tells us what shit to invest in, and look, it's working,' Mohsin said, shoving the stocks app into Amir's face again, 'I'm up like seventeen per cent since I started.'

'It's what we should have been doing this entire time,' Mohsin said, as if Amir had just been throwing his money down the toilet or out of car windows. 'Imagine if our dads had invested in Apple or Microsoft or Google back in the day, they'd be rich, we'd be rich, real money, they had no idea, none.'

Amir had flinched at the mention of his dad, of his dad's money, thinking of the house in Pakistan, the house that his father had spent two years building, a time in Amir's life, between eight and ten, when he'd been free. When his father had finally returned, he was darker than he'd ever been, and somehow bigger too, even though he had apparently been working every single day, regaling them with tales of digging the earth, laying the bricks, carving out the windows, just him creating this house from nothing. He also came back with a film he'd had made of the house, and he sat Amir and Bilal down to watch it, holding his breath as they watched, pointing out the gold plates on the sides of the gates, 'For my sons,' he'd said, and neither one of them had spoken.

The house was four times bigger than their house in Birmingham, and Amir knew that only his father's mother and his sister, with her three children, her husband dead, lived there. He didn't know how his father had afforded it but assumed that English money just went further in Pakistan.

Years later, when Bilal had graduated from university and returned home, working at Tesco, just before he was about to leave for the start-up, 'Good money,' Bilal said about the new job, 'really good fucking money,' and he'd told Amir how, when Bilal had told their father about his new salary, he'd asked Bilal to save his money, so that they could buy a new house. They'd been living in this house for such a long time, this small house, wasn't it time for their mother to have the house she'd always wanted? their father had said, and Bilal had laughed at first, thinking he was joking, but then realised that their father was being serious. Bilal had asked, 'Why did you spend all that money on a house in Pakistan if you wanted to buy your wife a bigger house here?' and their father had snapped, accused him of being disrespectful, disloyal to the family, and when Bilal hadn't given in, their father had ignored him for weeks. 'But it didn't cost that much,' Amir had said, 'the house in Pakistan,' and Bilal had looked at Amir like he was a child. 'That house cost us nearly two hundred,' Bilal said, 'money that he saved by making Mum run around with coupons, making us live off benefits, free school meals, blazers that were too big for us and then too small, that money, he could have easily spent it on us, bought a bigger house for Mum, if that's what he really wanted to do, but he chose to spend it back there, on a house no one lives in.'

So, no, his father hadn't been thinking about investing in tech companies from America. He had only been thinking about himself.

'Yeah,' Amir said, 'I'm on that app all the time.' He'd downloaded it that day, using Mohsin's referral code to get £100 for free, but only if he put in a grand of his own, and where the fuck was he going to get a grand from? The app had nudged him every week, telling him that his referral offer was going to run out, and then it had, and the app hadn't nudged him since.

'Good,' Mohsin said, 'I know it's complicated sometimes, but I've been reading about it, a lot, so just ask me if you need help.' He glanced at Amir before returning his eyes to the road. 'Our parents didn't have access to this shit, so I can't be too mad at them for not knowing about it, but we do, right, we have the internet and we can learn, so why not just do it?'

'Yeah,' Amir said, 'yeah, of course.'

'If you don't want the car,' Mohsin said, 'you should take the money from it.'

'What?' Amir said. 'What money?'

'When I sell it,' Mohsin said, as if it was obvious, 'I'll give it to you.'

'Why would you give me that money? It's yours.'

'Yeah,' Mohsin said, 'but it's not really, it's my uncle's money, and he doesn't want it. It'll be good for your portfolio, just throw it in there, don't even think about it. I'm not giving it to you to go spend on weed, just to grow your investment, that's all. You'll make it back easy, and then you can just give it back, whatever, it's no big deal.'

Amir said nothing. If this car sold today, it could go for

around fifteen grand, he knew, because he'd looked up how much it was worth online. *Fifteen grand*, he thought.

'We can talk about it,' Mohsin said, 'it's no big deal.'

'Yeah, sure,' Amir said, reaching for the spliff from Mohsin's mouth, putting it to his lips and dragging on it until there was nothing inside him but smoke.

Seven

When Amir stepped into the flat, the boys were already there. Nadeem, Omar, Abbas, Kamran, Zain.

Though Amir had known them for nearly two years now, he still thought of them as Mohsin's boys. He and Mohsin had met in their first class together, intro to civil engineering, where they'd sat next to each other. It was Mohsin who'd reached across the divide, introducing himself, hand stretched out to Amir, two rings, chain around his wrist, and Amir had taken it, giving his name to Mohsin, who'd said, 'You're from here,' and Amir, noticing the northern tilt of Mohsin's voice, said, 'And you're not.'

Their friendship had developed quickly. They were taking all the same classes, and Mohsin was easy to talk to, easy to listen to, easy to be around. But Amir made no other friends, and it was Mohsin who collected people, finding them on nights out, parties he attended, parties he threw, and Mohsin always invited Amir, throwing an arm around him, pulling him into clubs. That first year, Amir had insisted on leaving every party before midnight so he could get home on time, and Mohsin would mock him, shouting,

'Mummy's boy needs to leave,' ruffling Amir's hair, 'gotta go home when she wants him to, isn't that right?' and though Mohsin was often drunk whenever he said this, forgetting it the day after, Amir remembered, shame filling him, thick and hot, as he made his way back home. The boys had welcomed him, but no matter how much time Amir spent around them, he never felt like he knew them as well as they all knew each other. It wasn't just that they had the freedom to stay out as long as they wanted, but that they all disappeared over the holidays, Christmas, Easter, Eid, the summer, and Amir stayed. It was as if they were just passing through Amir, or maybe it was Amir who was just passing through them.

'Yo, yo, yo,' Zain said, the only one to stand up when Amir and Mohsin walked in, reaching across the glass table, a bag of weed on top of it, green spilling out onto the transparent surface. Amir took his hand, his grip strong, and, as Amir always was upon seeing Zain, he was struck by a familiar jealousy.

If Mohsin was the rich friend, Zain was the pretty one. The one who the girls looked at, the boys too, the one who sucked up all the attention in the room without realising it, or, at least, he said he didn't realise, but Amir had watched Zain look at himself in the mirror, fingers parting and moving and rearranging his hair, one finger running over his eyebrows, readjusting his jacket, had noticed the regularity with which he updated his profile online, with photos that were often taken by the girls he was seeing, sneaking a photo of Zain as he walked towards them, as he looked into the distance, as he sipped a glass of something, so that they could share the photo with their friends, prove that he was real, had noticed that Zain didn't eat as much as everyone else because his allure was partly the beauty of his face and it was partly how thin he was, like he might snap if someone pushed a little too hard.

Often, when Amir stood next to Zain, he felt wrong. Too tall, too dark, too much. But other times, mostly when there were other men around, he was glad that he was nothing like Zain, glad that no one would ever be able to snap him.

Amir went around the rest of the group, shaking hands with each of them, and then sat down too, more than enough space on the L-shaped sofa that took up half of the room, Mohsin proudly unveiling it to Amir in the first week of second year, the two of them putting it together, Mohsin telling Amir, 'You can just sleep here whenever you want, it's big enough.' Amir reached for the weed that Mohsin kept a good supply of, who never accepted anyone's money, waving Amir's hand away the first time they had hung out like this, reaching for his wallet, for the tenner that sat inside it, 'You don't need to pay for anything with me,' Mohsin had said, and though Amir had pushed the tenner at him, insisted on Mohsin taking it, he was relieved when Mohsin forced it back at him. Amir reached for the rizla, rolled himself a spliff, the crunch of the weed satisfying, and when he was done, he set it to his lips, flame wavering, white crisping to black.

'When's this party starting?' Nadeem asked Mohsin, who came and sat by Amir, leaning over the table, sweeping the discarded weed fragments into his hand to put them back into the bag.

'What's the time now?' Mohsin asked.

'Six.'

'I told everyone to get here for ten.'

'Sweet,' Nadeem said, leaning back into the sofa, burying his head into the soft cushion. 'Girls coming?'

'Of course, bro, who do you think I am?'

Eight

Amir's mother called him at eight. His phone was already in his hand, Amir watching a video that Mohsin had sent to him, a guy whose arms were bigger than Amir's head, skin stretched taut over muscle, veins pulsing their way to freedom, Mohsin telling Amir that this was his goal in the gym, patting his stomach, saying that he needed to get rid of ten, fifteen pounds before the summer, wanted to be shredded. 'You should come with me,' he said to Amir, 'I can get you in for free,' pulling at his arms, which were bone and fat, no muscle there, really, none that he had created in the gym the way Mohsin had at least, whatever was there was just from the way he lived. Amir kept watching this man, lifting more weight than Amir had ever weighed above his head, face straining, and then his mother's call appeared at the top of the screen. Irritation fizzed in him and he swiped it away. A moment later a text came through
Where r you son when r u coming home xx
and Amir ignored that too, as he always did, their conversation one-sided, his mother throwing questions into the void of his phone. He didn't know when he'd be home. Maybe he'd spend the night here.

Mohsin had offered him the place, time and time again, and Amir had said no, going home, no matter how late it was, until once, a few months ago, it had just been him and Mohsin left in the flat, everyone else gone, and Amir was sitting on the sofa, high, listening to Mohsin breathing in the other room, deep, heavy, and Amir had laid his head down on the sofa, because it felt good to, and before he knew it, he was asleep, and then awake, midday, sun coming through the windows. After that, the idea of sleeping in Mohsin's flat became normal to Amir. Once, Mohsin, drunk, had pulled Amir into the bed with him, and Amir, sober, because Amir didn't drink, he didn't like the way it burned his throat, couldn't turn off the voice in his head that told him it was too much of a sin, just lay still while Mohsin held him. Amir had stayed awake for an hour or two, Mohsin's arm around him, thinking of when he and Bilal used to share a room, years ago, before their parents had moved to the house they lived in now, the two of them sharing a double bed, Bilal sixteen, Amir ten, how they would spend entire nights talking about whatever it was that consumed them, and then the move had happened, 'Slightly bigger house, three bedrooms,' their mother had said, big smile, 'so you don't have to share anymore.'

The last time Amir had stayed over at Mohsin's, his mother had been waiting for him in the living room in the morning, and Amir could tell that she'd been up all night, had probably slept on the sofa, waiting for him, and he'd been angry at himself then, for not just telling her, 'I'll be home tomorrow morning,' what would that have taken from him? But then she had started asking, 'Where have you been?' saying, 'I've been worried, you shouldn't do this, don't stay out like this, without telling me, I worry about you, I worry about you both,' and whatever anger Amir had felt at himself readjusted itself to her. Hadn't he always come home? Hadn't he always been fine? Why was she so worried that something terrible was going to happen? Why couldn't she just let him be? But he didn't say anything, just stood, and she stepped over to him, grabbed his face with her hand, like he was a child again, fingers digging into his chin, asking, 'Where do you go? Where are you all the time? Why don't you stay at home?' and Amir moved his head away from her, told her that he was with a friend and walked past her to the bathroom, muffling the sound of her voice as she continued to speak, and Amir wished, desperately wished, that she would just shut up.

He was high now, after hours of sitting, hazy clouds around him, high in that pleasant way where the air felt thick and his reactions were slow and his body felt just out of his control. He pushed himself up from the sofa, whose soft cushions had been eating him slowly, walked over to the fridge, hands clumsy, took a bottle of water and put it to his lips, the cold flooding his chest. Mohsin's fridge was stocked full with bottles of water, Mohsin refusing to drink the water that came out of the tap, the water here was disgusting, tasted of chemicals, he said, 'and who knows what you Brummies are putting in it?' so he bought bottled water every week. Zain took the piss out of Mohsin for it, saying that he was destroying the world just because he had the money, and Mohsin told Zain not to be mad that he couldn't afford to do the same.

The rest of the boys were still sitting on the sofa, Amir watching them from the fridge. Omar and Abbas were playing *Mario Kart* on Mohsin's PlayStation, the sounds loud, the colours bright. Mohsin was on his phone, not paying attention. Amir had never seen Mohsin use the PlayStation, despite the set-up he had, PlayStation in its dock, soundbar under the TV, speakers on the walls, games neatly lined up inside the TV stand. Mohsin had told him that he'd only bought it for other people, to watch the boys play on it, and it was nice to have when girls came over, he said, because they inevitably wanted to play, and he liked how they pretended that they didn't know how to use it so that he could show them, pull their fingers over the joysticks, and once, he told Amir, leaning in, whispering, this girl, this white girl, she had stayed long past when everyone else had left, even as her friends stood up and said it was time to go home, and when they were alone, he had taken the controller, put it against her cunt, vibrations rocketing through her, and Amir had listened to him, not believing a word Mohsin was saying, because he couldn't imagine a girl, any girl, letting Mohsin do that to her, but the way Mohsin told the story, looking right into Amir's eyes, it felt true.

Nine

The others came around ten, some more boys that Mohsin knew and a handful of girls that Amir had seen before, but whose names he hadn't learned, no space in his mind for the carousel of people Mohsin invited into his life.

Some of these girls Amir knew from other parties that Mohsin had thrown, some he had even wanted to do something with, but the embarrassment stopped him. The embarrassment of knowing that if he did, if she was to slink her arm around his neck, if she was to press her lips against his, there was nowhere to take her. Mohsin had offered his flat to Amir several times. 'Just take her back to mine,' he'd said, 'you can fuck her in my bed, I don't mind,' a glint in his eyes, but Amir had refused.

It wasn't that Amir hadn't fucked. But that had been before, with Layla, and now, in the wake of her leaving, there was nothing. Girls were interested in him, yes, he had gone to clubs with Mohsin and had girls come up to him, telling him that they liked the look of him, pushing on his arms, pressing hands against his chest, and Amir would say nothing, and some of them, not to be deterred, would make it very clear what they wanted, and he'd back away, hands up, saying he had someone.

Once, Mohsin had heard him and had laughed, sharp, hard, and said to the girl, 'Is he using that line again? See, this boy right here, my boy right here,' Mohsin putting his arm around Amir's neck, bringing his face down and close to his own, 'he had his heart broken by a girl, just this summer, can you believe it? Who would say no to this?' pinching Amir's cheek, squeezing tight. 'So I think you,' Mohsin said to the girl, 'should take my boy somewhere and make him feel better, you know? Make him forget all about that girl.'

So she had, taking Amir's hand in her own, leading him to the disabled toilets, the wide door, wheelchair sign on the front of it, and when she'd closed the door, she'd got on her knees in a way that told Amir she had done this before, and Amir couldn't get hard, not when she pulled his joggers down, not when she took his dick in her hand, not when she put her lips around it, until, after a while of her trying, neither one of them looking at each other, not saying a word, she'd stood up, brushed down her dress, looked at herself in the mirror, adjusted her hair, taken her lipstick from her purse, reapplied it, and then turned to Amir, a polite smile on her face, as if they'd just arrived at the post office at the same time, Amir letting her go ahead of him, and he moved out of the way, and she slid out of the toilet.

He was glad, then, that she had left without saying anything, because he wasn't sure what he might have done if she had.

He hadn't got hard in months. He told himself it was the stress of his exams, but when he lay awake at night, staring at the sky through his small window, he wondered if it was because of Layla. Maybe his dick would only work with her, and though he knew that couldn't be true, he was too smart for that, the evidence spoke for itself. Maybe his dick had bonded with someone who wasn't coming back.

Mohsin went into host mode, guiding people to the drinks on the counter, red cups stacked, to the weed on the table, introducing them to the boys, who lazily waved hands as their names were said.

Amir watched Mohsin as he worked the room, and he noticed that Mohsin had changed clothes, was wearing a black shirt now, crisp, clean, buttons half open so that they could all see the lines of his chest, a small smattering of hair that had been shaved to look that way, Amir knew, he'd seen the different trimmers and razors Mohsin had in his bathroom, silver chain just visible underneath his throat, an earring in his right ear, one ring on his right hand, two on his left, black watch on his wrist, trousers tight enough that the shape of his legs was visible but not so tight that he couldn't move.

Casting an eye around the room, Amir saw that it wasn't just Mohsin. The boys were mirrors of him, though to a lesser extent, back-up singers to his lead, and the girls were all made up too, hair twisted, curls falling around their faces, lips red or purple or black, eyes covered in dark ink. Amir felt cheap. Like he had stumbled into a party he hadn't been invited to, but no one cared enough to kick him out.

He found himself in the middle of a conversation with Nadeem and a girl whose name he hadn't heard at the beginning, when Nadeem had introduced Amir and he'd shaken her hand. Nadeem was talking about politics, was doing a degree in politics, and he loved to talk about current affairs, it made him sound smart, he said, when he spoke about international relations between America and Britain, the sweep of the far-right across Europe, the consequences of Brexit, even though, he said, he didn't really give a fuck about politics, when had politics ever been good for people like us? But being able to speak about it made him sound worldly.

Amir listened to Nadeem go on, realising, in that moment, why Nadeem's ex-girlfriend had broken up with him earlier that year, how exhausting it was to listen to him. Amir excused himself, 'Gotta take a piss,' he said, and the girl looked at him, a look in her eyes that first said, *Take me away*, and then said, *Why are you here again?* but Amir had no interest in saving her or explaining himself to her, so he walked over to the bathroom, went in, door shut behind him, took a breath. There, in the muffled quiet of the room, he closed his eyes.

He stepped over to the sink, giant mirror facing him. Mohsin often took photos of himself in this mirror, top off, gaze directed into the phone he was holding, never at himself or at the phone's camera. Mohsin's electric toothbrush, skin creams and moisturisers, oils in small white vials. All the tools he used to shape himself every day.

Amir twisted the tap, waiting for the water to get cold, and then ran some over his face, wet hand to the back of his neck, reaching for a towel to dry himself off, soft in his hands the way towels should be, not stiff with age and use like the ones they had at home. He glanced at himself in the mirror before he went back out, hand through his hair, too short to do anything with, Amir pretending it was a stylistic choice and not because it meant he didn't have to think about it.

Who had the time? he asked himself, but the truer question was, *Who had the money?*

'There he is,' Mohsin shouted when Amir walked back into the living room, and before he could react, Mohsin's arm was around his shoulders, pulling Amir to him. 'This is who I was telling you about,' Mohsin said, 'the good boy who still lives with his parents, though maybe not so good, what were you doing in that bathroom, eh,' Mohsin laughed, running his finger underneath Amir's nose. Amir brushed him away, tense, looking ahead at the person Mohsin was speaking to, a girl whose face wasn't familiar to him.

Mohsin gestured to her, 'This is Farrah,' he said, and he lifted Amir's hand for him, inserting it into the gap between the two of them, 'and, Farrah, this is Amir.' Farrah took Amir's hand. 'It's Farrah,' she said, pronouncing it the way Amir's grandmother would have pronounced it, his grandmother, telling Amir, when he was younger, 'This is how you say your name, no other way, you understand? You don't let anyone take that from you.'

'Nice name,' Amir said, and Mohsin was already moving away, arm lifting from Amir, something else capturing his attention, and it was just the two of them, standing in the corner of the room, next to the big windows, the lights of the city pulsing underneath them.

Amir glanced over at the rest of the room, because he didn't know what to say, and he looked back at Farrah, at the drink in her hand, dark, bubbly, and he wondered, not for the first time, if he should just do it, just drink the alcohol. Clearly, it made everything easier, judging from the ease with which everyone else moved when they'd consumed it. Mohsin, putting glass after glass to his lips, white and brown and gold and pink and blue, commanded the room. But then again, Amir considered, that was who Mohsin was. What things came to him hard?

'How do you know Mohsin?' Farrah asked.

Amir turned his eyes back towards her face, dark skin, ring in her nose, black around her eyes, lips bruised with purple. 'We're doing the same degree,' he said.

'Oh, an engineer.'

'Civil engineering,' Amir said, correcting her, small smile.

'So you'll make bridges.'

'Bridges and buildings and something else starting with b,' Amir said. Farrah laughed, pride flaring in Amir's chest. 'What do you do?' he asked.

She looked away from him for a second. 'I don't think I want to tell you,' she said, taking a sip from her glass.

'Why not?'

'Because I think you'll have the same reaction my dad did.'

'Are you telling me I remind you of your dad?'

'Every boy in here reminds me of my dad,' Farrah said, waving her hand at the rest of them. 'You all have that same intense look in your eyes, like you're reliving the horrors of empire and taking it out on the women around you.'

'I don't do that,' Amir said.

'That's what every brown boy I meet says.'

'What degree are you doing?' Amir asked again.

She let out a small sigh. 'Film,' Farrah said, body slumping forward, looking up at Amir.

'First year?'

'Second.'

'What do you learn on a film degree?' Amir said, letting himself lean a little into her, drawn in.

'A whole lot of nothing.'

'Like?'

'Well,' Farrah said, 'I can tell you all about the French New Wave if you want, or we can talk about postmodernism, or I can spend an hour or two talking to you about the effect *Moonlight* had on the film industry.'

'*Moonlight?*' Amir asked, wanting to glance behind him, through the window, up at the sky, but stopping himself.

'You don't know *Moonlight?*'

'No,' Amir said, twinge of embarrassment.

'Oh,' Farrah said, surprise, disappointment maybe, he couldn't tell. 'You should, it's a good film.'

'I don't really watch a lot of films, I used to, when I was younger,' he said, 'but nothing that a film student would be into.'

'Try me,' she said.

Amir thought for a second. 'My brother and I used to watch horror films when we were younger.'

'Like what?' Farrah asked, leaning forwards, closing the gap again.

'You know, the old ones, *Nightmare on Elm Street, Jason X, Chucky, Evil Dead, Texas Chain Saw Massacre.*' The film titles came easy to him, swimming past his eyes.

'So just the good ones then,' Farrah said.

'Oh,' Amir said, grin wide, 'so you do have taste?'

'Listen, as much as I love an indie French film about a woman smoking cigarettes on a balcony, drinking coffee and wine, and having an affair, I also love horror, I spent a lot of time as a kid watching them when I wasn't meant to.'

'Me too,' Amir said, 'my brother and I used to just go downstairs when our mum was asleep, volume low so that she didn't hear,' Amir and Bilal, sitting together, quiet, Amir burying his head in Bilal's arm if things got too scary, watching everything the free channels had, and sometimes their uncle would bring them pirated tapes, clunky recordings from a cinema somewhere. Then, Bilal's school chose him to be given a free laptop, this chunky blue HP laptop, back of it dimpled, Amir running his fingers over it, and they started watching films there instead, the internet giving them freedom. But then it all stopped. Bilal disappeared to university, handing Amir that dimpled laptop, but Amir no longer felt the desire to seek out the films anymore. It was as if it had been another pair of boys, just someone else's story that Amir was telling.

'What do you want to do,' Amir asked, 'after?'

'After?'

'When you're done with the degree.'

'I don't know,' Farrah said, 'maybe directing, I guess, that would be fun.'

'That's big,' Amir said, 'right?'

'Too big?' she asked, eyes on his.

'I don't know,' Amir said, 'is it too big?'

'You don't get a lot of Pakistani Muslim women directors these days.'

'You don't get a lot of Pakistani Muslim anything these days.'

'Well,' Farrah said, slowly, 'I guess that's what I want to change.'

'What would you make?'

Farrah looked past Amir, out of the windows, to the cloudless sky behind him. 'I've always been interested in family, like, I don't know, my parents were born here but their parents, they were born back there, in Pakistan, came here all those years ago, barely older than I am now, did all that sacrificing, learning the language and how this side of the world works, away from everything they'd ever known, made enough for themselves to have children, gave their children enough, gave them an education so they could do better, so I could do better, so that I could stand here, talking to you, in this flat, so yeah, I'd like to make something about them, something real, something that spoke true to who they were, to thank them, I guess, for doing what they did.'

She said all of this not looking at Amir, and when she was done, she caught his eyes and then looked away, embarrassed.

'That's really nice,' Amir said, 'that you would do it for them.' He thought of his own grandparents, both his grandfathers dead, his grandmothers both alive, his father's mother in Pakistan, a woman he had only spoken to a handful of times, phone forced into his hand, and his mother's mother, who lived down the road from them, a woman who had filled his childhood as much as, if not more than, his actual parents.

He knew a little of his mother's parents' stories, how they had come over in the sixties, both working, had bought a house, had two children. But he didn't know more than that. Sometimes, Bilal would say they needed to get their history down on paper, asking their mother what she remembered about her childhood, telling her, when she got annoyed, when she asked him why it mattered, that it was important. 'To pass something on,' he'd say to her, and she'd tell him to leave her alone.

'What do your parents do?' Amir asked.

'My dad is a doctor,' Farrah said. 'I know, I know,' rolling her eyes, 'the cliché, but it was what his parents wanted him to be when he was younger, and he was smart enough and worked hard. He works for the NHS, always has, refuses to go private, even though he would make so much more money doing so much less work, comes home tired all the time. Sometimes, he'll finish his shift and something will happen, someone comes in that he needs to see or maybe one of his patients will start dying, so instead of doing ten hours, he does thirteen, fourteen, and then he'll come home, sleep, and be up to do it all over again.'

'Fuck,' Amir said. He thought of his own father, coming home from his shifts in the car, body clicking as he stretched out on the sofa, the curve of his spine, his head resting forward, sinking into his chest, the shape of his stomach. At the end of the day, all Amir's father could say was that he had driven someone from one place to another.

'I know,' Farrah said. 'It's hard to watch. He's not even that old, just forty-three, so it's not like he's heading to retirement any time soon, he has to keep doing this.'

'What about your mum?' Amir asked. 'What does she do?'

'She's a councillor.'

'What, like, with kids and stuff?'

Farrah laughed, 'No, no, like, she works as a Labour councillor, for our ward. What about you?' Farrah asked. 'What do your parents do?'

Amir considered lying, saying that he didn't have any parents, that he was like one of those little orphan boys that he'd read about in children's stories when he was younger, always saved by some nice person at the end of the book, they just had to suffer through a couple of atrocities first. 'My dad's a taxi driver,' Amir said, putting a hand to the back of his neck, looking away from her, 'and my mum doesn't really work, never has.'

'Never?' Farrah asked.

'Not really,' Amir said, and then, feeling protective of his mother, 'she got married straight out of school and then had us.'

'Us?'

'Yeah, me and my brother.'

'Do you think—' Farrah started to say, but then a girl appeared by her side, a hand on Farrah's arm, and her sentence was cut short, the ending somewhere in the air between them.

'Farrah, we should go,' the girl said, 'we've got that other thing to get to,' her eyes wide as she spoke, raising her eyebrows to Farrah. Amir looked around the room again and saw that things were different, people had left, the party was dying down. Mohsin and some of the boys were sitting on the sofa, unmoving, bad background actors. Zain was standing, talking to a girl who had her fingers in her hair, twirling a strand around and around, and from the way that they were standing, Amir knew that Zain was going to fuck her.

'Give me one second,' Farrah said to her friend, and the girl looked at her, then at Amir, asking who he was, and then she stepped away. Farrah turned back to Amir, 'You should have my number,' she said. Amir reached into his pocket, took out his phone, handed it to her, watched as she tapped in her number. 'Text me,' she said, handing the phone back to him, and when Amir took it, their fingers touched, briefly, 'I want to see you again,' she said, and she said it without hesitation or embarrassment or shame, her want so clearly put, and then she was leaving, heading for the door with some other girls, the same girl who had tugged at Farrah now tugging at the girl talking to Zain, who said, 'I'll come with you,' and he grabbed his jacket off one of the hooks near the door, said a quick goodbye to the room, winked at Amir as he stepped out the door, a big grin, and then they were gone, door closed, and all Amir could hear was the music.

Ten

Amir stayed the night at Mohsin's. By the time the others had all left, it was four in the morning, Amir's eyes hazy, and he considered walking back, no buses, an hour in the dark, so he looked at his phone, over ten pounds to get home in a taxi, Mohsin took Amir's phone out of his hands, said, 'It's fine, you can stay here,' and pulled Amir to his bed, muttering, 'It's fine, really,' and Amir let him, lying there, Mohsin asleep the moment he lay down, and when he woke in the morning, Mohsin was already up, the bed empty.

The room was dark, save for a sliver of light coming in from the door. Amir reached for his phone, saw the line of texts from his mother, all the way up until one in the morning, the several missed calls.

Amir put the phone down. Mohsin's bed was comfortable, moulding itself to Amir's body. Then he remembered what day it was, what had happened yesterday. He reached for his phone again, ignoring his mother's texts and going to his and Saqib's conversation. A small line at the top told Amir when Saqib had last been online, four days ago now. The last time they had spoken had been three years ago. An Eid text from

Saqib to Amir, who had replied asking him if someone had a gun to his head, Saqib asking him what he was going to do with the day, Amir saying he was going to their grandmother's house, would Saqib come too? And Saqib hadn't replied.

Amir scrolled up through the conversation. He'd already done this once, after his mother had told him the news, wanting to remember who they had been, to see where the crack had started. But there was nothing there. Texts to say that they had reached wherever they had decided to meet up, texts asking where the other one was, texts asking if the other one was going to come somewhere one of them was. No photos, no jokes. They'd shared everything in person. Even Saqib's profile photo was just of a sunset, with Saqib in the photo, back turned to the camera, or maybe it was someone else, hard to tell in silhouette.

After looking at his messages with Saqib, Amir went to his conversation with Layla, keyboard jumping up, his thumbs hovering over it.

He had spoken to Layla about Saqib, and Layla had understood because there were men in her family who were doing the same thing. Layla had been of the idea that people owed it to themselves to fix their lives, that to wait for other people to come and fix them, to heal their wounds, was weakness. When it came like that, she said, the cure would never last. Even though Amir knew she would blame Saqib for his death, she was still the one he had wanted to talk to.

He left her conversation, headed to the one online profile she had, a grid of photos. Her profile was a collage of photos she had found interesting, books she was reading, places she had been to, records she had bought, her recent obsession with physical media, Amir there for the start of it, following her from charity shop to charity shop as she bought Blu-rays, waving them in his face, saying, 'They'll never take these away from me,' books, music, she wanted it all physically. She didn't trust the internet, she told Amir, things could disappear at any moment, and Amir listened to her, but she would accuse him of not listening, and he'd say that he was listening but the one thing she couldn't get him to do was care, and then she would hit him with the book or record or disc she had just bought.

Amir turned off his phone, closed his eyes, took in a breath, held it deep in his chest, filling what felt like all of his lungs. He slid his feet onto the floor, pausing on the very edge of the bed, listening to the sounds of Mohsin in the kitchen, a kettle boiling, water being poured into a mug, spoon clinking. Amir reached for his phone again, this time to check the time. It was just gone nine.

Mohsin greeted Amir a touch too loudly, his eyes bright. He offered him some coffee, which Amir declined, Mohsin persisting, saying it was the fancy type, the one that he had ground himself, using a small machine that cost far too much money, something he had picked up once he had moved into this flat. 'No,' Amir said, 'I need to get home, I've got work to do,' and when Mohsin tried to wave that away, Amir just walked to the door. Mohsin stopped him, said he would drive him, but Amir shook his head, said, 'No, I need the walk, it's good for me,' and then, because Amir didn't want Mohsin to think he was angry at him, he hugged Mohsin, quick, short, and told him he'd text later.

The walk from Mohsin's flat to the bus stop was ten minutes, and as Amir walked, he wished he had at least taken a swig of mouthwash before he stepped out, his mouth grimy with sleep. He was aware of how he might look to people, old clothes, unwashed face, unclean mouth. Maybe they would decide he was just doing his walk of shame, leaving someone's flat, someone's bed, and in a way, he thought, he had done just that.

He didn't quite hear his name the first time, but he heard the echo of it the second, and he assumed it must be for another Amir, but the third time, the insistence of it, the closeness of it, told Amir that he was the one being summoned. He turned, ready to end the conversation before it had even started, and when he saw who was standing before him, his mouth went dry.

'Amir,' Adnan said a fourth time.

Adnan, or at least a version of Adnan that was both thinner and broader than Amir remembered, his face more defined, beard precisely shaped.

'Adnan,' Amir said, and when Adnan reached for him, hand out, Amir took it, Adnan pulling him in close, strong, his other hand going around Amir's back, and Amir remembered to keep his mouth closed, didn't want Adnan to smell the sleep on his breath, and then Amir thought about the way he looked, and when he pulled away, he let his eyes go down Adnan's body, to the chain that was hanging from his neck, to the shine of the Nike trainers he was wearing, the horse on his shirt, the thick gold bracelet on one wrist and what looked like a Rolex on the other.

'I've been looking for you,' Adnan said, 'since yesterday.'

'Yesterday?' Amir asked.

'Saqib,' Adnan said, 'I was at the janazah yesterday. I saw you, I wanted to come over, but you were with the family, so I didn't think it was right to.'

'Saqib,' Amir said. He hadn't seen Adnan there, but then again, Amir thought, there'd been no space in his mind for other people. He could only remember Bilal, his parents, Saqib's mother, the coffin. 'I didn't know you were there.'

'You were busy,' Adnan said, 'and it wasn't a good time. I'm sorry, for Saqib.'

'Yeah,' Amir said, not meeting his eyes.

'Young,' Adnan said, and he said it as though he himself was decades older than them, as if he wasn't the same age as Amir, the same age as Saqib.

'No younger than us.'

'And we're still alive,' Adnan said. He turned, looked behind him, then to Amir. 'You busy right now?' he asked.

'Nah,' Amir said, 'I got nothing going on.'

'Okay, good, come with me,' Adnan said, turning around and walking back in the direction Amir had just come from.

'What are you up to these days?' Adnan asked him as they walked. 'You're at uni, yeah?'

'Yeah,' Amir said, 'second year.'

'Second year,' Adnan said, 'that's good.'

'Yeah,' Amir said, thinking ahead to the exams that were arriving too quickly, to how little studying he had done, to how hard the work had become. Things that he'd had to just look at once to understand were now inaccessible to him. His brain was not the same as it used to be. 'What about you?' Amir asked. 'What are you up to these days?' What he really wanted to ask was, *Why do you look like this?*

Where did you get all this money from? How are you like this when I'm like this?

'A lot,' Adnan said, grinning at Amir, and Amir saw a gold tooth, his left upper canine, glinting in the light.

Amir waited for him to say something more, but he turned to look forward again. He took a breath, was about to ask Adnan why he was at Saqib's janazah, when Adnan stopped walking.

In front of them was a car, a Mercedes, sleek, and Adnan walked around it, to the driver's side, and Amir watched him, waiting for him to keep walking, but then the lights on the car flashed, Adnan pulled the door open, and Amir's vision went hazy with shock. He stared at Adnan, who caught sight of Amir's face as he got into the car, laughed, and said, 'Yeah, this is mine, get in.'

Adnan closed the door and Amir moved to the passenger side, opening the door. He lowered himself slowly into the car, the seat soft underneath him, *Leather*, he thought, feeling it with his hands, the stitches under his fingers, the dashboard, shiny, a screen set in the middle of it, that recognisable logo as Adnan turned on the car at just the push of a button. Amir reached over for the seatbelt, and when he pulled there was no friction, and as Adnan started to drive, Amir realised he could barely hear the engine underneath them, just the low hum of money.

'Fuck,' Amir said, as Adnan drove. 'This is really your car.'

'All mine.'

'Brand new?'

'Yeah,' Adnan said, and he looked over at Amir, one hand on the steering wheel, grinning, 'you impressed?'

'Fuck me,' Amir said, and he leaned back into the seat.

Adnan laughed, reached over to put a hand on Amir's shoulder, his fingers strong. 'It's mad, I know,' he said, 'I bet you never expected to see me drive something like this.'

'Nah,' Amir said, 'it's not that, it's just, I don't expect any of us to drive a car like this, no one that I know.'

'My brother,' Adnan said, 'these streets are paved in gold. You just need to know where to look.'

Eleven

Amir and Adnan had first met at primary school, placed together in reception, though Amir didn't remember that, it was just part of their story now. Adnan had an older brother too, the same age as Bilal, and though they weren't friends, it felt right that they knew each other too.

It wasn't until they made the move to secondary school, crossing the road from Nansen to Park View, that the differences between them became clear. Adnan, not as smart as Amir, was moved to the bottom sets, Amir right at the top, but they still hung out, even if they stopped seeing each other in class.

The two of them saw one another in a group that mostly consisted of Adnan's boys, who took the piss out of Amir for studying as much as he did, asking what the point was, and when Amir first told them that he wanted to leave with good grades, get into a good university, have a good job, make good money, buy a good house and a good car, they told him that was bullshit. 'Good lives like that', Adnan often said, 'aren't built for people like us.'

As the years passed, Amir spent less and less time with Adnan and his boys, started to find them grating, and when some of them started to deal drugs, Amir took no part in it, though he was always down to smoke weed if they had it, and if one of them wanted to pay for his burger and chips, he wasn't going to say no, but when they said that they were going to go run up on some boys, a job that needed to be done, Amir stepped away, went home, told himself he would not be like them.

It was when he met Layla, fifteen, Year Ten, that Amir stopped seeing Adnan completely. At first, it was because there was no space to feel anything but the burning joy that came from being around Layla. Then, there was guilt and shame that he had abandoned his boys for a girl, and when Adnan saw Amir in the hallways, he mocked him for it, not viciously, Amir never worried that it would turn violent, but it became clear, quickly, that Amir had stepped across a line, that there was no coming back. So when Adnan stopped turning up to school, his absences growing longer, and Amir didn't see him in the hallways, his name often called out with no response, Amir simply accepted that Adnan had become a ghost.

College came quickly, Amir taking those two buses to Joseph Chamberlain, and every so often, he would hear about Adnan from other people, and he didn't know what was true and what wasn't, but he paid it no mind. He forgot about Adnan. It was easy enough.

Because it was easy for Amir to step away from them, easy for him to stop thinking about them, easy for Amir to decide that their lives just weren't worth his time anymore.

Twelve

Adnan drove Amir into Sparkhill, pulling up into the driveway of a house that already had two other cars in it, another Mercedes and an Audi, both of them gleaming like they had just been driven off the shop floor.

The house was the sort that Amir's mother had always dreamed of having. When Amir was younger, she'd asked his father if they might move into a new house now that the mortgage was taken care of, maybe they could rent this house to someone, she said, and she could take care of that, maybe that could be her job, she wanted to move to Hodge Hill, she said, because that was where everyone else was moving to now, and while she talked, Amir's father said nothing, and when she was done, he asked her if she was finished and then laughed, asked her if she understood how hard it was for him to pay off the mortgage, did she? Did she really understand? If she really wanted a new house, she should go and get a job so she could have the driveway and the gates and the bigger garden and the two bathrooms and the five bedrooms, and whatever else it was that she wanted, and she could take her two boys with her too, maybe then he could find some fucking peace in this house he had worked so fucking hard to own.

Amir stepped out of the car, shutting the door lightly, tenderly, and followed Adnan into the house, the door already open, and where Amir was expecting the smell of weed, expecting the hallway to be littered with discarded shoes, dirt clogging the carpet, he was greeted with the smell of his own house, his grandmother's house. Clean, fresh air, slightly tinged with agarbatti, the kind of air that a woman was responsible for.

'Come through,' Adnan said, and they walked down the hallway, shoes neatly lined up on shelves attached to the wall, and when Amir followed him through into the living room, an old man stood up to greet them, brown flat cap on his head, snow-white beard tight against his face, and when he offered Amir his hand, Amir looked into his eyes and saw Adnan's, light-brown, almost gold, and Amir nearly said something then, of how long it had been since he had last seen him, but the old man let go of his hand and sat back down.

Adnan walked through into the kitchen, ripped from Amir's mother's dreams.

'You hungry?' Adnan asked, opening the fridge, Amir shaking his head no. 'I'm fucking starving,' Adnan said, pulling out some rice, 'you don't mind?' Amir shook his head again and watched as he warmed up the browned rice and chicken curry, pouring it over the rice, adding raita on the side and grabbing a Coke can, so cold that there was a chill on the surface of it, before sitting down at the island, gesturing for Amir to sit by him.

'Tell me,' Adnan said, 'what are you doing at uni?'

'Uni,' Amir said, hands in his lap, shoulders forward. 'Civil engineering,' he said.

'Civil engineering?'

'Yeah, like buildings and stuff,' Amir said.

'Don't do that,' Adnan said, mouth full, 'don't play down that shit, you got into uni, that's big for people like us, you gotta talk about that shit with pride.'

'Fuck off,' Amir said, grinning, but it was a misstep, Adnan's face shifting. 'I just mean,' he said, pulling back, 'it's a degree, I don't even know if I want to do anything with it.'

'Why not?' Adnan said, thick sip of the Coke, and as Amir watched him eat, he thought of how he hadn't eaten since yesterday morning, before he'd gone to the janazah, and even then, he hadn't eaten much, no appetite for it, and the weed never made him hungry, it just emptied him of the desire to eat. But now he was hungry.

'I don't know, what the fuck am I going to do?' Amir said, pulling his eyes away from the food. 'Go work for the council, build a bridge, make some blueprints, work in an office for the rest of my life? That's not for me.'

'Why'd you pick it then?'

'I don't know.'

'I don't know, I don't know,' Adnan said, mocking Amir, 'what do you fucking know?'

Amir bit his tongue, about to say it again. 'It just, it felt like the right thing at the time.'

'Why?'

'Why what?'

'Why did it feel like the right thing at the time?'

'Someone told me it was,' Amir said. Him, sitting on one side of the table, his maths teacher on the other, a small French man whose shirts were a touch too tight over his chest, buttons straining against his body, Amir hated the way his lips pursed when he spoke, but there was something about him that Amir also liked, and he had taken a liking to Amir too, told Amir that he should use this innate talent he had for understanding numbers. 'You get it,' he told Amir, 'in ways that others don't, don't waste it,' and Amir told him he had no idea what to do with himself, that university presented too many options for him, choices everywhere he looked, Amir envied those who knew exactly what it was that they wanted, 'Like my brother,' Amir said, 'he studied philosophy because he wanted to, I don't have that,' and he'd looked at Amir then, this French maths teacher, and asked if he wanted someone to tell him where to go, what to do, who to be, and Amir had said, 'Yeah, I do,' without thinking, and he had smiled at Amir, and Amir knew then that he had got it wrong, another question answered badly, he was meant to say no. Then his teacher had said, 'Maybe I can do that for you,' and he told Amir to study civil engineering. 'You'll learn interesting things, meet some interesting people, and if you absolutely hate it, you can always quit, but I have a feeling you might like it, and I have a feeling you'll be very good at it.'

'So what's changed now?' Adnan asked.

'It's not for me,' Amir said.

'That's bullshit,' Adnan said, 'tell me what's changed.'

But what was there to say? That at school it had all come so easily to Amir, all he had to do was listen to his teachers and read what they put in front of him, and he was good to go. The high grades he had achieved came as naturally to him as breathing, and yes, he did work hard, but he never felt like it was too much work. Then college had come, and that had felt harder, yes, but not so impossible, it just required him to sit with everything for a touch longer, to read a page maybe two or three times before understanding what it was trying to teach him, to spend more than just a glance on a maths problem. Then came first year of university, where it felt like a natural extension of everything at college. A touch harder, yes, but still relatively easy. Sometimes, it felt as if everything he was being taught was information that had already been in his head, he just needed to hear it again to free it. His exams were quick and clean that first year, and he spent the summer not stressing about what grades he would get because he knew that he'd be good, and he'd ended up with some of the highest marks in his class. Now, second year, it felt like the opposite, like everyone around him was suddenly speaking Mandarin and he was standing around, wondering what they were talking about and why he was even there, and maybe it was that second year was just harder, that's what everyone kept saying too, it's what Bilal had said when he came back home on those weekends from university, about all the essays that he had to write and the tomes he had to read, it's what Mohsin had said, it's what Zain had said, it's what their lecturers had warned them about before they'd started their classes that year, but maybe it was also that Amir no longer had it, the drive to work hard, which had been there in his first year, to learn what he didn't know, to push himself, and maybe that was all gone now and he didn't know where it had gone, didn't know why, only that it had and he had no idea how to court it back.

'Why don't you tell me' Amir said, 'how you can afford all this shit?' gesturing to the kitchen. 'The Adnan I knew barely had enough coins to get a burger meal from down the road and now you're driving that car, your house looks like this.'

'It's been a long time,' Adnan said, 'people change.' He picked up his plate, walked over to the sink, ran the water, reaching for the sponge shaped like a face, smile inserted in its middle, cleaned slowly, methodically. 'A lot has changed,' he said.

'What's changed?' Amir asked, getting up, standing just to the side of Adnan, arms crossed, leaning against that expensive marble, black, streaked through with lines of grey.

Adnan looked at Amir. 'You want the truth?' he asked, Amir nodding, 'I can tell you the truth, but I can't promise that you're going to like it.'

'Why don't you let me decide that?'

'Alright, big man,' Adnan said, turning off the tap and putting the plate on the silver drying rack next to the sink. 'Not here,' he said.

Thirteen

There was this family that lived at the top of Amir's road, in a house that used to be two separate houses before they demolished the walls that stood between them, Amir's mother watching every day as they worked on it, scaffolding creeping up the sides, and she'd mutter under her breath about how ugly it was, what a nuisance to look at, all she could hear were the drills, the constant drills, she didn't like the men that walked on her road now because of all this construction work, and maybe Amir might have believed that was why she was so annoyed about the work if she wasn't so transparent about it, one night, Amir sitting on the step of his room, listening to her talk to his father about maybe moving, maybe getting some work done on the house, if not a new one, she had always thought the bathroom could be extended to the back garden, didn't he agree? Wouldn't it be nicer to have a bigger bathroom rather than the small one they had now? And maybe if they extended it, they could have a bathroom upstairs too, and maybe they could extend this bedroom and knock the wall down, and she kept going, for longer than Amir thought she should have, knowing what his father was like, and when she was done, his father said nothing, and she asked him, after a few cold moments of silence, what he thought, and he said, 'If you want to change things to this house, you'd better go get yourself a job.'

After the work was done, months and months of it, Amir's mother had other things to say, that the money they had used was blood money, it wasn't good to have a big house like this, a driveway like this, cars like this, it was a sin to show your wealth like this, to be this prideful, and even if it wasn't, it all came from blood money.

'Blood money?' Amir asked her, when he was with her one day, interrupting her whispered rant, too young to understand what she meant.

'Blood money,' she said, turning and kneeling down to meet his eyes, 'the kind of money they spent on this house only brings bad things with it, do you understand? This is haram money, there is nothing good that comes out of this money, and no matter how much you have of it, no matter how happy it might make you feel when you're out there, in the world, spending it, nothing good ever comes from it, and when you're dead, when you're lying in that grave of yours, you'll know what I mean then, when your bones are being crushed by the angels, punishing you for what you've done.'

Amir, scared by the violence in her eyes and her words, said nothing, and when she stood up, grabbed him by the arm, pulled him along with her, he turned to look back at the house, with its nice cars and its paved driveway and its gold gates, and he wondered what could be so bad about money that could build something like that.

A few months after the house was finished, Amir's uncle befriended one of the boys of the family, Amir seeing them one day, walking down Alum Rock Road, Amir's uncle wearing what he usually wore, trackies that didn't match, a cap that fit oddly on his head, a touch too big, strange next to the son, who wore a shirt and trousers, clean, pressed, fitted to his body, the sort that would suit a person who had an office job.

'They sell weed,' his uncle told Amir, when he asked how they had so much money, 'weed, cocaine, ecstasy, heroin, all kinds of shit, they've been selling it for years, their dad was the one who started it, way back when, he was younger than me, in the streets, doing small deals on corners, and he got bigger and bigger and now all he does is sit in that house, surrounded by his money, lets his boys run shit now.'

Amir asked his uncle how he knew them. 'School,' he said, 'Park View was ours.'

'So why didn't you get into it then?'

'Why didn't I get into drug dealing?' his uncle asked, smacking Amir on the back of his head. 'Don't ask me a dumb fucking question like that, I didn't get into it because it's fucking stupid to get into shit like that.'

'But they have money.'

'They have money,' his uncle said, 'but that's dangerous shit, you never know who might turn up at your door and pop you right in the head,' he said, pushing his index finger into Amir's forehead, 'just because they feel like it, because they're tired of watching you and yours drive around in fancy cars and your nice house, they're tired of you having all that, they've decided it's their time now, they want it, I'm not getting into that shit,' his uncle said, shaking his head, 'even if it is nice, and of course it's fucking nice, the money that they have, all the shit that they can buy, I can't lie to you and say it's not, but it's not worth it, none of that shit is worth it.'

Fourteen

When Amir was nine, he had been walking home from school with Saqib, Saqib turning one way at a crossroads and he the other, and he decided to stop by the corner shop, using the money his grandfather had given him on the weekend to buy sweets. He stood in front of the chocolates, which sat at the very front of the counter, the old man that they called 'Uncle' watching him as he tried to make his choice. After several minutes of considering, he decided to go with a bar of Dairy Milk, the purple familiar and comforting to him, and he ate it all during the three-minute walk from the corner shop to his house, throwing the wrapper into someone else's bin, and when he turned the corner, he saw his mother standing at the door, looking out, concern on her face, and when her eyes landed on him, she shouted his name and waved him over, and when Amir got to her, she hugged him quickly, tightly, and then asked him where he had been. He said, 'Walking back from school,' and she moved him into the house, closing the door behind him.

She explained nothing, so Amir waited for Bilal, who, now in Year Ten, studying for his GCSEs, often came home late after working in the library, or so he said, Amir knew that he spent the time with his friends, sitting in burger shops, fries in hand, can popped open, and when he did come home, their mother asked him the same thing, and when Bilal came upstairs, Amir asked him, 'What's going on?'

There had been reports of a gun being fired, not once but four times, just around the corner from them, their mother hearing it as she hung out the clothes, thinking immediately of her two boys, her two children, who were not yet home. Could it have been one of them?

It was a scuffle between two gangs, no one hurt in the firing of the gun, at least, no one dead, and the police asked anyone who had been nearby questions, and Amir listened as his mother exaggerated the fear of that day, when things had happened, the panic that had eaten away at her heart, her two boys, she said, she had been terrified for her two boys, and when the police had asked to talk to them, she had said no, they weren't to speak to the boys, they had been at school, they had nothing to do with this, but the police insisted, and so a man, who had seemed so old to Amir at the time but must have only been in his twenties, asked Amir what had happened, so Amir told him about walking home, seeing his mother by the door, coming inside, not going back out, his brother coming home and the two of them waiting to see what would happen next.

Then, when Amir was thirteen, he'd been at his grandparents', and his uncle had said, 'Come with me,' and they'd left the house together, walking to the shop on the corner of the high street, which used to be a clothes shop, dresses hanging in the windows, but it had been bullied out of existence by other clothes shops that had popped up around it, offering the very same for a lower price, a race to the bottom that served no one, and now it had been turned into a dessert shop. When it opened, it was one of the very first of its kind, Amir could walk in and point to any chocolate on the counter, have it turned into a milkshake using high-powered blenders that roared in the background, but as time passed, it would fade into the background too, as other places opened up with the same foundation but with added extras, like American waffles and French toast, a whole world suddenly appearing.

Amir's uncle told him to get whatever he wanted and something for Bilal too, who had come back from university that weekend, and was helping their grandmother in the garden, so Amir got himself a Ferrero Rocher milkshake, his brother a Flake, and his uncle got a KitKat. Amir held his brother's shake in one hand, his own in the other, sipping as they walked back.

The walk from the dessert shop to his grandparents' house took just under two minutes. When Amir stepped out of the shop, he could see his grandparents' house, his uncle's car, the window of the spare bedroom, where he and Bilal slept when they were younger, staying up too late, looking out of the window at all the world passing them by.

The first boy who ran past them was young, Amir's uncle shouting at him to stop. Then there were three more boys, all running past, so Amir's uncle moved him to the side, and they stopped walking.

More boys ran, all of them after this one boy. They caught him just a few feet away from Amir and his uncle. The boys were shouting, though Amir couldn't make out what they were saying. A screwdriver appeared, like a magic trick, and was plunged into the boy's chest, who let out a yelp. Silence, a pause, and then the boys all ran, disappeared.

Amir's uncle pulled at him, but Amir's feet weren't working, they were stuck to the ground, his eyes on the boy, who had fallen now, whose eyes were closed, whose hands were around the screwdriver, whose chest was rising and falling slowly, and his uncle pulled at him again, and Amir moved, back to his grandparents' house, the shakes still in his hands, and when he walked into the house, his grandfather asked him what had happened, and Amir couldn't say anything, was aware of his uncle explaining what had happened outside, calling the police. Bilal came running downstairs, had heard what their uncle had said, asked Amir if he was okay, was he okay? Did anything happen to him? And Amir handed him his shake, which Bilal took, put to the side, asked him again, 'Are you okay?' and then Bilal, desperate with concern, looked over him, trying to see if he was hurt in any way, and then Bilal's eyes went down to Amir's shoes, and they stopped, and when Amir looked down, he saw that there was blood on the tip of his shoe, one single drop, like someone had put it there on purpose, and Amir started to shake, straw rattling in his cup, Bilal running to get some tissue, dabbing at the shoe until the blood was gone.

The police came, two officers, and asked them questions, Amir and his uncle together, his uncle speaking for the both of them, Amir still holding the shake in his hand, which had melted into liquid by now, forgetting what it once was.

The boy had died on the way to the hospital. There had been no saving him.

Then, when Amir was seventeen, his mother had come into his room, asked him, 'Have you heard?' and Amir had danced the dance with her, and she'd said, 'Do you remember Hamzah?' and Amir had said yes, slowly, and she'd reminded him of his cousin, through many various marriages and relations, who lived in Sheffield, who Amir had seen at Eids and weddings, who was three years older than him, who had gone to university but then dropped out in first year, who had got into selling drugs, hanging around with a bad crowd, Amir's mother saying, 'That's what happens when you don't have faith in yourself,' pulling Amir close to her, giving him a tight hug, saying that would never happen to her boy, her boy was good, her boy was smart, her boy was perfect.

'Well,' she said, 'Hamzah was in a car with one of these boys he hangs around with, you know, a bad man,' she said, using the term unironically, 'and another car stopped by theirs, and they shot the car, three times, one of them hit Hamzah,' she said, 'here,' she said, pointing at her neck, 'he's dead now, he's gone now,' and she closed her eyes when she said it, 'the janazah is tomorrow, me and your dad are going.' She just sat on the edge of his bed, her eyes closed, and then she said, 'I wish that we could stop being like this, I wish we could be better, I wish he didn't have to die,' and Amir watched his mother, not knowing what to do, but then the moment was gone, his mother opening her eyes, wiping them with the back of her hand and leaving his room.

Bilal came back from work that day and Amir asked him if he had heard about Hamzah, and Bilal had nodded, grimly. 'I knew—' Bilal started, but he stopped, shook his head. 'I knew that he was into that shit, his mum asked me to talk to him, when he dropped out of uni, I called him, asked him what was going on, and he told me that he knew what he was doing, and what are you supposed to say to that? I don't know him, I don't know anything about him, I can't tell him shit, so I just left it, and now he's dead.'

'It's not your fault,' Amir had said, and Bilal had smiled at his brother.

'Who says it isn't?' he said.

Then, then, then.

Fifteen

The warehouse Adnan took him to was one of many, he told Amir, but this was the closest, on the other side of Sparkhill, on a business estate that had dozens of other warehouses, all of them shut, metal pulled down, and when Amir stepped out of the car, when he walked in, it was as if he'd crossed over into a film, the kind that his uncle liked to watch, stepped through the screen, to find the wrapped parcels of cocaine, the bags of weed, the mountains of pills.

When Amir saw Ily, Adnan's brother, he didn't recognise him right away, a different person standing in front of Amir to the one who lived in his head. The Ily Amir knew had smelled like old cigarettes and sweat. The man standing in front of him, and Amir had to remind himself that Ily was the same age as Bilal, was clean, smooth.

'This is how,' Adnan told Amir, and when Amir asked for more, how this all worked, when they had started, how many warehouses he had, Adnan said maybe the details could come later. For now, Amir could just use his imagination.

Ily was more forthcoming, telling Amir that he'd been in this business for years, worked his way up the ladder, and now he was in charge of the whole thing. Or, at least, this part of it. He talked about it as if he was a manager at an Apple shop or HMV or PC World, explaining how he first applied for a sales job, on the floor, working diligently with an eye on the top.

'I want in,' Amir told Adnan the moment they walked back out, the sun bright in his eyes.

'Why?' Adnan asked.

'Because I don't want to be fucking poor anymore,' Amir said.

'What about uni?' Adnan asked, leaning against the car. 'I can't say yes and then have you telling me you can't sell because you have to revise for some exam, write some essay, whatever it is that you guys do.'

'Uni is no problem,' Amir said, 'we're at the end of the year, I can make it work.'

'Yeah,' Adnan said, looking at Amir, smile hovering on his lips.

'I'm in,' Amir said, 'I'm all the way fucking in.'

Adnan raised his hands, 'I heard you the first time, you're in.'

They swapped numbers, Amir's the same as it had always been, Adnan's new, and Adnan said he would call Amir, and he reached for Amir then, one hand around Amir's head, pulling him close. 'I got you,' he said, and then let him go, said, 'I'll take you home,' and when he reached his road, Amir told Adnan to stop at the top, fell out of the car, walked to his house without looking behind him and, as Adnan drove off, the car passing him and then disappearing around the corner, Amir's stomach was tight, as if wrung out between two hands.

MAY

Sixteen

'You'll be fine,' Zain said, he and Amir sitting at their regular, a chicken shop where the red tabletops were slick with grease no matter how often they were wiped down but the food was good and it was cheap.

Zain knew nothing about Amir's degree. He was the only one of them who was studying a subject that didn't come attached with a job to do after they were done. 'What can you even do with an English degree?' Amir had asked Zain when they'd first met, and Zain had shrugged, 'That's for later me to figure out,' he'd said. All Zain knew was that he loved to read, had always loved to read, and maybe one day he would write too, become one of those hot writers that get to fuck hot women because they're culturally valuable, he said, like Salman Rushdie, but Amir didn't know who that was. '*The Satanic Verses*,' Zain said, and Amir knew of that, because his mother had told him to promise her that he would never read it, and he had looked it up afterwards, eager to find out what this sinful book was about, but in the description, he found nothing that interested him. 'Look,' Zain said, showing Amir a photo, 'this is who he was married to.' 'That's his wife?' Amir asked. 'Not his daughter?' 'Nah, that was his wife,'

Zain said, laughing, 'he was fucking her, can you imagine?' Amir looked back at the photo, disgusted and impressed. 'I'll be like that,' Zain said, 'hotter, though, I'm never going to look like that, at least, not on purpose.'

'I don't know,' Amir said, pulling apart his chicken wings with his fingers, sliding the meat off, deboning them one by one, laying the meat on top of the thin chips that would collapse soon, losing their crispness and becoming a single soggy mountain of potato if he didn't eat them quickly enough. 'I feel like I don't get anything anymore, like my brain is broken.'

'I think that's just second year,' Zain said, 'I know Mohsin is finding it hard too.'

'Yeah, but Mohsin will be fine, even if he does fail, his dad will just pay for a tutor over the summer and he'll retake the exams, or he'll drop out and go work with his uncle, or his dad will get him an internship, they have money, they know people, he'll be fine.'

'Well,' Zain said slowly, 'yeah, but Mohsin doesn't want to just live on his dad's money forever, he wants to do his own thing.'

'I don't know why,' Amir said, 'he's living the perfect life right now.'

'Yeah, but he does have to think about how everyone just sees him as a daddy's boy, like he ain't got shit of his own, that's hard too.'

'Hard too,' Amir said, sharp laugh, 'yeah, sounds really hard.'

'Come on,' Zain said, reaching over the table, hitting Amir's hand, 'Mohsin isn't a bad guy, don't be a dick.'

'I'm not saying he is, I'm just saying, it's not the same for him as it is for me.'

'I know,' Zain said, 'don't forget, we have the same dad.'

'My idiot boy,' Amir said, putting on a thick Pakistani accent, 'why are you going to study the language that you speak? Don't you already speak English? What are you going to do for money when you finish? What kind of job are you going to have, my idiot, idiot boy?'

'Fuck off,' Zain said, throwing a small bone at Amir, which fell down Amir's shirt, through his legs, to the floor. 'I'll make money, it's easy,' Zain said, 'I'll write a book about a bunch of Pakistani boys at university, fucking around, and everyone will hail me as some great thinker of South Asian masculinity, *Wow, we've never seen this before, it turns out the brown boys are just the same as the black boys and the white boys.*'

'Do I get paid for being your inspiration?'

'Yeah, you can be the sad boy that stays at home with his parents, comes out to the parties and then goes home, like the good son he is,' Zain said, 'you can be our moral compass.'

'Oh, yeah, that sounds just like me.'

'Sounds just like you last year,' Zain said, grinning at Amir, 'what was it that you were always saying? We'll understand one day, when we're in committed relationships, like you and Layla.'

'Fuck off,' Amir said, looking down at the box in front of him, reaching for a chip, holding it tight, then letting it fall back into the box.

'I saw you talking to that girl,' Zain said, 'the other day, at Mohsin's place, what was her name?'

'Farrah,' Amir said, her name quick to his mouth. Her number was in his phone, waiting for him to do something with it.

'Farrah,' Zain said, 'you know, I think that's the perfect match, she's the you of that group.'

'What does that mean?'

'It means', Zain said, throwing a fry at Amir's head to get him to look up, 'that she doesn't put out the way the other girls do, at least, not to any of us, Mohsin has been trying to get with her for time, but she's not into him.'

'That was easy to see.'

'Yeah,' Zain said, 'I've just never heard of her being in a relationship.'

'So, not like me then.'

'Well, like you because you also don't date anyone, don't fuck anyone.'

Amir closed his mouth, teeth tight. 'You know why.'

'And I also know it's been nine months since it happened, you have to get over it.'

'Is that how long it should take me?' Amir asked. 'Nine months and it's done, four years disappeared, just like that?'

'I don't know,' Zain said, 'I've never had a girl for that long before, but you have to move on at some point.'

'Who says I haven't?'

'You,' Zain said, leaning back into his chair, and now his tone had changed, concern in his eyes. 'I mean, you this year is not the same as you last year.'

'Man, fuck off—' Amir began.

'No, listen, for a second,' Zain said, 'and I'm not saying it's a bad thing, I get it, she left, you didn't get a say in it, one day, you're together celebrating four years, she knows all your friends, she's hanging out with us all the time, she's taking the piss out of Mohsin the same way we all do, she's one of us, and then, she's gone, vanished, you can't even stalk her because she's not even in the same city as us anymore—'

'I wouldn't do that.'

'I'm not saying you would, I'm just saying you couldn't even do that, it's hard, I get it, but it has been nine months,' Zain said, 'and …'

'And?' Amir said, looking up at him.

'And, I don't know, man, it's different now, with you.'

'Different,' Amir said.

Now Zain looked away, down at his food, taking a wing, biting on it but with little enthusiasm, as if he was just doing it to have something to do. 'Yeah,' he said, 'different, like, not the same.'

'I know what different means.'

'I mean, I don't want to make you angry or anything—'

'I'm not angry.'

'Sad then,' Zain said, 'I don't want to make you sad, but you're distant, like you don't want to be here, sometimes, maybe, but Farrah seems like a good thing, and you know, she doesn't have to be anything, but I'm glad you talked to her, and it sounds clichéd and whatever, but we are here for you, me, Mohsin, the boys, always,' and then he grinned at Amir, who smiled back, nodded, ended the conversation there.

Seventeen

They were never going to get married. They both knew that. The girl from secondary school wasn't meant to be his wife, but when he and Layla left secondary school still attached, when the other relationships they had watched flourish at the same time as theirs broke apart, when Layla and Amir fucked for the first time, nice and slow, the second time, hard and fast, when they went to the same college and spent their lunches together, when it started to feel like there was something missing when her fingers weren't intertwined with his, when Amir told her every second spent away from her was an eternity and he meant it, he started to believe it would happen for them. Maybe they would be the exception.

Amir began, in his second year of college, to think about it often. Seventeen years old, he dreamed of their future, of coming home to his parents and telling them that he had this girl, this perfect Pakistani Muslim girl, whose parents lived down the road, who knew all the same people Amir's family knew. She was beautiful and she was smart and she was funny and she was kind, and beyond all that, she was a good person, and she made him feel like a good person when he was with her, so if they had a problem with it, Amir would say, if they told him that he was too young to get married or that Layla wasn't the right kind of girl or that they had someone else in mind for him, he would happily cast them aside for her. *Yes, he would say to his mother in these dreams of his, in answer to her question, I will leave you all for her.* It filled him with joy, this future that had yet to happen.

Their parents had been hounding Bilal for years, their mother, mainly, asking him, whenever he came back from university, if he had met someone there, the disappointment on her face when he said no, she never tried to hide it. Over time, she set up, with the help of other women across the country, dates for him to go on, to meet women his age, sometimes a little younger, rarely older, women with degrees and dreams and desires all their own, and Bilal went along to them, said yes to their mother whenever she asked him to. She would sit in the living room, looking at her phone, at the silver clock that hung over the fireplace that was covered up and replaced with a gas heater, asking Amir, 'Do you think they're having a good time? Do you think he's talking too much? Do you think he's not talking enough? He'd better pay for the dinner, he has to, it's no good asking the girl to split, I know some people do that these days, it's not right,' and at first, Amir answered all her questions, tried to comfort her that Bilal knew how to treat a woman, that she had raised her son right, until he realised that she was only interested in hearing the questions asked out loud, not in the answers that came. Then, Bilal would come home, and she would ask him, 'How was it?' and he would tell her, it wasn't quite right, she wasn't quite right, she didn't seem that interested in him, she was boring, she was flat, she wasn't into the things he was into, it just wasn't there, and their mother, exasperated, would throw her arms in the air. 'I give up,' she would say, 'I give up on you,' and then there'd be another date the next weekend, an endless supply of women for Bilal to turn down.

Amir loved to imagine the look on their faces when he brought Layla home, explained to them that he had managed to do the one thing their perfect eldest son couldn't do, had found someone without their help.

Then, first-year exams over, Layla told Amir, after four years of being together, that her family was moving to Edinburgh, that her father had got a new job, a really good job, she said, and she was moving with them, she was going to get her place from the University of Birmingham moved there, maybe she could skip a year or something, she didn't know, and before Amir could speak, Layla said, 'There's no way my parents will let me stay here without them, I'm moving too.'

All the while she talked, she said nothing about the two of them, and Amir wondered if he had even been factored into her plans, if she had even considered him, and when she finished talking, the only thing he could think to do was propose.

He said, 'I don't have a ring, I haven't bought one yet, this isn't planned, but I've been thinking about it for a while, doesn't it make sense? We both go so well together, we could carry this on, could do the thing that no one else does, and if we're married, if I was your husband, then you could stay here with me, because why would your parents say no then? It makes sense, doesn't it? What are we doing? Why are we just pretending that this isn't it, that we're not endgame?'

The desperation in his voice was sharp, clear, and he knew that he should stop speaking, he knew he shouldn't have spoken. Wasn't it obvious that she had made up her mind, that she had already decided?

Layla was quiet, looking down at her hands, fingers squirming over one another, thick worms in mud, and the two of them, sitting in a Nando's booth of all fucking places, waiter arriving with their food, sliding the plates across the table, brown chicken in front of them both, but Amir could only see her. Layla, silent, picking at her food. Amir asked her, 'Could you say something? Do you have anything to say about what I've just said?' Layla said, 'No, I'm not going to marry you,' the air tight around Amir, hard to breathe. 'Why not?' he said. 'Why not?' She said, 'Aren't we both a bit too young to be thinking about getting married? This isn't the right thing to do, this isn't the way, I'm moving with them, and maybe this is a good thing, really, maybe we've run our course, maybe this was coming to an end.' 'Not for me,' Amir said, 'not for me, I fucking love you.' 'Lower your voice,' Layla said, her head turning to the line of people at the tills, and Amir almost threw his plate then. 'Don't tell me to lower my fucking voice when you're the one ending this, breaking up with me.' 'I'm not breaking up with you,' Layla said, meeting his eyes finally, 'I'm just saying that we're done and it's felt like that for a while, you can't tell me it hasn't felt like that for you, we're not the same, not like we used to be, and that's okay, no one is to blame for that, not me, not you, but I don't think we should be holding onto whatever this is, fighting for it, just because it's been four years.' 'Just four years,' Amir repeated, and he laughed then, cold, bitter, 'just four years, just four years of being in love with you, just four years,' and Layla started talking more, about how it had meant a lot to her too, she wasn't trying to trivialise the time, only that it didn't mean that they should hold onto something that was no longer working, but Amir was done, 'I'm not listening to this shit,' he said, pushing himself up and leaving, not looking back at her as he moved past the people and out of the restaurant, and when Layla texted him that night, asking him if they could talk, he didn't reply, and when she called him, he didn't pick up, just listening to the voicemail after, eleven seconds of her asking him not to let her leave like this, and the day she left, Amir stayed at home, fists curled, eyes wet.

Eighteen

Bilal called as Amir and Zain were walking back to Zain's house, on the edge of the city centre, near the Cineworld on Broad Street, which he shared with three friends from his degree. Amir had met these friends a handful of times, but he didn't enjoy spending time with them. They, unlike Zain, seemed uninterested in Amir, asking him questions about authors, films that he'd never heard of, the low hum of soft music, guitars and hushed voices in the background. 'How do you spend time with them?' Amir had asked Zain the last time he had been in Zain's house, listening to two of his flatmates talk about a play, Chekhov something, in the kitchen, and Zain had said, 'They just have a different thing going on, that's all,' and Amir had wondered then if Zain thought he was an idiot too.

Amir reached for his phone, saw the name on the screen, debated whether to pick up.

'Yo,' Amir said.

'Where are you?'

Amir bit back the urge to hang up. 'I'm in town, what's up?'

'When are you coming home?'

'I'm with my friend,' Amir said, glancing at Zain, who was looking ahead, pretending not to hear the conversation.

'Can you come back now? I've got some news.'

'News about what?'

Bilal took in a breath, 'I've just got something to tell you, I want to tell you in person, before I tell Mum and Dad.'

Amir's chest tightened. 'What is it?' he asked. 'What's wrong?'

'Nothing is wrong, just, will you be home soon?'

'Something is wrong,' Amir said, 'otherwise you wouldn't be calling me like this.'

'Fuck,' Bilal said. He swore so rarely, it was as if he slipped into a different language. 'Okay, fine,' Bilal said, 'I'll just tell you, I wanted to tell you in person but, fuck it, fine, I'm getting married.'

Amir stopped walking, Zain was a few steps ahead of him before he stopped too, turning to Amir, questions in his eyes, raised eyebrows.

'Who the fuck are you getting married to?'

'Oh, thanks,' Bilal said, half laughing, 'that's nice.'

'No,' Amir said, 'I mean, I'm just, is this someone that Mum and Dad picked for you?' he asked.

'No,' Bilal said, 'it's someone from work, we've been seeing each other for a while, it's serious, I want to marry her, so I'm telling Mum and Dad today.' He stopped for a moment, took a breath. 'And I want you to be there, today, when I tell them.'

Amir glanced at Zain, who was still looking at him, waiting for answers. 'Okay,' Amir said, 'I'll head back now, I'll be there in an hour, I think.' Zain's eyebrows furrowed at him, and Amir shook his head.

'Get an Uber, I'll pay for it,' Bilal said.

'I'll just get the bus—'

'Get an Uber, I'll pay for it,' Bilal said again, firm, and then, after a moment, he said, 'thank you.'

'It's fine,' Amir said. Then Bilal hung up, and silence roared in Amir's ears, his face hot.

'Is everything good?' Zain asked, stepping towards Amir.

'Yeah, fine, just some family shit, you know how it is,' Amir said, and then, 'my brother's getting married.'

'I heard,' Zain said, 'mad.'

'Yeah, mad,' Amir said, 'he wants to tell our parents, so I gotta go.'

'Of course,' Zain said, pulling Amir in for a half-handshake, half-hug. 'I'll see you later, though, yeah, we'll figure something out.'

Zain turned to head towards his house, Amir watching him disappear before ordering an Uber, some guy who looked like he could be Amir's uncle, Ali, coming to get him in four minutes.

Nineteen

Amir's mother's, face cracked open in a huge smile, hands to her mouth, eyes wide, filled with tears, when Bilal told her the news. Amir had never seen her as happy, like a cartoon come to life, and when she stood to give Bilal a hug, holding him tight, she broke down, crying, unintelligible as she muttered things into his shoulders, and he held her back, laughing, and there were tears in his eyes too.

When their mother finally let go of Bilal, their father stood and hugged him too, tight, quick, and he joked how they had all been a little bit worried there for a while, because why wouldn't a young, good-looking man like him want to get married? he asked, fingers on Bilal's chin, gently pulling, they had all thought something was wrong, and even though none of them said it, it hung in the air, their fear of him being gay, and Amir held his tongue, didn't say it, didn't say anything. Bilal was perfect, of course this wedding was going to be perfect, let's sit down and think about timings, when shall we do the nikah? Would he want to do everything or just little bits here and there? Who should we invite? What are her family like? When can we meet them?

How quickly his father had forgotten all the ways in which Bilal was a disappointment.

She, the woman Bilal was marrying, Momina, was related to the family already. Not by blood, Bilal said, grinning, but by marriage, a distant cousin of theirs married to a distant cousin of hers. 'Isn't that funny?' he said to their mother, who agreed, 'Yes, yes, that is so funny, maybe we were at the same wedding together, how did you meet her?' so Bilal told them the story, how they'd both gone to a diversity meeting at work where their bosses had talked about ways to make the company better for all kinds of people, how Bilal and Momina had both volunteered to be on a committee to make recommendations for the company, how they had gone out for dinner to discuss the work, ended up talking for a long time about everything but the work, how the hours had stretched behind them, how he had fallen in love with her the second he had sat down at that table, menus laid out in front of them but neither of them looking away from each other, how they had been dating for a while now, two years, they wanted to make sure things were serious before they brought each other to their parents, and they were serious, he wanted to marry her, she wanted to marry him, she was telling her parents about him right now, and all the while he spoke, Amir felt sick, bitterness coating the back of his throat.

It was after, after they had talked about everything that their mother could think of, after she had reached over and touched Bilal's stomach, told him he had to stop losing weight now, he was going to look too thin at the wedding, run her hands through his hair, which had always been too long for her liking, telling him that he needed to get it cut properly, and maybe he should get his beard looked at, she didn't like the way he just let it grow like this, he could shape it, but what was she talking about, it was all too early to start thinking about those things yet, that Amir said, 'I can show you how to shape your beard,' and the room turned to look at him, three pairs of eyes landing on him, his mother looking at him like she had forgotten he was even there, his father blank, Bilal slightly confused, eyes falling to Amir's untouched stubble, and Bilal had laughed, said, 'Yeah, of course,' and their mother had asked, 'Are you happy for your brother?'

'Yeah,' Amir said, 'of course I am,' and he looked away from Bilal, the clear joy radiating from him. Jealousy raged in him, crashing, violent against his insides. 'I'm really happy for him, he met someone he loves and he wants to marry her,' Amir said, smiling at his mother in a way that he hoped was convincing, 'why wouldn't I be happy for him? I'm excited to see her,' and his father looked at Amir then, distrust in his eyes, and Amir didn't blame him, because even he didn't believe what was coming out of his own mouth.

'Me too,' their mother said, and she turned back to Bilal, started talking about when they might possibly meet Momina, both families should meet now, she said, it was only right, they could do it this weekend if Momina wanted to, would that be too early? And Bilal laughed, told her that he didn't know how the conversation had gone on her end but he thought that should be fine, and he reached for his phone to see if there were any updates, but there was nothing, not yet, he told their mother, 'But, yeah, we want both families to meet immediately, maybe they can come here,' and their mother said, 'Absolutely, that's what's right, they have to come here because we're the boy's family,' and then she turned her attention to their father, 'we'll have to get some clothes made, do you think Mumtaz can get everything quickly?' and their father said, 'Of course he can, we've known him for so long, once we tell him why, he'll do whatever we ask,' and their mother started preparing plans for Momina and her family as if they were a delegation from a foreign country, the food she would make, the clothes she would wear, she started talking about cleaning the windows, she hadn't cleaned them in so long, 'Maybe,' she said, thinking out loud, to herself more than anyone else, 'we can get that guy from down the road to come and clean them, you know, the one that's always around, asking people if they want their windows cleaned? And we know him, he won't charge too much.'

When Amir walked out of the room no one noticed, and when he went to his room, he closed the door softly, his breathing heavy.

Twenty

Farrah was already there when Amir arrived, sitting in one of the booths, on her phone, her head tilting up when Amir stood by the booth, her face shifting when she realised it was him, taking her headphones out.

'I didn't think you were going to text,' she said, holding onto her glass of Coke, black and fizzing.

'Why not?' Amir asked.

'Because it's been over a week since I gave you my number and nothing, I just thought, I don't know, that you were only talking to me because Mohsin said something.'

'That thing about me being a good boy.'

Farrah laughed, shook her head, 'He's an idiot,' she said.

'Mohsin just says that because I still live with my parents.'

'I bet your mum tells everyone that you're a good boy because of that.'

'I don't think my mum has ever told anyone I was a good boy.'

'Oh,' Farrah said, arms on the table, 'and why wouldn't she say that?'

'Because I stay out late and I don't tell her where I'm going and she always wants to know where I am.'

'That's not the worst thing, is it? Some parents don't even care where their kids are, it's nice that she cares enough to worry.'

'I guess,' Amir said. 'But it can also be real stifling.'

'That's just South Asian mothers, though.'

'Is yours like that?'

'My mum?' Farrah asked, Amir nodded. 'No, she's not like that, me and my sister,' she tilted her head, took a second, 'it's not that we grew up by ourselves, we live close to my grandmother, my mum's sister and her kids too, but she was always busy, Mum, always out campaigning, volunteering, she's always been very into politics.'

'Why?' Amir asked.

'Why what?'

'Why is she like that? Why does she care so much?' he said.

'Don't your parents?'

Amir laughed, sharp, 'No, my parents don't care about politics like that, my dad doesn't even vote, my mum does it for him, she gets the postal vote sent to our house and she fills it in for him, my brother is the one who cares about that stuff, he's always going on about the environment, the government, all the atrocities of the world.'

'He'd get along with my mum,' Farrah said, 'what does he do?'

'He works at a tech company,' Amir said, and when she looked at him, waiting for more, he said, 'I don't know what he does, really, he doesn't talk about his work.'

'Oh,' she said, her disappointment clear on her face but brief, gone quickly, 'but he's interested, that's good, it's good for people like us to be engaged.'

'People like us?'

'Young people, brown people, Muslims, I don't know, it's good for us to be engaged, I think it's too easy these days to become disengaged from the entire thing, you know? When everything is so bad, you start accepting that it's always going to be this bad, you just move through your life without thinking that it can be changed, because you don't know that it can be, and why would we? We're, what? Just twenty now, and we've already lived through a recession, houses are impossible to buy, everything is mad expensive, the government seems like its only aim is to make life as hard for us as possible, they're constantly raising the age that we can retire, cutting services, why would any of us think that there was a way out? So it's good that he's engaged.'

She sounded like Bilal, Amir thought, as he listened to her, but when Bilal talked like this, Amir's brain turned itself off, he left the room as quickly as possible, but with Farrah, it all seemed so obvious to him, right there, staring him in the face.

'Anyway,' Farrah said, 'my mum was always busy with that, and my dad was busy with his job, so we spent a lot of time with my grandmother and my aunty.' Farrah toyed with her glass, looking down into it. 'Sometimes,' she said, 'I wondered why she never wanted to be around us, it wasn't that she ever said it, and she came to everything she could, parents' evenings and stuff, but on the daily, she wasn't really there, and it's not that, I don't know, it's not that it ever felt like she didn't love us, but that she loved her work more.' She looked up, out the window, and for a second tears hovered on the edge of her eyes, but then she laughed, and they were gone.

They sat in silence, Amir watching her, Farrah looking away, until he said, 'My brother's getting married.'

'Oh,' Farrah said, turning her eyes back on him, 'that's exciting.'

'Well,' Amir said, 'weddings aren't really my thing.'

'Not even your brother's?' Farrah asked, and before Amir could speak, she said, 'I think it's nice, to get to celebrate the people you love in this big way,' running her fingers over the glass, tracing lines in the condensation. 'When is it?' she asked.

'Next year.'

'Plenty of time to figure out how you're feeling about it,' she said.

Another silence fell on them then, Farrah looking down at her drink, Amir looking at her. Then he said, 'What were you looking at, when I got here? You were looking at your phone.'

'Nothing,' she said, reaching for her phone, 'just some film stuff.'

'Tell me about it,' Amir said.

'Oh,' she said, this time surprised, 'it's just about the writers' strike in Hollywood.' Amir shook his head at her, waited for her to keep talking. 'All kinds of writers, film, TV, they're striking because they don't get paid as much as they should and there's a lot that's threatening their jobs, like AI and healthcare, it's all anyone in class is talking about.'

'Are they striking here too, the writers?'

'No, no,' she said, 'not yet anyway, they might, I don't know, it's only in America for now, but the strike means that nothing can get made, so everyone is sort of panicked, a lot of people aren't getting paid because of it, which, on one hand, is the whole point, that the industry is so precarious that if we don't sort it out, people are just going to be poor while they're working, but on the other hand, a lot of people are angry that the writers are striking when there are a lot of other people that don't get paid well either.'

'Because everything is fucked for everyone.'

'Because everything is fucked for nearly everyone,' she said, 'not the big guys at the top.'

'When has that ever not been true?' Amir asked. Farrah laughed, empty. 'Does it make you not want to work in film anymore?'

'What, the strike?' she asked, he nodded. 'No, it makes me want to work in it even more, we need more people like me, like us, to be there, to get in, to make the decisions, no, I want to get in there and change it.'

'Big job,' Amir said.

'It is,' she said, letting out a small breath, 'and I don't know, sometimes, I think about how hard it's going to be, like, I'm here, at the University of Birmingham, right, doing a film degree, but it's not the best school for the subject, it's not the best place for connections or the funding, it's not a name, so when I finish my degree, I'm going to have to work so hard, move to London, try to become a runner or an assistant or something shit, and sometimes it just feels like it's not fair that I have to work so hard to do something that I love so much, surely that should be enough? It should be enough that I love it so much, because that's the way it is for other people, they decide that they want to be a director or a writer or a producer and their parents know all of these powerful people who give them a job, get them into the room, while you and I, we're on the outside, banging on the door, trying to get in, and it's exhausting, I'm only twenty, I'm not even old, but I don't know, sometimes it feels like maybe I should listen to my parents and become a lawyer or a doctor or a teacher.'

'Nah,' Amir said, and the forceful way in which he said it made her eyes widen, 'there's no fucking way you think that, I've known you for five minutes and I know that's not you.'

'I mean, I do sometimes—'

'Nah,' Amir said again, shaking his head, leaning in closer, closing the gap between them, 'maybe you think that at the hard times, when shit feels like it's too much and it'll be easier to quit, but if it was easier to quit, you would have done it already, you wouldn't be sat here, reading an article about a strike in a country you don't even live in, you wouldn't know all the stuff you know, nah, nah, you're in it right until the bitter end, and you're going to make it, I can tell.'

Farrah smiled, eyebrows together, as if she was trying to work something out. 'You're not entirely wrong,' she said.

'I'm not wrong,' Amir said, 'at least, not about this shit.'

Twenty-one

Amir's uncle came around to the house three days after Bilal announced his engagement. Amir heard him downstairs, talking to Amir's mother, asking her what was on the menu today, and then, 'I hear we have news to celebrate,' and Amir's mother laughed, said, 'How do you know?' and Amir's uncle said, 'Don't worry about me, I know everything, where is he?' and Amir's mother said, 'At work,' and Amir's uncle said, 'Ah, fuck, of course,' and Amir's mother chided him for swearing in her house, and then his uncle asked about Amir, and his mother said, 'Upstairs, as always,' her voice heavy, 'where else is that boy going to be?' and then Amir heard his uncle climb the stairs, the heavy sound of his boots, because, unlike everyone else who walked through the house, Amir's uncle never took his off, saying, 'I'm just coming and going, why would I take them off?' and when he slammed open Amir's door, Amir looked at him, pulling up his duvet.

'What do you want?' Amir asked.

'Is that any way to greet your uncle?' his uncle said, reaching for the duvet. 'Come, we're going.'

'Going?' Amir said, exposed, quickly reaching for a shirt to pull on. 'Going where?'

'Out,' his uncle said, 'come on, quick, let's go, let's go.'

His uncle backed out of the room, went downstairs, and Amir got up from his bed, glanced at the time, just gone ten, this was late for his mother, who expected him to be up at seven every morning, as if he was still a child who needed to be made ready for school.

Amir changed into a shirt and trackies, and when he went downstairs, his mother and uncle were in the kitchen, his mother standing by the hob, a cup of tea in hand, his uncle standing, a cup in his hand too, and when Amir entered the room, both stopped talking and turned to him.

His mother gave him a look, wanting to ask him what time he called this, what he had planned for the day, was he going to go out that night, but she kept all the questions back, because there was another person in the house, and she couldn't bring herself to admit that not everything in the house was under her control.

Amir walked past her to the bathroom, closed the door, brushed his teeth, washed his face, ran his fingers through his hair, a little longer than he liked, but he'd leave it for now, and then brushed his facial hair, the beard that wasn't trimmed, wasn't cut neatly, the beard that was just hanging onto his face as if he had fallen onto the floor of his barber's and left the hairs where they stuck. There was a time, when Layla was around, when Amir had groomed his facial hair, nothing too much, but he cleaned his neck and his cheeks, shaved straight lines, made himself look good for her, but now, well, what was the point?

'Alright, let's go,' his uncle said when Amir emerged, downing his tea in one gulp and then heading out. Amir followed him.

Three years earlier, his uncle had been in a car accident. Not his fault, as he kept telling everyone, 'Hands up, swear to God, not my fault,' and it hadn't been his fault, he'd been parked at a traffic lights, waiting for the red to turn green, cigarette hanging from his lips, and a youth had rammed his car right into his uncle, who'd got whiplash, unable to turn his neck left or right for a week or two after the event. The car had to be written off, the insurance paying him what the car was owed, which happened to be more than he had originally paid for it. 'Such are the times,' Amir's father had said, when he'd heard the news, but offered no further insight into the matter. That same week, his uncle had bought the same lottery ticket he'd bought every week since his father had died, his father's birthday and the day that he died, and he'd won ten grand. That and the insurance money came to just over fifteen grand, and though Amir's mother and father had told him to save the money, invest it in something, set it aside for the future, his uncle had gone and bought himself a VW Golf, automatic, he told everyone, it had a sports mode, a smart screen in the middle of the car, didn't need a key to start, and when he first drove it to Amir's house, showing Amir all the features, guiding him through the car as if they were in a showroom, his uncle turned into a child again, giddy with excitement.

Now, the car was nothing to his uncle. Grimy on the outside, greasy on the inside, used but not cared for.

Amir got in, trying not to choke on the smell of weed and pizza, his uncle a delivery driver for a pizza shop, spending all the hours of the late afternoon, evening, night picking up cardboard boxes of food, settling them on the passenger side, driving to people's houses, walking up to doors, knocking, waiting, barely glanced at when whoever was inside took the food from him. He'd been delivering pizzas for years now, carrying cash with him in the early days, coins clinking in his bag, but not anymore, everything done online, small beeps from the machine inside the restaurant indicating a new order, so all he had to do was get there, hand the food over and drive back. It was easier, he told Amir, not needing to interact with anyone. Like a ghost, Amir thought, like he didn't exist.

'Where are we going?' Amir asked, unbuckling the seatbelt from underneath him and pulling it over himself. His uncle sat on his, hated the way seatbelts felt over his body, so he never wore one, Amir's mother telling him off for it, 'It'll take just one,' she told him, 'just one crash,' and after the car accident, she had refused to get in his car unless he wore a seatbelt, which meant she was never in his car.

'I found this place,' his uncle said, car started, taking off quickly, too quickly, Amir's body pulled back by the force, 'you'll understand when I get there, it's good,' his uncle said.

'Okay,' Amir said, waiting for more, but more didn't come. 'So, you heard about Bilal,' he said.

'You met her yet, this girl he's marrying?'

'Nah, not yet,' Amir said, 'they're thinking about getting the families to meet soon.'

'Makes sense, why wait around?'

'Yeah, why wait?' Amir said. He looked out the window, familiar streets rushing past. He tried to figure out their route but they could be headed anywhere, The Fort, Star City, maybe even out of the city.

'I'm glad for him,' Amir's uncle said, 'it's good that he's getting married, for a while there, I think we were all a bit worried,' he said, laughing, nudging Amir, the same hand that used to rest on the gear stick now free to do whatever it wanted. Amir laughed back. 'Nah, I'm joking, he's a good guy, your brother, I'm glad that he found someone, how long have they been together?'

'A couple of years,' Amir said.

'Must have been a while if they're serious about getting married, see, that's one thing that's changed these days, back in the day, you didn't need all this getting-to-know-each-other bullshit, you just got married to someone and you made it work.'

'Or not,' Amir said, glancing at his uncle, who was facing straight ahead.

'Or not,' his uncle said, hand a touch tighter on the wheel, 'but, mostly, you made it work, people wanted to be married, people wanted to have families with each other, you know? Now, it's like, oh, okay, this isn't working out before we even live together, before we even mean something to each other, let's just quit it and see what else is out there, because there's all this distraction out there, you know, like, all this stuff,' his uncle said, gesturing to his phone, which sat on the dashboard, screen black, 'and, man, I don't know, more and more now, I see our girls marrying white men, black men, even other Asian men, like Chinese and shit, I don't know what it is, maybe they see us as too much like their dads, but you know what I think?' he asked, Amir saying nothing, 'I think that they think they're better than us.'

His uncle glanced at Amir, car coming to a stop in front of traffic lights. 'Oh, yeah,' Amir said, 'why?'

'They go to their universities now, get their degrees, have their good jobs, and think that they're worth more than we can give them, right? That's what's going on, that's what's always going on, so I'm glad for your brother, glad he got someone,' his uncle said, and then, arm reached out to him, wrapped around his shoulders, pulling him closer, 'it'll be your turn soon, don't you worry, and if we can't find you someone like he did, we'll just get you married off to some cousin back home, you won't go alone, I promise you that.'

Red to green, and the car moved, arm slithering back to where it came from.

His uncle drove towards The Fort, but then stopped far before they reached it, turning into a road and then parking the car. There were three or four shops, none of which Amir could fit into an explanation for why they were there.

'Why are we—'

'Just come,' his uncle said, stepping out of the car, Amir following him, the two of them walking into a TV repair shop, busted TVs littering the floor inside, cracked screens spilling out their guts onto the floor.

A man appeared from the back, face flat, but when his eyes fell on Amir's uncle, he broke into a big smile, opened his arms, and his uncle hugged this man, quickly, and then they started talking, quickly, in Urdu, too fast for Amir to keep up with, Urdu one of those things that he looked like he should have access to, and once upon a time, he did, he and Bilal both able to communicate with the older members of their family, some who couldn't speak English and some who refused to, the elders smiling down on the two of them, ruffling their heads, saying to their parents, 'Aren't these such wonderful boys that you have?' but then Bilal went to university, and Amir stopped speaking at those places, stopped speaking Urdu, fell out of touch with the language, and now, even though Bilal was the one who disappeared, he was the one who could still speak it and Amir could only fumble with it, clumsy tongue.

The man went into the back and Amir's uncle followed him, Amir in tow. If the front of the shop was where TVs came after they were wounded, the back was where they were finished off. The empty remnants of them were strewn everywhere, and Amir could see that there was a table in the middle, light hanging over it, TV lying flat on the surface, in surgery, he thought, could imagine the man standing over it, poking and prodding at the thing, delivering the news to the TV's wife, to its children, that it never made it.

'Here?' his uncle asked, and the man nodded, and Amir's uncle turned to a pile of boxes, small electronic parts were spilling out of them. 'Grab one,' Amir's uncle said to him, so Amir did, the small box far heavier than he thought it should be. 'Back to the car,' his uncle said, so they walked back through the shop, towards the car, his uncle opening the boot, one-handed, and they put in the two boxes. Then they did it again, and again, and again, until the boot and the back of the car were overflowing with the boxes, electronic boards, green with circuitry racing through them.

They drove back to Amir's grandmother's house, where his uncle still lived, having never moved out. His uncle threw him the keys, and Amir unlocked the front door, stepping in. He breathed in, the smell of his grandmother, of his childhood, embedded in these walls. He said hello as he walked in, but there was no reply. 'She's out,' his uncle said, giving him a box. 'To the front room,' he said, and they started to unload the car, into the front room, his uncle passing him box after box after box.

Once they were done, Amir covered in sweat, the boxes heavy, and far too many of them, and his uncle had given him the harder part of the job, climbing the stairs into the house, down the hallway, into the front room, bending down to put the box on the floor, and then going back and doing the same thing over and over, while his uncle just stood by the car, box in hand, waiting for Amir, his uncle said, 'You hungry?'

'Yeah, starving,' Amir said.

So they left, locking the door behind them, his uncle pulling on the handle of his car to check that too was locked, and then they walked down the road, taking a right at the crossroads, past Dixy, past the fish-and-chip shop that used to be named Salim's, but ownership had changed, so the name had changed too, and they headed right towards Greggs, the only white-owned shop on the road.

Amir sat at one of the tables, his uncle getting them tuna sandwiches, two bottles of Coke and two biscuits for after, sliding Amir's across the table at him.

'Are you going to tell me now?' Amir asked.

'Yes,' his uncle said through three bites of the sandwich, his mouth full of food. Three weeks ago, he said, the TV in his room had stopped working, and he'd had the TV for a while, so he couldn't just go to the shop and complain about it, and besides, he wasn't sure if he had bought it or if his friend had given it to him, so he went online and tried to find out how to fix it, and after watching several videos, he realised the problem wasn't with the IR receptor, as he'd originally thought, but the motherboard. Something wasn't connecting, he said to Amir, putting his fingers together, so he had looked up the motherboard of the TV, couldn't find it on the official retailer's website but found it being sold by someone who'd clearly owned the same TV, so he'd bought it, and the seller, a decent guy, his uncle said, had told him how to fix the motherboard, so his uncle waited the three days for it to turn up and then dismantled his TV, a crazy scientist in his room, and when he'd put the motherboard in the first time, it hadn't worked, but he'd realised he hadn't connected a wire, so he went back in, and the second time it was as if it had never broken. 'So that got me thinking,' his uncle said, 'there must be loads of people who have old TVs who can't get the right shit for them because the companies have moved way on, they're, what, releasing new TVs every six months now?' so he'd gone on the hunt for a TV repair shop, and found this one, run by a man who turned out to be a cousin of a friend of Amir's uncle, and so Amir's uncle had asked him, did he have these motherboards? And the man had said yes, of course he did, but he threw them away at the end of the month, they were of no use to him, he had no space for them, and so Amir's uncle had asked, 'Do you know which ones are broken and which are fixed?' and the man said no but he could start to separate them, if Amir's uncle wanted, and so they had done it together, the two of them, late at night, talking about Amir's uncle's friend, about Pakistan, about the TV shop, how business was going, about the man's children, and Amir's uncle went back every night to sort through them, and now he had them.

'So now what?' Amir asked. 'How do you sell them?'

'Well,' his uncle said, grinning, 'that's where you come in, you and I are going to sort through all of those motherboards, take photos, tag them properly and put them online, and then the sales will come through, done, done, done.'

Amir picked at his sandwich, took a bite of it, looked out of the window to avoid looking at his uncle.

The first business idea Amir remembered his uncle coming up with was the garage. 'I can fix cars,' he told everyone, 'I've been doing it for years.' There was some truth to that. Amir's grandfather had been an avid car enthusiast, getting underneath his car and his van often, fixing small things here and there. He had taught Amir and Bilal how to change tyres, how to check the oil, how to replace the brake pads. 'Standard stuff,' he told them, 'that you should absolutely know before you buy a car.' Amir's uncle claimed to be the same sort of car enthusiast, but it was clear to the family that he just wanted his father to take him seriously.

So he'd decided a garage would be it, and he'd found the right place for it, and he'd managed to save up some money to pay for the first year of the garage, and the man who was renting it to him left all the tools there, he told everyone, so he didn't need to pay for those, but maybe one day he would buy his own. This, he told everyone, would be what he'd pass down to his children one day, that he would build it into an empire, maybe two or three of them across Birmingham, who knew?

He ran out of money in the third month, and by the fifth month he had given up on it, handing the garage back to the owner, who at least, kindly, gave him back half of the money he had paid at the very beginning. Amir's uncle had told everyone it wasn't the market for a garage, even as Bilal asked, 'But doesn't everyone have cars?' and they decided not to talk about it again.

The second idea came a couple of years after, a fish-and-chip shop that would also do kebabs and burgers and anything else unhealthy and deep-fried. Again, he found a place. Again, he paid up front, only six months this time, and told everyone only after he had signed the paperwork. This time, he decided to involve some of his friends in the matter, said that this would be their fortune, that they would branch out, franchise. It took four months this time before he had to give up, unable to afford to continue, suppliers not happy with his asking for more credit than they would give people they had worked with for a long time, let alone some young stranger who had decided, on a coin toss, that he wanted to own a fish-and-chip shop. This time, the man he had rented the place from didn't give him any of his money back.

The third idea came not from Amir's uncle but from a friend of his. 'A gym,' his friend said, 'don't you think? Someplace where men can work out and not think about women, a place where we can all come together and just be,' and so Amir's uncle, who had never stepped foot in a gym in his life, maybe at secondary school, maybe he had run around the football pitch a couple of times, maybe he had toyed with basketball and tennis, maybe he had flirted with badminton, but as an adult, it was as foreign a place to him as Iceland or Greenland or Finland, said yes, that absolutely made sense, let's do it, so he took what was left of his money, and he invested it into this gym, and he proudly told people that he was a co-owner, even as the photos that were put up on the walls were of three men who were not Amir's uncle, even as his name was nowhere to be found, even as they made decisions on monthly plans and discounts and classes without him. 'I don't have to pay to go to it,' he told people, and he did so with the look of a man who knew he had been conned, a man who knew he couldn't get his money back even if he tried.

It had been a while since the gym, and Amir's uncle had no more ideas, spending his days meeting his friends in the late morning and early afternoon before going to his job in the evenings. Maybe he had given up, Amir had thought, as time had passed and there was no more news, no mention of money or investment.

Now, here they were, Amir and his uncle, sitting on the floor of Amir's grandmother's front room, picking up a motherboard, looking for a serial number, putting it into a website, which would find exactly what sort it was, copying and pasting that information to another website, taking several photos of the motherboard, then reaching for packing tape, the sort that could be written on with a Sharpie, and so they wrote, endless serial numbers, and they put the motherboards into boxes, as organised as they could be, and when they were done, what had seemed like an ungodly mess before had now become something clean, something that they could search through if they wanted.

As they stood there, admiring the day's work, his uncle's phone went off, and he checked it, frowning for a moment and then grinning, turning the phone to Amir. 'First sale,' he said.

Twenty-two

Bilal was sitting in the living room when Amir walked in, laptop open, TV on low, because Bilal didn't like it when it was too quiet in the house when it was just him. When he saw Amir, he stood up, as if he'd been waiting for him, and when Amir saw the look on his face, he knew that he had, braced himself for whatever was about to come out of his mouth.

Bilal hovered for a second, then sat back down, and Amir mirrored him, opposite, waiting.

Bilal, coming to Amir's parents' evenings when Amir was younger, when Bilal was over the age of eighteen, coming ready with an excuse about why their parents couldn't be there, too busy with work, a death in the family, whatever came to his mind that day, because their mother had decided, for those three years that Bilal was at university, that she was no longer going to be a mother, spending her time at her parents' house, a few minutes' walk down the road, leaving just Amir and his father at home, coming to the house sporadically, mostly when Bilal came back, a weekend here, a week there, to see him, but the moment he was gone, she was gone too. Bilal, passing an eye over Amir's homework when he was back, signing detention papers, having the hard conversations with Amir's teachers about his behaviour over the phone. So Amir was used to this, used to Bilal standing in the place of their parents, and sometimes he thought it was because of the age gap between them, six years was a long time, of course he would act like Amir's guardian, it was only natural, but sometimes Amir thought it was just because Bilal liked being able to tell Amir what to do, and Amir wished he fucking wouldn't.

'I want you to meet her, Momina, before Mum and Dad do,' Bilal said.

'Why?' Amir asked.

'Because I think it would be good for you to get to know her,' Bilal said, voice low with hurt, 'and because she really wants to meet you.'

'You've told her about me?' Amir asked, hard to imagine Bilal spending any time talking to Momina about him, and even harder to imagine that Bilal talked about him on good terms.

'Of course I've told her about you,' Bilal said, and there it was, that confused look on his face like he didn't quite understand the parameters of the conversation they were having.

'I can do this weekend,' Amir said.

'Okay,' Bilal said, eyes on his laptop, as if it might hold some answers, 'I'll let her know, maybe we can go get some food or something.' He looked up at Amir, waiting for him to say something, but Amir didn't. 'It'll be good,' Bilal said, 'it'll be good,' and Amir didn't know if he was trying to convince him or himself.

'Yeah, for sure,' Amir said, and he stood, walked to the

kitchen, opened the fridge, even though he wasn't particularly hungry, it had gotten late enough with Adnan that day that the two of them had gone out for food, Adnan reaching out to Amir to stop him from paying, 'Don't disrespect me, put that away,' Amir's wallet disappearing back into his pocket.

'You good?' Bilal asked, following Amir, hovering at the edge of the kitchen.

'What do you mean?' Amir asked, staring into the fridge, at the small Tupperware boxes that his mother had lined it with, different curries sitting in each one.

'Are you doing okay?' Bilal said. 'You seem a bit …' He trailed off.

'I'm fine, man,' Amir said, stepping away from the fridge, closing it without taking anything out, 'I'm just tired, uni is hard this year.'

'Second year,' Bilal said, eyes lighting up, because this he understood, 'it's tough, I hear you, first year felt like a breeze to me but then second year came and it felt like I was speaking a different language to my lecturers.'

'Yeah, exactly,' Amir said, not looking at Bilal, just watching his warped reflection in the grey door of the fridge.

'You'll get through it, though, you'll find your rhythm, everyone does, it's hard but once you just push past it, everything will start making sense to you, you'll find your groove.'

'Yeah, absolutely,' Amir said.

'If you ever need help with shit like that, just tell me, I know that engineering and philosophy are nowhere near the same, but if you want, I can read through essays, help you with studying for the exams, memory shit, I can do all of that, you know that, right?' Bilal asked, and he reached out to

Amir, one hand on his arm, light, as if he didn't quite know if he should let his weight rest on Amir, who fought the urge to flinch.

'Yeah, thanks. I just need to get my head down and figure it out.'

'Exactly,' Bilal said, big smile, 'you'll be fine.'

Twenty-three

'You fuck her yet?' Mohsin asked Amir, both of them in Mohsin's kitchen, protein shake in Mohsin's hand, him shaking the plastic bottle, small ball tearing up the clumps of powder he'd dumped in there just moments before. Mohsin, wearing a shirt that was barely hanging together, his body exposed through the giant holes on either side.

'Who?' Amir asked, leaning against one of the counters, watching him.

'Farrah,' Mohsin said, and before Amir could say anything, he laughed. 'Don't lie to me, I know you met with her, she told Sana and Sana has the biggest fucking mouth I've ever known, if you know what I mean,' he said, winking at Amir, opening his shake, putting it to his lips.

'I'm not going to fuck her,' Amir said, pulling his eyes away from Mohsin, turning to look out of the windows, at the city, which seemed so small from up here, like one of those model cities from one of those films Amir watched when he was younger.

'Why, what's wrong with her?' Mohsin asked.

'Nothing is wrong with her, I just don't think she's right for me.'

'When has that stopped you before?' Mohsin asked, joining Amir, putting an arm around him, heavy, hot, gulping down the rest of the shake, throat tight, bobbing, wiping his mouth with the back of his hand when he was done.

'She's looking for something else.'

'Fuck her while she tries to find it.'

'Maybe I don't want to.'

Mohsin laughed, surprised. 'Tell me this isn't about Layla.'

Just the mention of her name made Amir tense.

'Because if it is,' Mohsin said, 'then I think we have to have that talk, and I don't think either one of us is going to like having that.'

'It's not about Layla,' Amir said, voice tight.

'Okay, good, because Farrah, she's fit as fuck, you know? I thought that she'd be good for you.' He pulled his arm off Amir, went to the sink, reaching for the sponge to wash the bottle. 'You, the good boy, she, the good girl, you'd be perfect together.'

'I'm not a good boy,' Amir said, closing his eyes for a second, frustrated.

'What my mum would give to have a son like you,' Moshin said, and then added, 'though,' Amir hearing the grin in his voice, 'you are an Alum Rockie so maybe you guys can't be good boys, no matter how hard you try.'

'My brother's doing that,' Amir said, ignoring the last bit.

'Doing what?'

'Being the good son, getting married.'

'Since when?' Mohsin asked, tap turned off, bottle stood up to dry.

'Turns out he's been dating someone for a while, and he wants to marry her now.'

'Muslim?'

'Yeah.'

'Paki?'

'Yeah.'

'Oh, I know your mum is dying over that.'

'She's never been happier.'

'Good for him,' Mohsin said, towel in his hands, brushing it over his face and down his neck. 'You think she'll move in with you guys?'

'Nah,' Amir said. 'I think they'll move, be by themselves.' He had no idea if this was true but, knowing Bilal, the things that he wanted from life, Amir could easily see him moving out, disappearing again, the two of them buying a house close enough that they could come by on the weekends but far away enough that they didn't have to worry about bumping into anyone they knew out and about, far away enough that they could pretend family didn't exist when they didn't want it to. That they were just two people walking around with no other context. How easy it would be, Amir thought, for them to just become two people in the world, no need to be part of anything anymore but themselves.

'You looking forward to that?' Mohsin asked. 'Just you and your parents?'

'Fuck no,' Amir said, 'I'll be gone by then.'

'Oh, yeah, and where are you going?' Mohsin said, walking around Amir, gesturing with a tilt of his head for Amir to follow him into his bedroom.

Amir walked behind him, watching as Mohsin took his shirt off, how his muscles played with one another underneath his skin. 'I don't know,' Amir said, 'but I'm not living with them without him there, it would be fucking awful, she already treats me like I'm a fucking idiot, can you imagine if he wasn't there? The golden son? Nah, I ain't doing that.'

'You should ask him to stay,' Mohsin said, walking over to his dresser, pulling out a shirt, pressing it against his body, deciding against it, reaching for another one. 'Convince him it's the right thing to do, your mum will love that, she'll take care of the baby, whenever it comes, and it's going to come, they always do, and he likes living there, right, at home? That's what you said,' Amir nodded, 'then he should stay there, but you should still move out, you should move in with me next year.'

'What?' Amir asked, not trusting his own ears.

'I mean it,' Mohsin said, facing him, 'I only have this place until the end of the year,' he reached to his side, pushed open the door to the bathroom, turning on the lights, 'I can either extend it to next year or I can get a different place, if you wanted to move in, you could do that, it would be easy.'

Amir stared at Mohsin, finding no words. How was he going to do that? How was he going to afford to live in a place that Mohsin wanted to be in? Amir knew if he said this out loud, Mohsin would wave it away. *Don't worry*, he'd say, *I can pay the rent, you can just help out with the food or bills or whatever*, and when Amir would push the point, that he had no money, that he didn't want to take advantage of his friend, Mohsin would tell Amir that it was his father's money, who cared how Mohsin spent it if his father didn't? And it was the least that his father owed him. *Just do it*, Mohsin would say, *just come and live with me.*

Amir could see it, could see himself living with Mohsin, sharing clothes, going to the gym with him, eating the food he ate, measuring out his protein shakes, wearing his jewellery and his cologne, going to the clubs together, brothers, almost. He wouldn't have to deal with his mother asking him where he was all the time, though he was pretty sure she would still ask him, it would just get easier to ignore her if he wasn't there all the time, and he wouldn't have to be around Bilal and his wife when she moved in, and he wouldn't have to tiptoe around his father. His space would be his space. He could just live the way he wanted to.

She'd never let him leave, though. His mother would rather die than let her other son move out. When Bilal had moved to Durham, she had begged him not to for weeks, Bilal listening as she talked to him, every hour of the day that summer, 'Don't go, you shouldn't go, there are bad things out there, the world isn't made for people like you, like us, you should stay here, where it's safe, why do you want to leave? Why do you want to hurt me and your dad like this? Have we done something to you? What could we possibly have done that is so bad that makes you want to leave us? Is there a girl? Are you leaving for a girl, is that what it is? What is it then? Why do you want to leave?' and Bilal, infinitely more patient than Amir ever was, especially when it came to their mother, told her it had nothing to do with her or their father, he promised, he wanted to go for his education, going to Durham would mean better prospects, a better future, and isn't that what she wanted for him? Didn't she want him to do better than everyone else, not end up like one of his cousins, with dead-end jobs, dying with envy at what everyone else has? Didn't she want him to have the kind of job that meant, one day, he might be able to buy her the kind of house she'd always wanted, and maybe their father wouldn't have to work so hard all the time because Bilal would earn so much money, he could go to Pakistan whenever he wanted? Wasn't that right? And as Amir listened to Bilal spin this world for her, he noticed how he was absent from the image Bilal was creating, and when she finally gave in, told him he should go, he was right, not knowing that Bilal had already confirmed his place there, had already sent all the paperwork over, and when he left, coming back every four weeks, like clockwork, spending every holiday at home, called her every other day and told her about everything that happened in his life, she told everyone how special her son was, going to such a prestigious university, wasn't he so smart? Wasn't he so brilliant? And he loved her so much, he came home all the time, called her constantly, could barely keep away from her, even as she only came back to the house whenever he was back, disappearing the moment he had left again.

But maybe it didn't matter what Amir's mother wanted anymore.

'Just think about it,' Mohsin said, before stepping into the shower, water running, door still open.

Twenty-four

Adnan ordered, in a way that told Amir he came here often, and the guy behind the counter nodded, not writing anything down, and when it came to pay, the guy told Adnan it was on him, don't worry about it, and the way Adnan pulled out his wallet, took out notes, placed them on the counter, slid the money across, told Amir that he had done this before too, that this was a game that they played with one another, an endless back and forth.

The two of them sat in one of the red booths, ripped at the edges where kids had pulled at the fabric with their restless fingers, the table between them wiped down, gleaming in the strong white lights above.

Adnan pulled a phone out of his pocket, an old Nokia, like the one Amir's father had way back in the day, Amir asking him if he could play Snake on it while he waited, when Amir's father took him to the garage when the MOT was due on his car, Amir sitting in the waiting room, trying desperately to get that pixelated snake not to touch its own tail, to eat and to grow until it filled the entire screen, but Bilal was the only one who could get that screen to fill up entirely, square after square eaten until the snake was finally satiated.

Adnan passed it over to Amir, this phone, said, 'This is yours now, this is where shit will come through, I'll call you if I need you, you never call me,' and Amir nodded, holding it in his hand.

'What's first?' Amir asked.

'What's first?' Adnan repeated, but before he could say more, the food arrived, two spicy chicken burgers, Adnan had ordered for Amir, the coating on the breasts red, fries, cans of Coke, wings on the side, sat right next to chilli and mayo and ketchup dips, the kind of food that Amir had grown up on, but he didn't reach for anything, let Adnan start first. It was only when Adnan had pulled some food to himself, when he'd taken a bite, that Amir began too. 'You do what we all did,' Adnan said, mouth full.

'What's that?'

'You sell.'

Amir looked down at the burger in his hands. 'Sell?' he asked, his mind conjuring up all the things he had seen in films and on TV, deals done in the night, hands tight around small bags, handshakes masking the passing of money.

'Yeah, everyone sells first.'

'Is that what you did?'

'Didn't I just say everyone?'

'Ily too?'

'Ily started selling when he was eleven.'

'Eleven?' Amir said, looking up at Adnan, expecting to see a grin.

'Yeah,' Adnan said, putting his burger down, wiping his mouth with a tissue.

'Did you know, that he was selling?'

'Not back then, not for a while, but yeah, he sold, didn't

sit no exams, got no GCSEs to his name, but the fuck does he need them for now? He's made.'

'When did you start?'

Adnan looked at Amir, eyes narrowed, 'What is this,' he asked, 'an interview? You got a wire?'

'Just interested,' Amir said, thinking of himself at eleven, how small he'd been, nine years ago, he couldn't imagine himself standing on the street, selling drugs to grown men.

'Fifteen,' Adnan said, after a second.

Fifteen, around the time Amir had met Layla, how young he had been then too, all that time they had spent together, sitting in the library at school after the final bell had rung, pretending to study, laughing together quietly, walking home, his hand in hers, how safe she'd always say she felt around him, how all the nothingness made sense when she was around.

'Do your parents know?' Amir asked.

'They know,' Adnan said, 'but they don't ask any questions, but why would they? It's a nice life that me and Ily have given them, they don't need to know any more than they do.'

'Are you not worried?'

'Worried about what?'

'Worried that people might find out.'

Adnan laughed, 'And what happens if people find out?'

'I don't know,' Amir said, 'you know what our people are like.'

'Afraid,' Adnan said, 'that's what our people are like, all those white mans on TV, the way they talk about us, that we're fucked up inside, that we're violent, that we like to do crimes, but that's all fucking bullshit, truth is that we're the ones who try so hard not to be like that because it's all we've ever been told, all our parents have ever been told, all our lives, so we try to fit in, but we're never going to be good enough, that's the thing that our parents don't get, but me and you, we get it, right? We understand that we can do all the shit that they want us to do, wear the clothes, talk the right shit, look how they want us to look, and it's never going to be enough, because what they want, really, is for us to be underneath them, that's how they get their fucking kicks, that's how they stay powerful, if we keep believing that we're not worth anything, if we keep fighting their arguments that we're nothing, if they keep us distracted enough, if they make us think we have to spend our whole lives fighting to look good, then we'll never take power away from them, but I'm not going to do that, we're not going to do that.'

'How?' Amir asked.

'By doing this,' Adnan said, spreading his arms wide, 'by taking back control, taking their money, you know how many white mans come to us, giving us their money for something that's so fucking easy to get but they're scared to do it themselves? All the money I have is from white mans, that's what taking power looks like, not just walking down the path that they made for us, hoping that maybe, one day, we might be able to have the job or wear the suit that makes them respect us, nah, that's not the fucking way, this is the fucking way, because at the end of the day, respect is one thing, but power, that's a whole other fucking thing, you get me?'

Adnan's eyes were wide, manic almost. Amir recognised the look in them, the same one that his father got whenever he talked about Pakistan and India, whenever he talked about politics back home, whenever he began his conspiracy speeches, how the British had destabilised the entire world, if it wasn't for them, he would be back home in a country as powerful, maybe even more powerful, than the UK and the US, how Muslims should be respected more, how, in all of them, there was power for more, and hunger for power.

'It's just like women,' Adnan continued.

'What is?' Amir asked, wondering, for a moment, if he had misheard.

'Women,' Adnan said, as if that was answer enough, but the blank look on Amir's face told him it wasn't. 'They've spent all this time, women, yeah, talking about how they want jobs and they want independence and they want their own power, but at the end of the day, what they want, at least the ones who want men, I don't fucking know what the other ones want, they want to come home to a man, and they don't want to just come home to any man, they want to come home to a man who earns more money than them, who fucks them the right way, a real fucking man, not these fucking simps we keep seeing, not the men who lick their arses and say all the right things, going on about being feminists, but they can't admit they want that because now it's bad to admit anything like that, it's bad to admit that you want to be taken care of, that you want a man to hold you up, but there's nothing wrong with that, this feminist shit, I'm telling you, it's gone too far, it's the same shit, the white mans tell us we're too violent so we try hard not to be but that's exactly how we get our power, that's what we're meant to be doing, women tell us that they want men who can talk about their feelings and cry, when what they really want is a man who knows how to be a fucking man, not a man who's fucking confused, but we can't say that we're violent because then we're adding to the narrative, or whatever the fuck, and women can't say that they want a man like that because it's not the right thing to want.'

Adnan stopped for a moment, opened his can, the fizz of it loud, gulped it down, throat convulsing, looked back at Amir. 'You get me, right?' he asked. 'You understand what I'm saying, yeah?'

'Yeah,' Amir said.

'You'll get it,' Adnan said, 'once you start actually paying attention to what's around you.'

Amir said nothing, took a bite of his burger, teeth through the bread, the lettuce, the tomato, the chicken, it all rested on his tongue, a melody of flavours, and he asked, mouth full, 'When do I start?'

'When do you want to start?'

'Right now.'

Adnan laughed. 'Finish your food first.'

Twenty-five

Bilal was tapping his fingers on the steering wheel as he drove, unable to keep still. His nerves came off him in waves, hot and sticky, and they rubbed off on Amir, neither of them talking. The car he was driving belonged to their mother, Bilal was on the insurance just in case he ever needed it, their mother joking, years ago, that she was going to make him drive her around wherever she needed to go, when in truth Bilal barely touched it.

They were meeting Momina in Nando's at Star City, because it was close to them and it was halal and, Bilal added, embarrassed, it was where they went for their first date, outside of anything to do with work, they went to the cinema to watch a superhero film he could barely remember, Momina was into all that kind of shit, and they'd sat at the booth for a long time after their food was finished, empty plates, and the way he talked about it made Amir's chest hollow with longing for Layla.

Momina was already there when they arrived, standing when she saw the brothers walking in, waving them over. She was taller than Amir had imagined, nearly as tall as Bilal, her black hair impossibly straight, like something from an advert, her leaping up from underneath a waterfall, wide smile, shampoo in hand, her face long and thin, and when her eyes landed on Amir, she smiled like they were old friends coming together after years apart, and it occurred to Amir then that she had seen photos of him, that Bilal had told her everything about the family, and it made him feel odd, off kilter, the relationship immediately unbalanced.

'Hey,' Momina said, Bilal kissing her on the cheek, and then she looked right at Amir. 'Hey,' she said again, letting out a small chuckle, 'shall we hug?' she asked, and Bilal looked at Amir, gave him a small nod, encouraging, so Amir said, 'Yeah, sure,' and then they hugged, quickly, Amir stepping away from her almost immediately.

'He's told me so much about you,' Momina said, sitting opposite Amir, Bilal next to her, so that Amir felt as though he was with his parents, celebrating something, or maybe they were about to break some awful news to him, like they were getting divorced, over spicy chicken, the Nando's meant to make the news hit a little sweeter.

'I bet he has,' Amir said, looking at Bilal, whose face had become slightly red, slightly shiny, his hands trembling. He was scared, Amir realised, scared that Amir might say something stupid, like Amir was a dumb fucking kid.

'Nothing bad,' Momina said, 'but I'd rather hear about you from you.'

'You have questions?'

'I have some,' Momina said, laughing, 'but maybe we should order some food first.'

'It's on me,' Bilal said, pushing a menu towards Amir, and though Amir knew what he was getting already, half a chicken, rice, garlic bread, wings, he looked at it as if he'd never been there before, staring at the menu until he heard Momina telling Bilal what she wanted, and then he gave his order too, Bilal taking the menu from him, standing up, leaving to go join the queue.

'How long have you guys been together?' Amir asked, reaching for an easy question. Her eyes, he noticed, were such a dark brown that they almost melted into her pupils.

'I thought I was the one with the questions.'

'I might have some too.'

'Not long,' she said, 'nearly two years.'

'And you're sure that you want to get married to him?'

Amir said it as a joke, but Momina looked at him seriously. 'As sure as I've been about anything,' she said, voice still, 'you sound like you're trying to get me to not.'

'I don't think there's anything I could say to you that would stop you from marrying him.'

'No, there isn't,' she said, 'but I think the better question is why you would say anything like that in the first place.'

'I don't know, I'm the younger brother, isn't this what I'm supposed to be doing?'

'I don't know, I don't have a younger brother.'

'Older?' Amir asked.

'No, I don't have any brothers, only child.'

'Only child,' Amir repeated, and he looked over her shoulder at Bilal, who was looking right at them as he waited, three people ahead of him.

'My parents' favourite child,' Momina said.

'Ha,' Amir said, looking back at her.

'Why did you come?' she asked.

'Come here?' Amir asked, she nodded. 'Because he asked me to.'

'And you always do what he asks you to?'

'No, but I thought this was important, it is important, to him.'

'That we meet?'

'Yeah.'

'So then maybe you should try.'

'Am I not trying?' Amir asked.

'It doesn't seem like you are.'

Irritation pulled at him. 'So why don't you tell me how to try then?' he said.

'I don't know, ask me a question.'

'What kind of question?'

'Anything, ask me anything you want to know.'

'Why are you marrying him?' Amir asked.

'Why am I marrying your brother?' she asked, small chuckle, surprise spilling from her lips. 'That's a big one.' She looked over at him, turned in her booth, then looked back at Amir. 'I guess I'm marrying him because he's a good person and he's kind and he makes me feel loved, and I think that marrying him is going to make me happy, and I know that marriage is hard and filled with compromise, and you shouldn't look to one person for happiness, and I also know that happiness isn't a constant, it's something that comes and something that goes, but I think that your brother is the kind of person who is going to bring a lot of joy to my life, so I guess the answer is that I'm selfish, I'm marrying your brother because I can't bear to think of my life without him.'

She didn't break eye contact with Amir as she spoke, and it twisted his stomach, made him want to crawl up inside of himself. 'Good answer,' Amir said.

'But not the answer that you wanted.'

'It's not about what I want.'

'But it is,' Momina said, leaning a little towards him, laying her arms on the table, 'because our parents will get along, my parents are good people, yours are too, and we're already related,' she said, 'through marriage,' she added, 'a cousin of mine, a cousin of yours,' she said, waving her hand above her head, 'so it's perfect, they'll meet each other and our mums are going to say very nice things about the clothes that they're wearing, my mum will bring a gift, compliment the house, the cooking, our dads will go sit in another room and talk about Pakistan and politics and cricket and try to size each other up, it'll all go fine, but it's you, you're the one that's still a question.'

'Why am I a question?'

'Because you're the younger brother, you're the one I have to win over.'

Amir was filled with the desire to leave, it would be so easy to just stand and walk out of the restaurant, there were so many other things he'd rather be doing, so many other people he'd rather spend his time with. 'So win me over then,' Amir said.

'Okay,' Momina said, 'I'll ask you some questions and all I ask of you is that you answer them honestly.'

'Sure.'

'What are you studying at university?'

'Civil engineering.'

'Do you like it?'

'Enough.'

'Is enough enough?'

'It'll get me a good job at the end of it.'

'And is that enough?'

'What did you do at university?'

'I studied biology.'

'Biology?' Amir asked. 'But you work with him.'

'As a product manager, yeah, it pays more and it's less hours and it's easy to do, so why wouldn't I?'

'Why did you do biology then?'

'I wanted to become a scientist.'

'What happened?'

'I realised that becoming a scientist is hard and I don't want to spend the rest of my life looking at things in vials under microscopes, getting wrapped up in academic bureaucracy, why do you want to do civil engineering?'

'It felt like the right choice.'

'But not now?' Momina said.

'Well,' Amir said, shifting in the booth, pushing himself further back into the fake leather, 'I don't know, I didn't really know what I was going to do at university, just knew that I wanted to do something, that I had to do something.'

'You're in your second year, right?' Amir nodded. 'How are you finding it?'

'Hard.'

'Second year is hard,' Momina said, and it was like Amir was talking to Bilal now, knew this conversation, 'but you just have to work through it,' she said, 'remind yourself of why you're there.'

'Yeah,' Amir said, looking back over at Bilal, who was now standing at the till ordering, gesturing to the menu, taking his wallet out of his pocket, 'I don't know, maybe I'll just end up like you.'

'Working for a tech company?'

'Doing something different.'

147

'What would you like to do?'

'Something that makes me money.'

'Oh,' Momina said, chuckling, 'what kind of money?'

Amir looked back at her, 'A lot of money,' he said, 'the kind of money where my kids' kids don't have to worry about doing anything because they know they have all this money that'll be there forever.'

'That's a lot of money.'

'That's the kind of money I want.'

'And what if you don't get it?' Momina asked. 'What if it doesn't come to you?'

'Then I keep trying.'

'Even if it ruins your life?'

'How would it ruin my life?'

'If all you're doing is thinking about how much money you don't have all the time, it'll ruin your life.'

'All I do is think about money,' Amir said, and Bilal appeared, receipt in his hand, that crisp white paper with black lines running over it.

'What are we talking about?' Bilal asked, slipping into the booth by Momina and shuffling over, Momina moving a little too, so now Amir was facing them in the middle again.

'Nothing,' Amir said.

Twenty-six

When Amir heard his uncle's voice downstairs, he thought of the motherboards in the boxes. He wondered how many his uncle had sold, if he had finally landed on an idea that worked. It didn't take long after hearing his uncle's voice for Amir to hear his footsteps on the stairs, sitting up under his duvet, his day not yet begun, ready to ask his uncle how it was all going, but when the door slammed open, Amir knew immediately that something was wrong.

'What is it?' Amir asked.

His uncle walked in, closed the door behind him, sat on the bed close to Amir. 'Tell me it's a fucking lie,' his uncle said, 'tell me it's a joke that I just got told my nephew was hanging around Adnan and Ily, tell me whoever told me is making shit up and I'll go fuck them up, teach them not to lie to me about you ever again, tell me it's all a lie.'

Amir's mouth went dry, his chest tight, 'I don't know what you're talking about,' he said.

His uncle laughed, hollow, 'It's a lie, yeah?' he asked, and Amir nodded. His uncle looked away from him, closed his eyes, disappointment etched into the lines of his forehead. 'Why were you with them?' he asked.

'I wasn't—'

'Don't lie to me again,' his uncle said, interrupting him. He stood, turned back to the door. 'I'm only telling you this because you're my nephew and I love you, and my sister would fucking kill me if anything happened to you and I could have stopped it, those boys are dangerous, there's a reason why they drive around in cars like that and it's not because they're selling a bit of coke here and a bit of weed there, they're into some rough shit, and you know that, because I know they took you to the warehouse.'

'The warehouse,' Amir said.

'Yes, the fucking warehouse, I know where you went, you can't hide shit from me, not here, you went to the warehouse, you saw the shit they're doing, but whatever they showed you, I promise you, it's just the tip.'

'What else are they doing?' Amir asked.

His uncle took a breath, hard. 'What does it matter?' he asked. 'What does it matter what else they're doing? Why the fuck are you hanging out with those boys?'

'I'm not hanging with them.'

'I told you, don't lie to me.'

Amir took a breath of his own in the hope that filling his lungs might calm him down. 'I bumped into Adnan in town,' he said, 'he was there, at Saqib's janazah, it's been years since I've seen him, we thought it would be good to catch up.'

'And he told you about all the money he's making, yeah, asked you to come in, maybe you can have some of that too, if you work for him?'

'He didn't say shit like that to me,' Amir said. No, Adnan hadn't said anything like that to him, Amir had to beg for it, if Adnan had even hinted at it, Amir would have been there the second Adnan had called his name.

'Sure he didn't, because he's a good guy and he warned you off, right? Showed you all the money he has, that nice car he got for himself, that nice house he got for his parents, and then told you that none of this was good and you were too good for this world,' his uncle said, shaking his head, 'you're not stupid, you know that shit is dangerous, why would you even want any part of it? You're at uni, you're doing the right thing,' he moved to the bed again, sitting close to Amir, 'you're doing the thing that I never did, that none of us did, don't you think that if I was your age again, I would make different choices? I would have done something else.'

'No, you wouldn't have,' Amir said.

His uncle laughed, 'If I was half as smart as you or your brother, I would have gone to uni, got a degree, got a good job, that money, it's no fucking good, someone's always after you, there's no fucking rest, someone coming after you, there's no fucking rest there, but what you're doing, what you and Bilal are doing, working hard, what you'll do after, that's what counts, that's where you need to be.'

Amir's hands, tight fists under the duvet, to stop him from shaking. 'It's not as easy as you think it is, that life,' he said.

'I never said it was,' his uncle said, softer now, 'nothing is easy, not for people like us, but you're doing it, you're trying, that's what counts.' He stopped, took a breath. 'Look,' he said, 'I can't make you not do something, I can't hold a knife to your throat, you're too old for all that shit and you'll go do whatever you're going to do anyway, God knows I did when

I was your age and everyone told me not to, you think you know everything when you're that young, all I can do is just tell you, I did all of that shit and more when I was your age, and now I'm nearly forty years old, driving pizzas around in a fucking car. That's no life, Amir.'

Twenty-seven

When Adnan called him, Amir was at the library, sitting with Zain, books in front of them, headphones in. He'd been reading the same page over and over again, none of it going in, a chorus of voices inside him, all demanding his attention. Zain, opposite him, had been typing on his laptop steadily for over an hour. He, working on his research project on Zadie Smith and postcolonial identities, didn't have to sit any exams, and though Zain sat there with Amir, complained about all the writing he had to do, all the reading, how he often went to his lecturer to talk through his project to find his lecturer disengaged, having not read anything Zain had sent to him, Amir envied him for having all this time, for not having to balance the year's success on a handful of exams.

Amir reached for his phone, buzzing in his pocket, screen cracked, phone falling out of his grip when he'd stepped off the bus heading back from town last week, and there, amid the spiderweb of cracks, was Adnan's name. Amir stared at it for a moment, thinking of the other phone he had, the one that he kept in his bag so that he didn't have to explain it to other people.

He motioned to Zain, gestured at the phone, and then stood, walked to the other side of the room, out into one of the balconies looking over the city centre, and answered.

'Yo,' Amir said, keeping his voice level.

'You got the phone on you?' Adnan asked.

Amir glanced back through the window at Zain, at his bag. 'Yeah,' he said, 'why?'

'Come through tonight, I'll send you the address.'

'Tonight?' Amir said. He'd said he would come with Zain to Mohsin's after, just to hang out, after a day's worth of studying, they had earned the high and the time.

'Tonight,' Adnan said, and then, without saying anything else, he hung up. Seconds later, a text came through on Amir's phone, telling him the address, telling him to get there for eight.

He glanced at the time. It was just gone five. His hands shook as he put the phone back in his pocket, and when he took a breath, it was shaky, not entirely filling his lungs. He had studying to do, he thought, but the studying was being done right now, but it wasn't being done right now because he was too busy thinking about this, well he didn't have to think about this anymore, did he? Because he knew where to go, when to be there, but he would miss Mohsin and Zain, were Mohsin and Zain going to give him money? Mohsin would, if he asked, but he wouldn't take it, not from Mohsin, not ever from Mohsin. He pressed himself against the railing, looking down. He wasn't far up, Birmingham Library wasn't that tall, but from here, he thought, if he let his legs go, if his body swung up and over the railing, if he aimed his head down, like an arrow, he'd die, skull caved in, brain smashed, blood pooling.

Amir went back into the library, Zain taking a headphone out, asking if anything was up, and Amir said, 'Nah, it's all good, I just have to get home tonight,' and Zain asked, 'So you can't come tonight?' 'Nah,' Amir said, 'it's the whole wedding thing, my brother,' and Zain looked at him oddly for a second, like he didn't quite believe him, but then he nodded, said, 'Yeah, I bet your mum is losing her mind,' and Amir grinned, said, 'Yeah, all her dreams have just come true, why wouldn't she be?' and then the two of them returned to their books.

Whatever Amir read in those two hours, before he and Zain both left, handshake turned into hug, was gone from his brain the second he sat on the bus, heading out of the city centre, towards Sparkhill, towards this house, which he'd looked up on his phone. He didn't know what he was expecting, but it was just a house on a road, sitting between two other houses, like his parents' house, like every house he'd ever walked past.

There was a short walk from the bus to the house, and Amir realised how hungry he was, not having eaten since the morning, because he'd known that if he could wait until the evening, once he got to Mohsin's, Mohsin would order food, and there would be that game again, of Amir saying he would pay for it, Mohsin rejecting his offer of money, Amir reaching for his wallet, Mohsin telling him it was fine, really, stop, Amir finally relenting, saying he would get the next one, but both of them knowing that he didn't have the money for the next one, that if Mohsin had said, *Yeah, fine, go ahead, pay*, Amir wouldn't have been able to, that this game was to save Amir's pride even though it exposed the hard edge of his shame.

He passed a chicken shop, thought about going in, but there was no money for that. There was money in his account, of course there was, even when things were hard, Amir wouldn't allow himself to have nothing, but there wasn't money for this, a frivolous expense that he didn't need, so he carried on to the house, and when he reached it, he looked up at this normal house, stomach twisted, swallowed his nerves and walked up to the door, which he saw was already open, so he pushed on it.

He walked into a hallway, carpet fucked by people dragging their feet over it, completely flattened but also curling up at the sides, small strings jumping up for freedom. The walls had been white at one point but were now yellowed with age, maybe smoke too, Amir thought, because the house smelled like he had just stepped into a lit cigarette.

There were stairs ahead of him, going up, and then a door to his right, and he could hear something low coming from behind it, so he took a breath, pushed on the door, and when it swung open, he saw the TV first, shiny, new, big, the curtains closed, the room airless, and then he saw the man, sitting on the sofa, just a couple of years older than Amir, who glanced at him. 'Amir,' he said, and Amir nodded, and the man slapped the sofa next to him, 'come,' he said, 'sit.'

Amir hesitated by the door for a second, but then moved across the room, sat by the man, who was leaning back in the sofa, phone in hand, watching videos. Amir waited for him to introduce himself, to tell Amir what he was doing there, but the man said nothing, so they sat in silence, Amir looking at the TV instead, which was playing a nature documentary, a rainforest so green that it seemed unreal, small creatures moving in slow motion.

He thought about texting Adnan, to say that he was here, at the house, but he wasn't a child, he didn't need to check in with Adnan, he was here, on time, and he was ready to do whatever he needed to do.

So Amir sat, unsure of how much time was passing, no clock on the TV, no clock on the walls, and he didn't want to check his phone, embarrassed by the cracks on the screen. All he had to track the passing of time was the short videos the man was playing, small bursts of sound, someone talking, some music. He didn't laugh as he played the videos. It was as if Amir didn't exist.

Then the man put the phone down, reached for another, Amir watching him without turning his head, holding a phone just like the one Adnan had given Amir. He looked at the screen and stood. 'Come on then,' he said to Amir, who mirrored him. The man walked back out of the room, turned right at the hallway, further into the house, into another room, the kitchen, small, the sort that would be hard to cook in, no space, cramped corners, not that any cooking happened here, Amir thought, looking at the growing pile of takeaway boxes in the corner, yellow and brown, paper bags stuffed into them, the smell of rotten food sweet in the air.

'Here, grab this,' the man said, throwing him a small bag, which Amir caught, the look and feel of weed distinct and familiar. The bag had come from the counter, which Amir now saw was stacked high with other bags like this, some with weed, some with pills, some with powder.

They left then, the man heading to a car parked right outside the house, Amir following him, sitting in the passenger side, and as he sat, he noticed that the seatbelt was buckled already, the way his uncle did, so he unbuckled it, put it around himself, and if the man noticed, he didn't say anything. They drove in silence, a four-minute drive, and when they stopped, the man said to Amir, 'It's that guy,' and gestured with his hand to the window. Amir turned, looked out of his window, saw a man standing on the road, hands shoved in his pockets, watching them. 'It'll be twenty,' the man said, and Amir looked down at his own hand, at the bag in it, and he forced himself out of the car, forced himself to walk across the road, where the standing man looked at him, waited for Amir to say something, but Amir said nothing, and then the guy said, 'Weed, yeah?' and Amir said, 'Yeah,' and showed him his hand, and the guy offered him his own hand, a twenty in there, and they exchanged, Amir quickly turning around and heading back to the car, heart hammering in his chest.

Amir expected the man to say something, to congratulate him on his first time, but the man just drove them back to the house, Amir following him back inside, car locked behind them.

That was all it was, Amir realised, as the night passed. He'd had visions of standing on street corners, of carrying a knife with him, a bat in his back pocket.

He sat on the sofa from eight until just past two in the morning, and they barely talked, Amir and the man. He seemed content to be on his phone, and after a while, out of boredom, Amir turned to the TV, started to flick through the channels. He wished he had brought his laptop with him, so he'd have something to do. The man's phone buzzed, they left, Amir always the one to get out of the car and hand over the drugs. His hands stopped shaking, his throat not so tight, his chest not so hollow. He started demanding the money first, before handing the drugs over, started to see himself as someone else.

When the night was over, Adnan came to the house, 'My boys, my boys,' he said when he walked in, handshakes to both of them. He took the money first, from the man, who had held onto every note, and he sat on the sofa, counting through it, and then handed the man a stack of notes. 'Only once, yeah?' the man said, looking at Adnan, and Adnan nodded. He left then, the man, and it was just Amir and Adnan, Amir standing away from Adnan, hands crossed over his chest because he didn't know what else to do with them.

'Faraz,' Adnan said, 'normally works alone, doesn't like the company, not like the other boys,' Adnan said, shaking his head once, 'I don't know why but he gets shit done, I asked him if he would take care of you today, was he good?'

'Yeah,' Amir said, Adnan looking up at him, 'quiet,' he added, 'doesn't talk much.'

'Nah, Faraz doesn't talk much, but that's fine, he gets it done.' Adnan moved, patted the sofa next to him, Amir walking across the room to join him. 'Alright, here you go,' Adnan said, sliding a stack of notes across the table to him, 'this is your take for the night.'

Amir looked at the notes, and for a moment he thought Adnan was fucking with him. Just by guessing, without counting, he had nearly two hundred there. Two hundred, in one night, at Foot Locker, that would have taken him four or five days, and all he'd had to do was sit and wait, get in a car, drive somewhere, hand someone a bag, come back, do it all again until the hours passed.

'You good?' Adnan said, and Amir said quickly, 'Yeah, I'm good,' and Adnan looked at him, grinning. 'You good?' he asked again, and Amir grinned back at him, said, 'Yeah, I'm fucking good.'

Twenty-eight

Amir's mother was discussing the evening's events with Bilal, talking through every detail, about what Momina's parents had been wearing, what Momina's mother had said about the food, what she might have meant by this comment that no one else had even heard, what Momina's father had meant when he said this one thing about the front garden. Amir was there, forced to listen to the whole thing, even though no one had asked for his opinion yet, Bilal sitting right by her, answering all of her questions, letting her talk for as long as she wanted, their father already gone, disappeared into the back garden to smoke, to call his friends, the low growls of his voice floating into the room.

Their mother had been obsessing about the visit ever since Bilal had confirmed it with Momina and her parents. It had been decided they'd arrive on Saturday, one week after Amir had met Momina in Nando's, Bilal asking Amir to wait for him, Amir standing by their car, watching as Bilal walked Momina to her car, the two of them talking, and then they hugged, and when Bilal walked back, he waited outside the car to watch her drive away before he got in, before he told Amir that Momina had liked him, a lot actually, and that she thought he was a good guy and she wished she had a brother like him, except now, Bilal said, laughing, she would have you as a brother, and Amir said nothing, just smiled along with him, told Bilal he had liked her too, let him have the win.

Instead of buying food, instead of ordering in from any one of the local Pakistani restaurants, their mother decided she was going to cook. It was important, she said, that they make the right impression, so she bought all the ingredients on Saturday morning, Friday evening spent obsessing over her shopping list, checking and rechecking cupboards as if something in there might have changed since the last time she had looked. Saturday, she headed out with Bilal to buy everything, Amir listening to them downstairs when they came back, the crinkle of bags, the slamming of cupboards, the clink of cutlery, and then she had started to cook, standing in the kitchen all day, making three different mains, just in case, she said, answering a question no one had asked her, 'Maybe they might not want to eat meat, we didn't ask,' she fried samoseh and pakoreh, 'And if they want dessert,' she said, 'then we can go out and get that, I don't want to assume they'll want something, what if they don't like kheer or rasmalai? No, it's better to just say we'll go out for that,' and when Amir headed downstairs, she made him help her, Bilal out, running other errands for her, picking up different drinks, soft, fizzy, taking her car for a wash even though there was no need, Bilal joking that she was worried Momina's parents were going to peek inside it, cleaning the house when he got back. So Amir stood beside her, in the heat of the kitchen, windows cracked, back door open, listening to her panic about the dinner, what if they asked these questions? she asked, What if she wasn't able to answer things that they wanted to know? She was thinking of inviting their grandmother, her mother, wouldn't that be nice? Her eldest grandchild getting married, but their grandmother had already said no, it wasn't appropriate, it was times like this, their mother said, that she missed her own father, he would know what to do, he was the one out of her parents who liked people, and he definitely would have wanted to be here, for Bilal, for her, 'He'd be stood right here,' she said, 'in this kitchen, helping me cook, making me laugh, like he always did,' and she got upset then, stepping away from the oven, wiping tears from her eyes, and she put a hand on Amir's face, kissed his cheek, told him that she was glad he was here though, she would always have him.

Moments before they arrived, their father launched at their mother, telling her that all of her flittering around was panicking him, this was what she did, always, all the time, he said, directing his comments at Amir and Bilal, as if they had suddenly stopped being the children, her children, and were strangers, as if he expected them to be on his side, she panicked over the smallest of things, he said, and she made other people feel panicked, and over what? This was just a dinner to get to know the parents, 'They've already agreed,' he said, 'the fuckers have already said yes, that they'll let her marry him, otherwise they wouldn't be coming today, so what are you so nervous about? Why are you asking all of these questions? Why are you stressed out about the way the plate looks on the table? Stop being such a stress on me,' and then he walked out, into the back garden, slamming the door behind him, and when they arrived, gently knocking on the door, he wasn't there.

Not that their mother needed him to be there. She was the one who was good at these things, at making people feel comfortable in her presence, just the right mix of adoring and cool, of asking questions and listening attentively, and Momina's parents knew exactly what they were in for, Momina's mother trained for this, just as their mother had been, similar ages, the two women, and they swapped information, my parents are from this village back home, they came over in the sixties, my mother worked in this factory, my father in this one, my father died at this point, my mother died just last year, we go back to Pakistan every so often, we need to go back more, I'm worried for my children, that they'll lose all touch with that part of themselves, that they'll grow up too Western, too white, and as the two women spoke, Momina's father barely said anything, and when their father came back in, the two men went to the front room, the mothers in the kitchen, preparing tea, Momina's mother insisting that she help, their mother insisting that she didn't, leaving the three of them in the living room, alone, Momina and Bilal whispering to one another about how they thought it was going, and the whole time, Amir felt as if he was just watching, part of some larger audience, trapped.

'I thought they had a good time,' Amir said, interrupting his mother, who turned to him, head swivelling like she was an owl. 'I mean,' Amir said, 'I don't know, it seemed like they were having a good time.'

'When?' his mother asked, and before he could answer the question, she said, 'There are things, Amir, that you didn't see, that you probably don't know how to see, because you're not there yet.'

Amir looked at his mother, then to Bilal, who shook his head a fraction. 'Okay,' Amir said.

'Okay,' his mother said, turning back to Bilal, 'we need to start thinking about dates, who we're going to invite, do you know how many people they're going to invite on their side? How much they're going to want to pay? How much we're going to have to put down? Do they know people the way we do? They don't live far from here, right? They're in Solihull, you know, when I was younger, we thought about moving there, to Solihull, but then Dad went and he saw how white it was and he decided against it, better to stay here, he always said, where we knew everyone, but he did want to move out at some point, maybe to a different city, he has friends who live in Manchester, that was something that he talked about sometimes, but I guess it's hard to move when you've got roots somewhere, when it's all that you've known, scary to just up and move,' she said, talking to herself more than to Bilal, who watched her as if she was performing a monologue on the stage, or Amir, who took her mutterings as an opportunity to leave.

Twenty-nine

Amir was sitting in Mohsin's flat, just the two of them and Zain. Mohsin was busying himself in his bedroom. When Amir had arrived, he'd been in the middle of rearranging his clothes, saying that they needed to be put elsewhere, 'but sit, sit, Zain will be here soon,' and then Zain had arrived, coming to sit by Amir.

The two of them had a running joke that Mohsin found it impossible to be by himself for longer than a gym session. If he wasn't calling Amir over, he was calling Zain, and if it wasn't Zain, then he had Nadeem or Omar or another of the boys, and if they were busy, then he would dive into his phone, find a girl to spend the night with, and then tell them all about the meeting the day after, details often exaggerated, and if he couldn't do that, then he would take himself out to the clubs, find a group of people to hang with, because it had never been hard for Mohsin to make friends for a night.

'You good?' Zain asked, nudging Amir. 'Ain't seen you in a minute.'

'Just busy,' Amir said. Since Amir had left Zain to go to the house for the first time, he had been there every night for two weeks. His days had become something of a routine, waking up around midday, coming home in the middle of the night, closing the doors quietly, inching upstairs, hiding the money in his room, in a hole under his windowsill, a brick he'd carved out when he was younger, putting his birthday and Eid money there. Now, it was filled with the money he made with Adnan, and he knew he should take some to the bank, make a deposit, but he liked watching it grow, the stack becoming taller and taller. Two weeks, and he had made nearly three grand. Three grand. He'd have to work three months to get that sort of money at Foot Locker, and that was if he could work all the shifts that they had, if they gave them to him, and if he hadn't been forced to give most of it to his father. Or it was two terms of student loan money, which needed to stretch to five months of living. This, he had made in just two weeks, and it was all his money. None of it needed to go to his parents, because they didn't know he had it, he didn't need to pay any to the tax man. No, it was all his.

Last night, Amir had sat in front of the hole looking at the money, counting it again. It had just reached over three grand then, and he thought about all the things that he could do with it. He could replace all of the clothes he had that were fraying, coming apart with age, the shoes that needed to be thrown away. He could buy himself a membership to the gym. He could book classes with a personal trainer. He could invest it.

Amir had done this as a child, spending days thinking about what he might buy with his birthday money. What could this twenty from his uncle get him? What would it be best spent on? But he wouldn't know what to do with it, wouldn't know where best to spend it, so he wouldn't make any choice, keeping the money, only to then spend it on something trivial, like food or a toy that he didn't particularly want or some sweets from the shop, and he'd look at the thing he'd bought with this money, this money that had felt so important on the day, and he'd fill with shame at his own actions.

So he did nothing with the money. He let it sit there, in the hole, because he wanted to see it grow, because he didn't know where best to spend it. There was also, in the back of his mind, a fear that if he did spend it, if he decided to buy the clothes, invest in the stock, replace the phone, that Adnan might turn around and say he was done, that Adnan didn't need him anymore, and the money would stop coming in, and he'd have nothing to show for it.

'You down for Mohsin's plans?' Zain asked.

Mohsin had sent the idea in the group chat a couple of days earlier, saying he wanted to do a boy's trip, he was going to Europe for the summer, had decided that he didn't want to sit at home as the weeks dragged on, and he wanted them to come with him for some of it. Amsterdam, he'd suggested, close by, not that expensive, 'and I've been there before,' he'd said, 'so I can show you all where everything is.' The boys had all said yes, bar Amir, who had stared at the message, wondering if he could go, could he take the time from Adnan? Would it show Adnan that he was just doing this for a short infusion of cash, to spend on nothing? Would Adnan let him back in?

'I don't know,' Amir said, 'there's a lot going on, the wedding.'

'The wedding,' Zain said, looking at Amir as if he was telling a joke, 'what are you doing for the wedding? Isn't it happening next year?'

'Yeah, there's just a lot to do, like, she came over the other day—'

'His wife?'

'Yeah, she came over with her parents, so it was this whole thing, we made all this food, you know how it gets, and there's going to be other stuff like that too—'

'But you don't need to be there for that, do you?' Zain said. 'I mean, it's his wedding, so he'll be there, but you can take a week or two, come to Amsterdam, what are your parents going to do, say no?'

'Yeah,' Amir said vaguely, though that was part of it for him too. He couldn't imagine going to his parents and telling them that he was planning to go to Amsterdam with his friends for a week. His parents, whose only holidays had been to Pakistan for the summer every other year, who saw driving to Sheffield for a funeral or a wedding as something big, who wouldn't dream of spending their money on a fanciful holiday like that. What would be the point, his father would ask him, if you have no family there? What are you going to see? What are you going to do? Then there would be the questions of why Amsterdam, what he'd be getting up to while he was there, the strippers and the cocaine and the weed.

'You should come,' Zain said, nudging Amir, 'and if it's about money, I don't know, let Mohsin just spend his money on you, who gives a fuck? If he doesn't, why should we?'

'I'm not letting Mohsin pay for me,' Amir said. Mohsin had offered, as a joke, in the chat, that he could pay for them to come if they couldn't afford it. 'Fuck it,' he'd said, 'it's not my money anyway, let's do it,' and the boys had all laughed with him about it, about letting Mohsin's dad pay for their fucking around, but the thought of it stuck in Amir's throat. Some weed here, a pizza there, that was fine, but to pay for a plane, for a hotel, for everything he ate, everything he did while he was there, that was too far, a chain around his neck. He didn't need it, anyway, he thought, picturing the stack underneath his windowsill. If anything, Amir thought, if they planned to go in August and it was only May now, he could earn enough money to pay for all of them. How satisfying would that be, he thought, to come to Amsterdam, with stacks and stacks of cash in his bag, to tell Mohsin, *Nah, I got this one,* see the look on his face?

'I'm letting him pay for me.'

'What?' Amir said, looking at Zain. 'He's paying for what?'

'Yeah,' Zain said, 'I can't afford to go to Amsterdam, I told him straight when he asked, I don't have the money for it, what I'm not spending here on food and going out and books and all the rest of it, I've saved up, and that money isn't for fucking around in Amsterdam, so Mohsin said he would pay for me, and I said fine, go ahead.' Zain gave Amir a look. 'What's the other option?' he asked. 'I spend all this money that I've spent months, years even, saving up, and it's all gone, just like that, or I say no and then spend the summer at home with my family, watching you guys get fucked up without me? Nah, I ain't doing that.'

'So you'd rather let him pay for you?'

'Yeah, like I said, Mohsin doesn't give a fuck.'

'He doesn't give a fuck because it's not his money.'

'So what?' Zain said. 'So what if it's not his money? No one is going to come to collect at the end of the day, and if his dad turns around one day and cuts him off, which I don't think will happen, look at this place, but let's say his dad does, says he's spending too much money, it'll be our turn to help him, as much as we can, but that's not on us either, it's between him and his dad, and if Mohsin wants to spend some of that money on me going with him on a trip, I'm not about to be all proud and say no.'

'Proud,' Amir said, 'it's not about being proud, it's about having some self-respect.'

'Ouch,' Zain said.

'No, I mean,' Amir said, and he turned his eyes back to the TV, blank, black, 'I just mean, I can't do it.'

'That's you,' Zain said, 'but what then? You just gonna stay here over the summer, get a job, work, and then come back September, you're back at it again, money all spent on buses and food and books, studying all the time? And third year is gonna be even worse, that's when all this shit starts really counting for something.'

'I don't know, man,' Amir said, 'it's hard to think about next year when we're still in this one.'

Mohsin, finished with whatever he was doing in his bedroom, arrived at the sofa, launching himself into it, feet up, next to Amir, looking at them both. 'What serious shit are we talking about?'

'Amsterdam,' Zain said.

'Yeah,' Mohsin said, and then he nudged Amir with his elbow, 'you coming or what?'

Amir swallowed his annoyance, said, 'I don't know.'

'You don't know.' Mohsin sat up, turned to him. 'What do you mean, you don't know?'

'I don't know, man, I've never been—'

'I told you, I went, when I was seventeen, just before I came here, it's a good time, it'll be beautiful in the summer, and there's loads of things to do,' Mohsin said, and Amir waited for the jokes about the fucking they'd do, the weed they'd smoke, all the shit they'd get up to, but Mohsin never said any of that, just added, 'It's a great place, you should come, I want you to come.'

'Alright, alright,' Amir said. With Mohsin on one side and Zain on the other, it was as if they were holding him there. 'Let me think about it.'

'There's no thinking,' Mohsin said, leaning back on the sofa, 'you just do it, you can't keep telling yourself you won't do things because of, I don't know, money or parents or family or duty, or whatever the fuck is going on in your head, you just have to do it, there's no right choice, there's only the choice and then the commitment to the choice.'

'Shit, we got Oprah over here,' Zain said, and Mohsin told him to fuck off, and then asked if they were hungry, and Zain said yeah, and the conversation moved on to what food they were going to get, and Amir said little, just nodding his head, saying, 'Yeah, I can go for shawarma,' when the option was presented to him.

Thirty

Amir's uncle turned up at the house one day, Amir waking to the muffled sound of his voice downstairs. His uncle had never learned how to whisper, talking to Amir's mother, Amir unable to make out what they were saying to one another, but something told him it was about him, and when his uncle climbed the stairs, turned to his room, opened the door and shouted his name, Amir hated that he was right.

'Get up,' his uncle said, pulling the duvet off him.

Amir stared up at him, took a breath, held it, and then moved. 'Back to the TV guy?' he asked, his uncle saying nothing, just watching as Amir reached for a shirt and slid it on, standing before him.

'Get dressed,' his uncle said, before leaving the room.

Amir did, and when he went downstairs, his mother was sitting on the sofa, TV on with the volume turned down, a habit she had picked up from Bilal, or maybe Bilal had picked it up from her, her phone in her hand, and when she looked up at Amir, it was only for a second before she was back on Facebook, looking at bullshit conspiracy posts written by strangers or bots, sharing them with everyone she knew, warning them about pig products in Rubicon Mango or microchips in vaccines or harmful radiation from 5G towers. Amir walked past her without saying anything.

'Where are we going?' Amir asked his uncle, sitting in his car, opening the window all the way to release the smell of weed, trying to ignore the way the seat underneath him felt sticky from the grease of the food he delivered in the evenings, all the way into the early hours of the morning.

'Don't worry about where we're going,' his uncle said, foot jammed on the accelerator, car speeding along. His uncle had always loved driving fast, telling distant family members he only met at Eid or weddings how he went up to 120mph on the motorway, zooming in and out of cars, how he could have been something if he had learned to drive earlier, he could have been in races, he could have been an F1 driver, and those who listened looked at him, short, shirts struggling to keep in his stomach, yellow teeth, eyes worn out by life, and they said nothing, just smiled and nodded as he talked through his delusions.

He drove out of Birmingham, stopping at a petrol station just before the turn onto the M6, where he stepped out, jammed the hose into the car, Amir reaching for his phone, a few messages in the group chat, Mohsin wanting to throw a party before he left for the summer, exams done and coursework handed in, and everyone was saying yeah, that would work for them, before they disappeared too, and now it felt like the summer was right in front of Amir, this long stretch of nothing, his friends gone home. Where would he be? Who would he be with? He didn't have anyone.

His uncle came back, threw a Lucozade at Amir, a cigarette between his lips, and they were off again, hitting the motorway, his uncle immediately veering to the right-hand lane and staying there, undertaking cars that he deemed too slow, moving all the way to the left to come all the way back, like they were playing a game. Amir's window was still open, the wind roaring in his ears, and his uncle didn't move to close it so Amir didn't either, sensing that it was some sort of test, and he didn't open the Lucozade bottle, let it fall to the floor in front of him, and every time his uncle moved into another lane, the bottle rolled between his feet.

An hour. That was how long it took for them to get to their destination, Leicester, a city Amir had never been to, though he knew he had cousins there, cousins who got married and moved out of Alum Rock, out of Birmingham.

They stopped at a random street, houses that looked like home, a corner shop with vegetable and fruits at the front, cars that went unnoticed for how mundane they were. His uncle got out of the car and Amir followed him, waited for him to stop at a house, to turn in, walk up to a door, but he kept going, then turned off the road into a park, people walking around, some runners, and his uncle kept walking, with a familiarity that told Amir he had been here before.

He finally stopped in the middle of the vast green space. A group of boys passed a ball among themselves nearby, while other groups of teenagers clustered together, the girls looking at the boys, the boys pretending they weren't looking at the girls, families who were there to spend a weekend afternoon in the sun. Amir thought about the last time his family had done something like this, when his father's sister had lived near them, her and her four kids coming with Amir and Bilal and their mother to Ward End, the two of them sitting with all of the other mothers, scarves loose on their heads, watching their children from a distance, Amir and Bilal and those four kids running around, trying to climb the spider net, waiting for the swings, running up the slope to get to the top of the slide, Amir careful to point his feet because the soles of his shoes would trip him up on the descent down the shiny metal, walking back home with ice creams in their hands bought from the vans parked up near the exits, the children saying goodbye to one another when their paths split, Amir and Bilal coming home and washing themselves with the hose in the back garden, spraying one another, chasing each other with buckets of water, painting the concrete tiles a dark grey. All that came to an end when their aunty moved, deciding that Alum Rock was no longer enough for her and her family, 'She's gone to Hodge Hill,' their mother said, envy souring her words, and even though Hodge Hill was no more than a ten-minute drive away, they rarely saw them again, and when they did, it was as if the four people they met only looked like the children they used to be.

'What are we doing here?' Amir asked, looking at his uncle.

He said nothing, looked around for something, what, Amir didn't know, head up, like a dog sniffing the air, and then he spotted it, walking over to the line of trees, Amir behind him.

'Here,' his uncle said, brushing his hand over a tree, and Amir looked at it but saw nothing, just the wrinkled bark of a tree. 'Here is where I got this,' his uncle said, pulling his cap off, pointing to the scar that ran on the left side of his head, this crooked line that curved around his skull.

'I thought you got that in a car accident?'

'I was a fucking idiot,' his uncle said, and by the way he said it, Amir knew his uncle had rehearsed whatever was about to come next, 'I was just a little older than you, twenty-one, twenty-two, this was where we used to come, all the way out to Leicester, we had beef with some boys in Cov so it was never worth going there, we'd come out here to fuck around, smoke some shit, take some shit, and then drive back, sometimes we'd bring girls with us, fuck around with them for a little bit, once, one of my boys, you don't know him, Adi, he brought over this prostitute, fucked her right in front of us, then offered her around, but none of us took her, so he just let her go, didn't even pay her, and she was screaming at him in some other language, Romanian or Polish maybe, and we just laughed at her, watched her walk away, I think Adi threw something at her, a bottle maybe, smashed against her back, he's gone now, Adi, dead, overdosed, a few years back, but that's what we did, we just came here and we fucked around and we made noise, too much noise, because then the lads from here, they heard of us, these Brummie boys fucking around in their ends, so they came through one night, to see who we were, told us not to come back, this was their land, and they were older than us, nearly thirty, I think, and I could tell that they were being serious, but we didn't listen, who the fuck is going to listen to someone telling them not to come back and not backing it up? So we came back, waited for them, we brought bats with us, had them all lined up, we were going to show these mans who we were, then they came, and they came with knives, and we got into it, they didn't even wanna talk, they stabbed P, right in the side, he's only got one kidney now, fucked with the rest of us too, and we were all talk back then, didn't know what to do, panicked, and they knew exactly who they were, exactly what to do, and one of them, this guy, not even that big, came up to me, took the bat right out of my hands, and smacked me round the head with it, and when I fell, he hit me again and then I was gone, and when I woke up, they were carrying me and P, we were the ones that were fucked up the most, drove us back to Brum, dropped us off at a hospital, and we lied, me and P, said we didn't know what happened, we were jumped somewhere, can't remember where, they took his kidney, stitched me up, I was in there for days, Mum and Dad asking me what happened, and I think they knew, you know, that I'd been up to some shit but it was easier for them to pretend that I wasn't up to nothing, that I was just an innocent guy, walking around, and someone had jumped me, that I was the victim, but we shouldn't have gone back, we thought we were the biggest mans in the world, thought no one could touch us, and there we were, lying in that hospital, the pain I was in, I couldn't even open my eyes because it hurt too much, and I remember, when I left, looking at myself in the mirror at home, in the bathroom, I'd seen myself in the hospital bathroom but that didn't feel real to me, you know, standing there in those hospital clothes, that white gown that ties together at the back and shit, that never felt real to me, felt like I was just looking at someone else, but when I was there, at home, in my own bathroom, looking at this ugly fucking line across my head, the stitches, the way they'd shaved my head, I'm never going to forget that. I thought I was dead.'

His uncle's eyes were glazed over, looking at something that Amir couldn't see.

'You'd think I would stop,' his uncle said, 'that after what happened to me and P, we'd all stop, but nah, I was angry, real fucking angry, I wanted my revenge on those mans, so I went out again, beat the shit out of anyone who looked at me wrong, built a reputation for myself, showed them that they shouldn't fuck with me, and I came back, back here, hoping to find these mans that had fucked my head up, but I never did, I don't know what happened to them, I never saw them again.'

He looked at Amir. 'Do you understand what I'm telling you?' he said. 'Do you understand why I'm telling you this?'

'I'm not you,' Amir said.

His uncle laughed. 'You are exactly me,' he said, 'who the fuck else are you going to be?'

'I'm not you,' Amir said again.

'That's my point, you idiot, you don't have to be me, you're better than me, so this shit that you're playing with, this shit with Adnan that you're doing, it isn't for you.'

'But it was for you.'

'But it wasn't for me,' his uncle said, voice low, 'that's my whole point, I played that game, for years, I sold drugs, I took them, I got beat up, I beat other people up, for years, I was on those streets, acting like I was the biggest man around until someone bigger than me came around and beat me down, but I jumped back up again, I did that, and look at me now, what the fuck do I do? What is my life?'

'I'll do it better than you,' Amir said, and the second he spoke, his uncle's face shifted, turned ugly.

'Oh, yeah?' his uncle said. 'How?'

'I know how to make it work.'

'You know how to make it work,' his uncle said, slowly, softly, nodding his head, 'okay, you know how to make it work, because you're not just better than me, you're better than everyone else, yeah? Better than all the other boys out there, better than Saqib, yeah, better than him too?'

Saqib's name made Amir tense. 'Maybe I can learn from what happened to him.'

'And what did you learn?'

Amir closed his mouth, hard, teeth smashed against each other, 'I guess I learned to be smarter than he was.'

'Yeah, you got it all figured out, smart boy, smartest boy,' his uncle said, and then he slapped him, hard, on the face.

'What the fuck?' Amir said, voice filled with shock, stepping back, away from his uncle. 'What the fuck are you doing?'

'Hit me back,' his uncle said, stepping towards Amir, 'defend yourself.'

'I'm not going to hit you.'

'Hit me back,' his uncle said, 'hit me.'

'I'm not going to fucking hit you,' Amir said, stepping away from him, backwards, face stinging, red.

'Then what?' his uncle asked, moving a step forward for every one that Amir took back. 'What are you going to do if someone comes for you out there, if someone pulls out a bat or a knife or a gun? Are you going to stand there and ask them to be nice to you? Are you going to tell them that you're smarter than them, better than them, hope that stops them?'

'I'm not going to fucking hit you,' Amir said, his breath short, fast.

'Yeah,' his uncle said, stopping, and Amir stopped too, 'you won't hit me but you're going to fuck up your life, all because you're angry, real fucking smart.'

Thirty-one

Someone pulled at Amir's arm and he turned, body ready to fight, but it was only Farrah, and Amir was surprised at the joy that ran through him when he saw her face. 'What the fuck are you doing here?' he asked, pulling her in for a hug without thinking about it.

'I'm a student, just like you, remember?' she said, shouting over the music that was pumping through the speakers. 'Snobs is where we live,' raising her glass to her lips, movements clumsy, and Amir realised she was drunk, her body slow and jerky.

'You here alone?' Amir asked. Farrah shook her head, gestured to her right, and he turned to see some of the girls from that night at Mohsin's there, around Mohsin, Zain, Kamran, Abbas and Omar.

'I didn't see you at first,' Farrah said, leaning in so that Amir could hear her, her hair brushing against his cheek, 'I thought maybe the good boy was at home with his parents, but then I looked over here and saw you all by yourself, why are you standing here all by yourself?'

'I'm not by myself,' Amir said, 'I was just coming back from the toilets,' but that was a lie. It had reached the point in the night when the other boys were all too drunk to even speak to, thrusting glasses in Amir's face, telling him to drink, only one, it wouldn't hurt, no one was going to tell the big guy upstairs, so he'd been about to leave the club, walk a little through the city centre, he liked it when it was like this, quiet and dark. It felt like it was just him and the city.

'You look sad,' Farrah said, her lips close to his ears.

'I'm not,' he said into her neck, smelt her perfume, light, fruity, sweet, 'not now that you're here.'

Farrah pulled back her head, laughing, 'That's so fucking corny.'

'Did it work?' he asked, grinning.

'Maybe,' she said, and then she took him by the hand, into the thrum of people, and when Zain saw Amir, he laughed, shouted something that was lost into the air, and Mohsin noticed, shouted something too, and suddenly, Amir was back in the middle of them all again, Mohsin putting his arm around Amir's shoulder, holding him close, and Farrah still had her hand on his, and she pulled at it, telling Amir to dance with her, 'However you want,' she said, 'just dance with me.' So he did, moving his body a touch, just in line with the beat of the music, heavy around him.

Farrah downed her drink, giving her glass to one of the other girls, and then she leaned into Amir, moving from side to side, and then she turned around, grabbed Amir's hand, curled his arm around her waist, somehow moved even closer to him, pressing herself into his body, and something twitched inside him, something familiar, and when he pressed himself into her, when he let his hand wander, when he put his face to her neck again, hair brushing against his skin, when he touched his lips to her soft flesh, he was hard.

It wasn't long after that Amir was kissing her, searching the inside of her mouth with his tongue, the alcohol bitter but he didn't care, not long after that he was walking out of the club with her, pulling her close to him, 'It's not far,' she said, 'like fifteen minutes, ten if we're quick,' her swaying from side to side, Amir holding her close to him, so she didn't fall into the side of the road, and every so often, he stopped walking to kiss her again, Farrah mumbling words against his lips that he didn't understand, and when Farrah put her hand on his body to push him away, he pulled away and kept on walking, only to stop again to kiss her, her body felt so fucking good pressed up against his, his hands on her back, her legs, he wanted to pick her up and push her against a wall, and when they reached her house, the keys were shaking in her hands so Amir took them from her, put the key in, and Farrah told him to wait, hand on his chest, she needed to use the bathroom, and when Amir closed the door to the flat the world went quiet, there was no else here, he realised, just the two of them, and he waited outside the bathroom, patiently, and when she came out, she laughed when she saw him, opened her mouth to say something and Amir kissed her again, and this time, he pulled at her jeans, button open, zipper down, put his hand down, felt her wet, and she let out a moan into his mouth, and he was so fucking hard, so he unzipped himself, took it out, took her hand, placed her fingers around him, thick and hot, and he couldn't take it anymore, he pressed himself against her leg, and she said, 'Wait, wait,' and she walked away from Amir, upstairs, and he followed her, Farrah going into her room, reaching for her drawer, the sharp crinkle of a condom, and Amir took it from her, ripped it open with his teeth, slipped it on, and then he turned her over on the bed, face down, put one hand under her, under her shirt, held her breast tight, her nipple hard, and fuck, he wanted this so bad, she said something, Amir barely heard her over the blood in his ears, and he put his dick in her, and she tensed, her leg moving in a way that Amir didn't like so he pushed it back with his hand, pressed his face into the back of her, and when he came, he let out the roar that had been inside of him for too long.

Thirty-two

Amir woke and when his eyes opened, when he took in the light blue walls around him, the sunlight that was coming in from the wrong side of the room, confusion bloomed in him, he had no idea where he was. Then he heard a sound from his left, turned his head, saw Farrah standing, back to him, and the events of the night before poured through him.

'Hey,' Amir said, pushing himself up, 'what time is it?' His shirt was off, down by the edge of the bed, he'd taken it off when he'd decided to sleep there, too late to go home, he was too tired to trek across the city.

'Eight,' Farrah said.

'Eight?' Amir repeated. 'What time did we get back last night?' he asked.

'I don't know,' she said, moving from the bed over to the windows, where she stopped, tense, tight, arms wrapped around herself, like she was holding herself together.

Amir understood that something was wrong. 'What is it?' he asked, standing up, reaching for his phone, which was on the floor next to his wallet, next to his trousers, next to his shoes. 'What's wrong?'

'I think you should leave.'

'Well, I wasn't going to stay around for the whole day,' he said, saw the condom on the floor, he hadn't tied a knot in it, his cum, thick, off-white, 'but, you good?'

'I'm good,' Farrah said, still not looking at him, 'but you need to leave.'

'I'm going to leave, Farrah.'

'Good.'

'Good,' Amir said. Now he was getting angry. 'What's wrong?' he asked, she shook her head, arms tight, 'Look,' he said, 'I don't know what's going on—'

'I said no,' Farrah said, turning around to face him, her eyes red, dark, mascara smeared, lipstick wiped onto her cheek, 'last night,' she said, 'I said no, and you, you came in here, you fucking came in here and you—'

'No, you didn't,' Amir said, 'you didn't say no.'

'Yes, I fucking did,' Farrah said, her voice shaking, 'I said no, I said no and you still fucking, you still, I said no and you didn't listen to me.'

'I never,' Amir said, then he stopped, searched his mind, coming into the flat, following her upstairs, it was her who had led him, her who had taken the condom out of the drawer, when did she say no? He couldn't remember. 'You didn't say no,' he said.

'You need to leave,' Farrah said.

Amir looked at her, silent, and then said, 'Sure,' reaching for his trousers, for his shoes, and when Farrah told him to delete her number, never to text or call her again, Amir said nothing, turned to the door, and as he walked out of the room, another door in the house opened, one of the girls, looking at him, her hair standing up from sleep but her eyes clear, and Amir knew she had heard every word.

Thirty-three

By now, Amir had been introduced to the boys that he'd spend his nights with. After that first night with Faraz, who Amir had never seen again, he had been slowly introduced to them all. There was Frosty, tall and thin, called that because his skin was so pale, Sparks, who was always playing with his lighter, no matter what he was doing, the click-click of it enough to drive anyone crazy, he couldn't stay still for longer than five seconds, Tabby, because he was like a large cat, round and cuddly, Michelin Man come to life, and Slick, because he always turned up at the house dressed as if he was about to fuck, hair back, beard neatly trimmed, tight shirt and tighter trousers, Frosty always taking the piss out of him for being so small.

Amir didn't have a nickname yet, 'But that'll come soon,' Frosty told him, 'Adnan will see something in you and he'll give you something,' but for now, Amir was just Amir.

Tonight, Amir was with Slick, who sat with him on a sagging sofa, Amir falling into it, like a child in a bouncy castle that had started to deflate, walls collapsing around him. There was a PlayStation attached to the TV, which Tabby was always on, he told Amir every time he saw him not to fuck with his saves, it would be the last thing he did, so Amir hadn't touched it. Amir's mother would lose her mind if she stepped in there, would reach for her gloves, start cleaning, but not before she told them all to get out, worried that Amir would catch something by simply breathing the air.

Slick was watching videos, scrolling past them quickly, small buzzes of sound interjected with pauses as he moved on to the next one, video loaded, another burst of sound, another pause, another burst. Amir wasn't even sure that Slick knew he was there.

Amir held onto the phone in his hand, tight, ready to leave the second it vibrated. He had hoped that Adnan might have been there tonight, not that Adnan spent every night there, but he'd been there a few times, sitting with the boys, controller in hand, playing with Tabby. Amir got the sense that he liked coming there, that there was some kind of escape in it from the rest of his life, that these boys really were his boys, that he chose to come to this house out of all the others there were, but not tonight.

A video played on Slick's phone, a voice Amir had heard before. He glanced over at the screen, a man whose accent was odd, British but not, American but not, foreign but not, whose face looked to Amir like it might be black, it might be brown, it might be some kind of white, his head shaved, gleaming. In this video, he was sitting with a microphone in front of him, looking away from the camera, at someone else, speaking.

'What do women want, really, when you think about it, when you really think about it? Take away all the politics bullshit that they keep trying to force down your throat, think about it, what they really want is to be protected, to feel safe, to know that the men they choose to spend the rest of their lives with are going to be able to protect them from danger, to provide for them, that's what they want, they don't want anything else but that, and it's our duty, our fundamental duty, to provide that.'

Slick's finger hovered over the screen, shared it to a group of his own boys, adding some text, and then went back to the app, scrolled to the next video, another one of this man, now sitting in a different room, dressed in a tight suit, his arms unreal, like a cartoon man, seams stretching as the clothes struggled to contain him.

'They want to put me away for telling boys, for telling men, to take care of themselves, to look after themselves first, to live their lives the way they want to, not the way they're told to for others, to make money for themselves, to protect women, to build family and community, and that's why they want to put me away, because that's scary to them, because breaking down men is how they get ahead, making us feel small is how they get more power, but that isn't their power, it's our power and it's time we took it back.'

Slick scrolled through another few videos and then turned to Amir, who was still watching alongside him. 'You know who this is?' Slick asked.

'No,' Amir said.

'He's been banned,' Slick said, 'but his videos get reposted everywhere, he speaks the truth, about taking back what belongs to us.'

'Yeah,' Amir said, looking back at the phone, at the man on the screen.

Slick took it back, hitting another video, then said, 'Has Sparks told you about his girl?'

'Nah,' Amir said. He'd only had a couple of nights with Sparks.

'He's been with her for years,' Slick said, 'three, I think, and now she wants to get married.'

'Yeah?' Amir asked.

'Married,' Slick said.

'What's wrong with that?'

'Have you seen Sparks?' Slick asked. 'He can't sit down for two minutes, she's talking about getting married, buying a house, giving all this up, selling his cars, wants him to stop being with all of us, really do the whole thing, family, kids, maybe a cat, school runs and changing nappies, can you imagine a man like Sparks doing all that?'

Amir thought of Sparks, just four years older than Amir himself. 'I don't know him as well as you do,' Amir said, 'but if it makes him happy—'

'Trust me,' Slick said, 'I've been around him for a long time, I know that man like he's my brother, that's not the life he wants, he talks about it sometimes, but he doesn't mean it, he's not made for it.'

'My brother's just got engaged.'

'Oh, yeah?' Slick asked.

'Yeah, he met someone at work.'

'Office, yeah?' Slick asked, and Amir nodded. 'Yeah, see, that's the sort of person who wants that life and is made for it, he goes to work, she goes to work, they're into the same shit, they want the same shit from life, they'll have kids, she'll stop working for a while, maybe she goes back, they get a house, get a pet, two cars, yeah, that's how it'll be for your brother, how old is he?'

'Twenty-six,' Amir said.

'Twenty-six, perfect time for it, makes sense, Sparks ain't that, Sparks isn't about to get a job like that working at some office, and he isn't about to go working anywhere else either, he's been doing this for too long.'

'How long?'

'Years,' Slick said, 'years and years, he's twenty-four now, so nearly ten years, he's been here, selling shit, and he likes it, he knows how to do it, he knows how to take care of himself, no one's ever going to get a lick in on Sparks, he's wily as fuck, it makes him good money, fuck, it makes her good money, he buys her everything, she's at uni now, yeah, but he's the one paying for everything, so I don't get it, she wants him to give this up and for what? So he can go sit in a home she pays for, working some dead-end job that won't pay him shit? She'll have the better job, she'll pull in the money, everything will be hers, and what then? His own kids will grow up not respecting him, trust me, you can't see your dad living like that and have any respect for him, nah, it'll kill him if he does.'

Amir said nothing. It was wrong, he thought, to talk about Sparks like this when he didn't know him as well as Slick did, and it was wrong, too, that Slick was talking about Sparks like this to someone who'd only met him a handful of times. But more than that, Amir was struck by how angry Slick was, at Sparks, at Sparks's girl, at something.

Amir's phone buzzed and he looked at it, a text for weed, and Slick asked, 'Got something?' and Amir stood, said, 'Yeah.'

Thirty-four

When Amir got home, his brother and mother were in the living room, deep in conversation, he could hear their voices through the closed door and turned away from it to the stairs, to make his way to his room, when his mother called his name, told him to come inside. 'What do you think', she asked Amir when he opened the door, 'of your brother having his nikah months before the walima?'

Amir looked to his brother for an answer but couldn't read his face. 'I don't know,' he said.

'It would be good to have it separate,' his mother said, Bilal speaking at the same time as her, 'She wants us to have it months before the actual wedding.'

'Don't interrupt me,' their mother said, gently hitting Bilal on the knee, 'I'm just saying,' eyes back to Amir, 'it's what all the kids are doing these days, splitting them up like that, and it means that we get to have two big bits.'

'We're already going to have so many big bits, I don't know why you want us to have the nikah this year.'

'You have the nikah this year,' their mother said, turning to Bilal, 'right at the end of the year, November, maybe, and then that part of it is done, you're married, done, you don't have to worry about it, and then we can plan for the walima next summer instead of rushing the whole thing and panicking about when to do what and how.'

'You're the only one panicking,' Bilal said, mirroring their father for a second, his voice tight.

'You should be panicking too,' their mother said, turning back to Amir, 'do you hear him talking about how I'm the only one panicking?' she said, as if Amir was on her side. 'We should all be panicked, you, her, her parents, all of us, this is a big thing, my son is getting married, it's a big thing.'

'Mum,' Bilal said wearily, and he looked at Amir, rolled his eyes, and Amir might have felt some sympathy for him if he didn't let her do this to him, if he didn't just sit there and take it all the time, if he told her the truth, that he didn't want her to get involved in everything, that it was exhausting to be on this end of it all the time. 'It'll be fine,' Bilal said. 'Let me check with Momina, don't forget, her opinion counts too.'

'Check with her, trust me, she'll want the same thing, I'm telling you, it's all the rage these days, have your nikah a few months, a year, two years even, from the walima, get married, have a big small party, and then you have the walima, your big big party, you invite everyone, you plan this huge thing, you know, your cousin, Salma, she did this very thing, she had her nikah and then a year and a half later, I think, she had her walima.'

'Salma from Pakistan?'

'Salma from Pakistan,' their mother said, hitting her own leg, 'in Pakistan they're doing this and we're not going to do it here, in England, we're doing it, speak to Momina, see what she thinks, but we're absolutely doing it, it just doesn't make any sense not to.'

'Fine, fine,' Bilal said, raising his hands at her, 'I'll do it, I'm going to see her now anyway,' he said, standing up.

'You are?' their mother said, standing up too. 'At her house?'

'No, not at her house,' Bilal said, the strain in his voice clear.

'Oh,' their mother said knowingly, 'a date.'

'Mum, don't be weird,' Bilal said, reaching for his shoes, slipping them on, 'I'll be back later.'

'Where are you going?' their mother asked, and Bilal gave her a look, repeated himself, 'I'll be back later,' and then he stood by Amir, waited for him to move out of the way, which Amir did, and then he was gone, door closed after him, and Amir stayed where he was, his mother sitting back down on the sofa, turning on the TV, reaching for her phone, and Amir waited for her to say something to him, to acknowledge his presence in the room, to ask where he'd been all day, wanted her to ask him where he'd been all day so that he could tell her, *It's not where I've been, it's where I'm going, to a fucking drug den, just like you've been scared of all this time, just like you warned me not to do all those years ago, I'm going to sell drugs today, sit in a car with one of Adnan's boys, drive to drop them off, small bags of weed in my hand, take their cash, do you know how much cash I have upstairs? Do you want to know how much? The sort of money you don't even know exists in this world, I don't need you, any of you, for shit*, but his mother didn't even look up at him, not as Amir turned away from her, made his way up the stairs, to his room, door closed behind him.

Thirty-five

Amir's days became strained. Between studying for exams, which he often did in the library with Zain, hanging at Mohsin's flat, running away every night to go sit in the house and wait for the texts to come through, heading home in the middle of the night, stack in his pocket, falling asleep on his bed, only to wake and do the same thing the very next day, it was as if he was living one endless day, falling asleep only to wake like he'd never closed his eyes.

But his exams were just weeks away, the days creeping up on him, and then he'd be done, for a few months at least, until September came back around and then he was trapped inside it again. And what then, he thought, when he had to go back to university, back to classes, back to feeling like he didn't know anything?

That first night he had sat in that room with Faraz, who said nothing and paid him no attention, when Adnan had handed him the money, that big, thick wad of notes, when Amir had come home and put them underneath his windowsill, when he'd checked them the following morning just to make sure that they were still there, that he hadn't dreamed them up, that his imagination hadn't run wild, he'd wondered if he even needed to go back.

When he laid it out to himself, being at university made no sense. Yes, he was good at maths, yes, he understood the way that the numbers interacted with each other in a way that Bilal never did, that his parents never did, his uncle or grandparents, yes, there was something in him that spoke that language, but civil engineering was not something that he would say he was dying to do, and the idea of donning a suit and tie after his graduation, applying for graduate schemes, interviewing with people who thought less of him because of where he was born, the way he spoke, what he knew, wasn't giving Amir much hope that his future was in any way stable. And if he got the job, what then? Years and years, endless time, of sitting in an office, in front of a computer, emailing, stuck in meetings, aiming for promotions that might never come his way. It itched at him, this version of life, made him want to rip off his skin.

But this, what he was doing with Adnan, this was just the beginning. Sitting around, waiting for a text to come through, exchanging small bags for money, this was nothing, and yet he was making more money than he'd ever thought he would. He was smart, smarter than the others, who all struck Amir as the sort of boys that Adnan had surrounded himself with at school, boys who didn't quite take life so seriously because they didn't seem to have the brains to do so, who would break bones in a second but had no thoughts about the future. That's what they were, and Amir, well, Amir was the sort who worked hard, who wanted more.

So, yes, sometimes Amir sat in front of the papers and the mock exams, and he read them, and he marked himself, and he saw the grades in front of him, the low grades, the sort of grades that he knew would mean he would end his third year with a degree that no one would take seriously, that he would be passed over for jobs by people who spoke the right way and had the right grades, the ones who looked like they would fit right in, and he would be relegated to, what? Working as a pizza delivery driver? No, Amir thought, no, that wasn't going to happen.

If Adnan could do it, then Amir could do it. He could wear those clothes, drive that car, buy that house for his own parents. At night he lay in bed and thought about the look on his father's face when he handed his mother the keys to the sort of house she'd wanted all her life, the sort of house that made people stop and stare as they walked by, that would make other women stop their children in the middle of the road and say, *That house was bought with blood money*, because it was all they could say to hide their own envy for whoever lived inside. He'd pay for Bilal's wedding, because he could. He'd pay for their honeymoon too. He'd buy them all cars, send them on holidays, whatever they wanted.

That was what Amir wanted.

Thirty-six

Mohsin invited the boys to a party at his, the last blowout before exams descended on them and they all disappeared for a week or two, pens scratching in exam halls, sweating with the weight of their futures in their hands.

Amir came early, Mohsin opening the door, towel wrapped around his body. 'I'm just about to shower,' he said, before glancing at the time, 'you're here early.'

'Yeah,' he said, 'I needed to get out of the house.'

Amir had woken up later than usual, past mid-afternoon, and Zain had already gone to the library to work on his essays. Amir had started to get himself ready to head into the city centre, join Zain, but midway through putting on a shirt, he thought, what was the point of staring at his books for hours? So he told Zain he would meet him at Mohsin's.

For the first time in a long time, it felt as if the day was just his. There were no lectures to go to, no exams to prepare for, no study, no mock exams, no marking of his own work, no friends to meet. Even the house was empty, Bilal and his father at work, his mother out somewhere.

So Amir made himself breakfast, boiled eggs cut into neat

segments and placed between two slices of toasted bread, a flurry of salt on top, and when he was done, he decided to go to his grandmother's house, not calling ahead first but just turning up, knocking at the door, and when she opened it, she was surprised to see him there.

This house, a place where Amir used to spend so much of his time, he and Bilal coming here when they were children, to spend weekends and school holidays there, because they weren't the kind of people who went on holidays, unless the three or four times their father took them to Pakistan counted as a holiday, weeks spent in another country, sitting in the house their father had grown up in and nowhere else, this was where they came for fun, this was where they came to escape, where they felt joy, especially when their grandfather was still alive, looking in his pockets as if he didn't already know what was in there, feigning shock when he pulled out pound coins, giving them to Amir and Bilal secretly, behind closed doors, telling them to spend the money wisely, not to tell their parents where they'd got the money from, 'Especially not your mother,' he would whisper to them, 'she's always been weird about money,' and Amir and Bilal would go to the corner shop, eager to spend their money but always unsure of what to spend it on, Amir too scared that he might buy the wrong thing, and he would watch Bilal, to see what he got, what he spent his money on, because it might just be the thing that Amir should get too, and whatever they got, they'd have to consume it right then and there, outside the corner shop, no matter the weather, not able to take it back to the house, because it wasn't just their mother who had a problem with it, it was everyone else too, berating their grandfather for spending his money on the kids when he could be doing something else with it, as if a few pounds every other week was going to mean the end of him.

'Your uncle is out,' Amir's grandmother said, turning back into the house, Amir following her in, 'but he's left all his stuff here, have you seen all this stuff he's brought into my house?' she said, waving her hand to the front room.

'What stuff?' Amir asked, pretending that he didn't know, that it wasn't him who had sat there with his uncle, sorting through all the motherboards. He peered into the front room as he passed and saw that his uncle had bought even more boxes, looking unruly next to the organised ones, and that there were packages there now, sellotaped, addresses written on top of them, ready to take to the post office.

'This new idea of his,' his grandmother said, walking through the living room to a small room that sat between it and the kitchen, a dining table there, only three chairs around it, the fourth sacrificed because there wasn't enough space to have them all out, one side of the table pressed against the wall. She sat herself back down at the table, and Amir sat by her. 'Your brother is getting married.'

'He is,' Amir said.

'Is she nice?' she asked, and then, before Amir could answer, 'Your mum seems to think so, she told me the other day all about this nice girl and her nice parents, told me that we knew them, that they're related to us through marriage, that's nice, I think, nice to know them, nice to know they're not bad people.'

'Yeah,' Amir said, and then he added, 'I met her.'

'Momina,' his grandmother asked. He nodded. 'What was she like?'

'Smart,' Amir said, 'smarter than him, and she knows exactly what she wants.'

'Good,' his grandmother said, 'good, we need more women like that, the last thing I want is for him to marry some little girl who has no idea what she wants and just lets him take charge, men like your brother, they need a strong woman, someone who's not going to be afraid to come in and show him what to do.'

'No, she won't be afraid of that,' Amir said, and he laughed, thinking back to when he had met Momina. She would make a good partner to Bilal, he thought, and part of him was glad for his brother, happy that Bilal had found someone.

'So,' his grandmother asked, 'why are you here? What do you want?'

'Can't I come spend some time with my Nani?' Amir said.

'You don't usually come here unless your uncle is bringing you or you want something,' she said, 'not like when you and Bilal were younger, here all the time, that never happens now.'

'I had some time,' Amir said, ignoring her words, because to focus on them would be to make him upset, 'and I wanted to come and see you.'

'Good,' she said, 'because I need your help.'

'Oh, you need my help,' Amir said.

'Yes,' she said, 'let me finish my food and then I'll tell you.'

When she was done, she pointed him to some black bags filled with clothes and other old things she was clearing out, and he carried them down and out for her, through the back garden, down the alley, out by the road, ready to be collected the next day, and when he was done with that, she asked him if he wouldn't mind moving her bed for her, she wanted it in a different position, she'd asked his uncle, but you know what he's like, she said, always running off to do something, and so Amir moved the bed for her, from one side of the room to the other, and when she was happy with it, he rearranged the rest of the furniture, bedside table, dresser, bookcase, and then she told Amir to go get her some ingredients for the curry she was going to make, and he was welcome to sit and eat it, so he went to the shop for her, buying exactly what she told him to get, because his grandmother was an exact person, the money she had given him could only be spent in the way she needed it to be, and when he came back, she set him on cutting vegetables, dicing onions and peppers, and grinding chillies and garlic and ginger to a paste, set him on stirring the pot while she deboned the chicken, and while they were in the middle of that, his uncle came back, clapped a hand on Amir's back, said, 'Are you training him how to be a good wife, now that Bilal is getting married? It's time this one did too, isn't it?' and Amir's grandmother gave his uncle a reproachful look, and then his uncle said, 'Come, I need your help,' and Amir glanced at his grandmother, who waved her hands at him, said, 'Go, go, I'm fine,' and so Amir went into the front room with his uncle, his uncle picking up all the packages, telling Amir, 'You're good with this, yeah? Just like last time,' and so Amir took out his phone and started to take down serial numbers again, and his uncle came back, helped him, and Amir got so into it that he didn't realise how late it was until his grandmother called, said that the food was ready, and he saw the time, said he needed to go home, he had somewhere to be later, and his grandmother said, 'Not without eating,' forcing him to sit, and the chicken curry she had made was perfect, as it always was, his grandmother joking, 'Hasn't your mum got it right yet?' and Amir said, 'No, she hasn't,' and when he was done, he stayed another five minutes, cleaning the dishes, then raced out of the door, heading back to the house, so he could quickly change before he caught the bus into the city centre, to Mohsin's.

When he got home, Bilal was standing in the kitchen, glass of water to his lips. He'd been for a run, it looked like, his face glossy with sweat, shirt and shorts different colours, his sweat turning the grey into black. 'Hey,' Bilal said, panting slightly, 'sorry, I didn't know anyone was here.'

'Mum's out,' Amir said, having not seen her car parked outside when he'd come back, 'probably wedding shopping.'

'Yeah,' Bilal said, looking up at the ceiling, 'I knew she'd be into it, I didn't know she'd be this into it.'

'You didn't think she'd be this into her favourite child getting married?'

'Don't,' Bilal said, shaking his head, 'it's exhausting, and we have so much time left, we're not even getting married until next year.'

'Unless you have the nikah this year.'

'Unless we have the nikah this year,' Bilal said, downing the rest of the water and putting the glass in the sink, reaching for the sponge. 'You good?' he asked.

'Yeah,' Amir said, 'I'm just going out to a friend's.'

'Cool,' Bilal said, water running, soap slipping down the side of the glass, 'before you go,' he said quickly, 'I was talking to Mum today, she wants to do the whole thing, seven days, a whole week, I'm trying to talk her down to four, maybe five at most, Momina hates all of this stuff, always has, she'd rather we just signed the marriage certificate and were done,' he said, smiling at Amir, 'but Mum wants a lot, and so do her parents, really, so we're just thinking about everything, and you know, Momina doesn't have any brothers and sisters, it's just her, so ...' Bilal said, dragging the word out, and Amir could see exactly where this was going, what Bilal was going to ask next, to be his best man, to be involved, to help plan, to execute, and for a second, Amir felt like cutting him off, saying, *No, I don't want to be your best man, I don't want to sit around with Mum and listen to her talk about clothes and food and music, I couldn't think of anything worse*, but then he thought about it for a second longer, how he and Bilal had been the best men at their uncle's wedding, how fun it had been, to be together like that, and sure, that had been years ago, things had changed now, things were different, but maybe they could do it again, here, maybe things could be the same again.

'I'll do it,' Amir said, 'be your best man,' and he smiled at Bilal, whose face flickered, eyebrows flinching in confusion.

'Oh,' Bilal said, 'no, I mean, that's kind of you, but no, we don't, I asked someone else, my friend, Imran, you remember him? From university, we lived together, he said he would, he lives in London now but he'll come up here for it,' Bilal said, and Amir stared at his brother, his chest hollow, the smile slipping from his face.

'Yeah, I get it,' Amir said. He took a step back, away from the kitchen.

'No, I mean, there are so many other things that we want you to do, I just thought—' Bilal said, panic on his face, 'I didn't think that you'd want to—'

'I get it,' Amir said, 'I have to go, but we can talk about it later,' and then he left the room, heading upstairs before Bilal could say anything, and he changed quickly, had thought about showering but now just wanted to get out of the house as quickly as he could, and when he went downstairs Bilal called his name, but Amir pretended not to hear him.

'I need to shower,' Mohsin said, 'I'll be, like, five, ten minutes.'

'Yeah, yeah, that's cool,' Amir said, 'don't worry about me.'

Mohsin headed off to his room, leaving the door open as he did, the sound of the shower turning on echoing through the flat. Amir went to the sofa, sat down, reached for the remote, turned on the TV, but all Mohsin had were streaming apps, each throwing up endless things for Amir to watch, not like when he was younger, he and Bilal just jumping channels, landing on whatever was best, even if it was already halfway through. Now, there was too much, hard to decide, so he gave up. He stood up, walked over to the window, looked out over the city. From up here, people were so small, like ants that he could reach out and crush if he wanted to, all it would take was one carefully placed step and they'd be wiped out, one swing of his hand and buildings would fall, one forced breath and everything would collapse.

'Sorry, man,' Mohsin said from behind him, Amir turning around to see Mohsin wearing the same towel around his body, hair wet, 'I just got back from the gym.'

'It's fine,' Amir said.

'Let me put some clothes on, the others won't be here for a while, you hungry?'

'Nah,' Amir said, 'nah.'

'I gotta eat, though, is that cool?'

'Yeah,' Amir said, 'of course.'

'Do you mind doing me a favour?' Mohsin asked. 'There's

some chicken in the fridge with some rice, can you warm it up for me, just in the microwave?'

'Yeah,' Amir said, and Mohsin thanked him before heading into his bedroom. Amir walked to the fridge, took the food out, plastic container, plated it, put it in the microwave, watched the food go around, took out the plate and stirred the rice with a fork, returned the plate to the microwave, watched the seconds count down, wondering all the while what he was doing, when had he turned into this person?

'Thanks, man,' Mohsin said, putting a hand on Amir's shoulder, then reaching around him for the plate. 'I just need to eat before tonight. You staying, yeah?'

'Yeah,' Amir said. He had told Adnan the night before, just before he'd been given his portion of money, and Adnan had said, 'That's fine.' Amir explaining exactly why he couldn't be there, and Adnan had laughed, said, 'You don't have to tell me everything, you know, I'm not your dad, I'm not going to get angry if I don't know where you are, just tell me when you can't do a night, there's always someone who can take your place.'

'Good,' Mohsin said, 'you've been disappearing on us lately.'

'Family stuff, you know, the wedding.'

'The wedding?' Mohsin said, talking around the chicken and rice in his mouth. 'Your brother's wedding, that's why you've not been around?'

'Yeah, it's busy,' Amir said, 'they want me involved.'

'Say no,' Mohsin said, 'you ain't gotta do shit.'

'He's my brother,' Amir said, 'I can't just not do anything.'

'Why not?' Mohsin said. 'Just because you're brothers doesn't mean you owe him anything.'

'What?' Amir said, 'We're family.'

'Yeah, but isn't that how they get you?' Mohsin asked, leaning against the counter, plate in his hand, shovelling the food into his mouth like he'd never eaten before. 'They say all that shit about family, about loyalty, about how they'll always be there for you, but they just want you to be a certain way and the second you stop being that, it's all, *You're not my son anymore, you're not part of this family, you need to change your ways*, same old story.'

'Yeah, maybe,' Amir said, 'but I should be there for him.'

'Should be, not want to be?' Mohsin asked.

No, Amir wanted to say, *want to be too*, but he shook his head, said, 'It's just a bit busy.'

'Well,' Mohsin said, one hand reached out, on Amir's shoulder, squeezing a touch, 'just know you can say no, if you want to, and if they kick you out, you can always come here, and besides, you're living with me next year, right? We're sorted with that.'

'Sorted?' Amir said, Mohsin taking his hand back, needing it to continue eating. 'What do you mean, sorted?'

'I mean, I've found a place, here, let me show you,' Mohsin said, taking his phone out of his pocket, swiping quickly and then turning it around. Amir took it from him, a flat even bigger than the one they were in now. Amir quickly swiped through the photos but then went down to the price.

'Two grand a month,' Amir said, looking at Mohsin.

'Yeah,' Mohsin said, taking the phone back, 'it's here, in this building, a couple of floors above us, so not much difference, same view, same gym, same everything.'

'Mohsin, I can't afford two grand a month.'

'It won't be two grand a month,' Mohsin said, 'you're not paying for all of it.'

'A grand then, I can't afford a grand.'

'I'm not asking you to,' Mohsin said, 'I'm paying seventeen-fifty for this now, it's just two-fifty more a month, my dad won't even notice.'

'Mohsin—'

'Amir,' Mohsin said, 'it's done, it's sorted, don't worry about it.'

'Mohsin, I'm not—'

'Why not?' Mohsin asked.

'I'm not—' Amir started to say, but then he thought about the stack under his windowsill. *A grand*, he thought, *it would just be a grand a month*, and he could make that money in five days with Adnan. Five days, and he could live here. Five days, and he wouldn't have to live at home anymore. Five days, and he'd have a place of his own. 'I can't let you pay for it all.'

'Okay, then you can pay the extra two-fifty,' Mohsin said, 'if that'll make you feel better about being here.'

'Nah, I'll pay the grand.'

'How?' Mohsin asked. 'I don't want you to—'

'Don't mind how,' Amir said, 'I can make the grand.'

Mohsin looked at him, opened his mouth as if to say something, then changed his mind, said, 'So you're in?'

'I'm in,' Amir said.

Mohsin let out a shout, reached for Amir, plate pressed in between them, laughed, said, 'Well, then, fuck, we need to celebrate tonight.'

Thirty-seven

Amir's father was waiting for him when he came down the stairs. It had just gone past midday, Amir awake for a while, lying in bed, fighting his bladder until he couldn't stand it anymore. He had been waiting for his father to leave, just the two of them in the house, Bilal gone to work and their mother out somewhere, Amir listening to her leave in the morning. He'd been waiting to hear the front door open and close but it hadn't.

His father didn't say anything when Amir stepped into the living room, walked past him, to the bathroom, where Amir closed the door, washed his face as slowly as he could, brushed his teeth for longer than he normally would, all in the hope that when he walked out, his father wouldn't be there, but when Amir opened the bathroom door, he saw his father's reflection in the kitchen tiles, sitting on the sofa, peering at his phone.

'Sit,' his father said, when Amir entered the living room. Amir turned to look at him. His father, still looking at his phone, gestured to the space next to him. 'Sit down,' he said again. Amir took the other sofa instead, sitting opposite him, and waited for him to speak.

When Amir was younger, he often tried to guess what his father wanted from him, not letting him finish his sentences because he was sure he knew what his father was going to ask, what he wanted, so eager to please, and his father would get angry, his hand tight on Amir's face. Amir became used to the slaps, became used to not talking.

'Your brother is getting married,' his father said slowly, 'finally, we waited too long with him, twenty-six is old, not too old, but it's old, I told her, we should get him married sooner, but she was convinced that he had someone, that we should give him the choice, so we did and, lucky for her, it worked out.' Amir's father paused, and Amir stayed quiet. 'It's going to cost a lot, and we need everyone to contribute.' Amir's stomach tightened. 'Your exams are over, yes?'

'Not yet,' Amir said.

'But they will be soon.'

'Yes.'

'Then you need to get a job,' his father said, 'your brother is getting married and it can't all rest on me.'

Amir didn't look at his father, just stared at the wall opposite him, hands tight by his sides.

'Are you listening to me?' his father asked, looking at Amir.

'You want me to get a job so I can pay for Bilal's wedding,' Amir said, not quite asking.

'Help pay,' his father said, 'of course you should help pay, you're his brother, that's what brothers do for each other, that's what I did for my sister, I paid for her wedding, paid for her to come over here, helped her buy a house, it's what family do for each other.'

'Is that what Bilal wants?' Amir asked. 'For his younger brother to pay for his wedding?'

'What does it matter what Bilal wants?'

'It's his wedding.'

'Yes, it's his wedding, and we're going to pay for it.'

'So he won't then?' Amir asked, looking at his father. 'Bilal won't be paying for anything?'

'Bilal will be paying for some,' his father said, looking at Amir with confused eyes, mouth open with exasperation, 'a brother, a son, contributes to the family.'

'And what if I don't want to?' Amir said.

'You don't want to?' his father asked, taking off his glasses. 'You don't want to help,' his father said, nodding slowly, 'okay, you don't want to help, but you're happy to live here without paying for anything, happy to eat the food in the kitchen, to sleep in that bed, to go out with your friends, not tell anyone where you're going, you think that's okay, you think that's right.'

'What am I supposed to pay with?' Amir asked. 'What money am I supposed to give you?'

'You get a job,' his father said, voice tight, 'that's what people do, that's what everyone does, people work and they earn money and they contribute to their families.'

'I told you—'

'You told me that you couldn't work because university was too hard, well, your exams are nearly over, the summer is coming up, you had a free ride—'

'A free ride,' Amir said, and he almost laughed then, caught himself.

'Yes, a free ride,' his father said, 'has anyone asked you for anything this year? Has anyone asked you for a single thing? No, we've left you to whatever you want to do, but enough is enough, you are a grown man, things need to be paid for.'

'Oh, things need to be paid for,' Amir said, 'sure, sure, and did things need to be paid for when Bilal was at university?'

'That was different.'

'That was different?'

'Bilal wasn't living here.'

'So if I leave then,' Amir said, 'that means I don't have to pay for anything?'

'Leave?' his father said, reaching for his phone again, putting his glasses back on. 'Where would you go? Who would take you in?'

His father's eyes lowered on the phone, no longer looking at Amir, who sat, his skin fizzing with anger. 'I'm not paying for Bilal's wedding, he has a good enough job and I know you have money.'

'Oh?' his father said, looking up at Amir, eyes narrowed. 'And what do you know about my money?'

'That big fucking house in Pakistan, I know you robbed your own children to pay for it, I know this house doesn't have a mortgage, I know you have money,' Amir said, the words spilling out of his mouth, too quick to catch, too hot to hold back.

'You don't know anything,' his father said, 'and you'd better be careful how you speak to me in my house.'

'Your house,' Amir said, 'and what if I do leave, what then?'

'Who would take you?' his father asked again.

'That's none of your fucking business,' Amir said, standing, and his father mirrored him, the two of them standing before each other, and even though Amir towered over him, it still felt as if his father was the taller one. But even as Amir spoke, he didn't know where he would go, everyone was going to leave for the summer soon, Zain, Mohsin, Nadeem, Omar,

Abbas, Kamran, all leaving to go back to their homes, to their families, and Amir resented them for it, and he envied them too, that they could escape, that this wasn't their fucking home, that there was somewhere else in this world that they could return to.

His father moved, his hand around Amir's face, thumb on one cheek, finger on the other, squeezing tight, Amir's cheeks stretching. 'I'll tell you what my fucking business is,' he said, voice low, Amir pulling at his fingers, at his hand, at his wrist, 'you're my fucking business and I've told you what you're doing, you're not grown, you're nothing, and you're going to listen to me, that's what good sons do, so be a good fucking son.' His father let him go, and Amir moved back, pain pulsing on either side of his face. 'Be a good fucking son,' his father repeated, 'and do what I say.'

'Fuck you,' Amir said, and his father moved again, but before he could get to Amir, Amir made for the door, rushing through it, up the stairs, to his room, door closing behind him.

Thirty-eight

Amir stood outside the house, waiting for him to arrive. Amir had called him straight from his bedroom, asked if he could come over, and he asked nothing of Amir, told him he was out but he'd be there in twenty minutes, was that fine? And Amir told him, yes, threw on his clothes, grabbed some things, his money, and then raced down the stairs, out of the front door, his father shouting at Amir to wait a minute.

Amir ran all the way to his house. By the time he got there, he was drenched in sweat, the kind that made the heat of the day unbearable, so he pulled off his hoodie, his shirt, sat down on the front step, not looking up at any of the people who passed by, who gave him curious looks.

Amir was aware of how he looked, tall, dark-skinned boy, sitting outside someone's door, wearing joggers and nothing else. He told these people to be scared, to go ahead and look at him, but only when he wasn't looking back, because if he caught them staring, there would be hell to pay. He knew what people saw when they looked at him, just another brown boy with violence in his eyes. He was a threat to them. He was always going to be a threat to them.

Amir's uncle pulled up in his car, parked, threw his keys at

Amir as he walked around the car, Amir catching them and opening the door, thankful to get inside. There was safety inside this house.

'What happened?' his uncle asked as Amir walked straight to the kitchen, pulling the fridge open, his uncle, addicted to Coke, red cans lining the fridge. He reached in for one, pulled it open, cold in his hand, put it to his lips, downed half the can right there, even as it burned the back of his throat, made him cough when he put the can down, wiped his mouth with the back of his hand, sugar smeared on his skin, thick.

'What do you think?' Amir said. 'My dad is a fucking dickhead.'

'Don't,' his uncle said, 'don't talk like that in front of me.'

'Am I wrong?'

'I'm not saying that,' his uncle said slowly, 'but I'm just saying, don't talk about him like that in front of me.'

'Why do you always act like he's such a good guy?' Amir asked, frustration bubbling under him.

'He is a good guy.'

'Why? Why does everyone say that about him?'

'Because he's here,' his uncle said, walking past Amir to the cupboard, swinging open the door, reaching for a jar of sweets, purple and red and green and orange and brown and silver, offered the jar to Amir, who shook his head. 'Because he's here,' his uncle said, 'and not somewhere else, with some other woman and a thousand other kids, you know what men are like,' crinkle of the wrapper as he opened it, put the soft between his teeth, 'you know how they run off with some white woman who wants to fuck a brown man, thinks it's fun to have a Muslim man, even better if he's still married with kids of his own, it's exciting for them, but your dad has never done that, he comes home every day, he's still here.'

'He's still here,' Amir said, 'he's still here, so I'm supposed to ignore everything else that he does and think that he's the best dad in the whole world?'

'No one is telling you to do that.'

'He's not.'

'He's not what?'

'He's not the best fucking dad in the whole world,' Amir said, 'just because he stayed, it doesn't mean that he's great or good or even okay at being a dad.'

'Okay,' his uncle said, gesturing at Amir to follow him into the other room, his uncle taking one seat at the dining table, Amir sitting opposite him. 'So what happened today?' his uncle asked.

'He told me he wants me to pay for Bilal's wedding.'

His uncle's face shifted, confused.

'He told me that good brothers, good sons, contribute, and that I needed to get a job and help pay for it. He's obsessed with money,' Amir said, 'obsessed with having it, with hoarding it, from everywhere.'

'He worked hard for his money,' Amir's uncle said, 'you know he came from—'

'Has he fuck,' Amir said, and when his uncle opened his mouth, Amir shook his head, said, 'no, don't start telling me that I should appreciate how hard he works, because that money was never for me and Bilal, it was all for him, all for that big house in Pakistan that no one lives in.'

'That was his dream,' his uncle started.

'So we had to grow up poor so that he could achieve his dream?'

'It was his money,' his uncle said, 'you wouldn't let anyone else tell you what to do with your money.'

'I don't have kids,' Amir said, voice raised now, on the edge of shouting, 'I don't have any children, he did, he has two of us, and he let us live in poverty, that's what we were fucking living in, Mum always having to ask you guys for money, telling me and Bilal not to say anything to him because he was so proud, he'd rather we starved than ask for help, running from shop to shop with all her vouchers to make sure that we had enough, all so what? So he could go back there, build this big house that no one is ever going to live in so that all those people back there, all those people that he left, can look at it and remember what a big man is, what a big fucking man he is, robbed his own kids for it, yeah, that's a real man, nah, that's a real fucking man.'

'You have everything,' his uncle said, looking at him blankly, 'you've never needed anything.'

'Are you fucking kidding me?' Amir said. He put the can down on the table, because he didn't want to crush it in his hand, the can teetering on the table for a moment from side to side. 'You have no idea,' he said, 'he was never there, always working, and I always thought it was because he wanted to make sure that we had everything we needed, but he was only doing it for himself, and now, now after all those years, never looking at us, never talking to us, reminding us of what disappointments we are to him, he wants us to, what, turn around and give him everything we have, we're meant to just say, "Yeah, sure, Dad, because you've given us so much, here we are, every bit of us, for you."'

'You have no idea', his uncle said wearily, 'of the kinds of dads that are out there, the ones who fuck around with other women, the ones who drink, do drugs, gamble all of their money away, the ones who beat their wives and their kids, the ones who don't come home one day, leaving their wives and their kids to figure things out, you're sad because, what, he didn't come home every day and tell you that he loved you or ask you questions about what you did at school? He did everything else, made sure that you had a roof over your heads, made sure that you had clothes, that you didn't starve, you're at university, think, for a second, about what that means to him, his two sons educating themselves in a way that he never could, does that mean nothing to you, or are you so stupid that you can't see any of it?'

'I'm not stupid,' Amir said.

'Then stop acting like it, you might not like him, and no one is telling you that you have to, but nothing is black and white.' He stopped, took a breath. 'Look, stay here, I'll go to your house, I'll get whatever you need, clothes and stuff, you just tell me what you need, and let me talk to your mum and dad, figure out what's going on, and if he really doesn't want you back there, and I don't think he'll say that, then you can stay here, there's always space here for you and your brother.'

Amir looked away, down at the red can, put his fingers around it. He wanted, so much, to be able to say no, to say that he didn't need any of them anymore, that he was going to carve out a space in this world for himself by himself, that he could live a life without them, that they needed him more than he needed them.

'Okay,' Amir said.

Thirty-nine

Amir's grandmother came back to the house a couple of hours later, found him sitting at the dining table. She looked at him with gentle surprise mixed with joy, asked him what he was doing there when he was just there the other day, putting a hand on his head as she walked past him into the kitchen.

Amir stood and asked her if she needed help, reaching for the thin blue bags that she was carrying, the plastic stretching to ripping point, and she said no, pulling the bags away from him, 'I don't need your help, I've managed this long without needing you to hold my bags, I think I'm fine for another little while.'

She moved with the ease of someone who had lived in this house all her life, for nearly fifty years, she had existed there, in that house, refusing to move even when her friends moved, even when her sister moved, taking all her daughters with her, disappearing to Sheffield, even when Amir's grandfather died and she went to Pakistan for nearly an entire year, his mother and his uncle not knowing if she was going to come back, but then she did, slipping back into her life as if she'd never left.

'What are you doing here?' she asked. 'Is your uncle around?'

'No,' Amir said, 'he's gone out.'

'Out, out, out,' she said, shaking her head, 'that boy is never at home, but then again,' she said, looking at Amir, 'neither are you from what I hear.' Amir looked away, shame forcing his eyes away from hers. 'Are you staying to eat?' she asked. 'Will your uncle be back for that? I've got some fish in the fridge, but I can make something else.'

'Well,' Amir said, and all of his bravado was gone as he stood in front of her, shifting on his feet, the years melting underneath him. He was six years old again, caught with his hand in her purse, two pound coins gripped in his fingers, closed tight over the metal, looking down at the floor as she asked him what he thought he was doing, Amir mumbling that he just wanted to go to the shop to buy something, a chocolate or something, his grandmother forcing his hand out of the purse, opening his fingers, slowly but her grip on him strong, taking the coins, and then slapping Amir, hard, on the face, only once, but it was enough for him to remember never to do that again. 'I'm here to stay,' he said.

'Stay?' she asked, looking at him. 'Stay here?'

'Yes.'

'Why?' she asked, and then, before Amir could answer, she said, 'You can stay, no one is saying no to you, no one will ever say no to you, this is your home, you know that, but you haven't stayed here for years, you or Bilal, why are you staying here now?' and before Amir could even open his mouth, 'Are you fighting with them?' she asked. 'With your dad?'

Amir nearly laughed, then caught himself. 'Not fighting,' he said.

'But fighting,' his grandmother said, nodding her head slowly. 'What is it now?'

'Nothing,' Amir said, but that was the wrong thing to say, her eyes narrowed at him. 'They just, they don't want me to be there.'

'Your dad doesn't want you to be at your own home?'

'No,' Amir said, words suddenly slippery, 'he just, my dad wants me to help pay for Bilal's wedding.'

'Pay for it?' Amir's grandmother said, soft chuckle, but then her face shifted as she realised Amir wasn't joking. 'You shouldn't,' she said, 'and Bilal would never ask you to, your dad,' she said, shaking her head, 'I don't think he's ever going to learn, it's going to take something big for him to get it through his head, that his children are not just his children, that you both are always going to do what you want to do, like when Bilal left and your mum came here, I told her, day after day, "What are you doing here? Go home, go home to your other son," but she didn't want to go back, not until Bilal was back, she wouldn't listen to me, and your dad is the same, they will never learn.'

She stopped speaking then, as if she'd just realised who she was talking to, turned her face away from Amir.

'So can I,' Amir asked, pulling the conversation back, 'stay here?'

His grandmother nodded, said, 'Always, always, you never have to ask,' and then she chuckled again, 'next thing you know, he'll be telling you that you need to get married, I remember when your mum had it in her head that Bilal needed to get married, sent him on all those meetings with those women, time after time, coming here, asking me what was wrong with her son, and I kept telling her, "Things are different now, give him some time, he'll come to you when the time is right," and she was convinced that there was something wrong with him,' his grandmother, closing her eyes for a second, 'and you know, they might think the same thing about you,' she said, pointing a celery stick at Amir, 'but you don't need to get married, it's not going to fix what's in you, it's just going to ruin the life of whoever they find for you.'

'Fix?' Amir asked. 'Fix what in me?'

'The thing that was wrong with your uncle, getting married didn't fix that for him and it won't fix it for you either.'

Anger flared inside Amir, anger and hurt. 'What's wrong with me?' he asked.

'The same thing that's wrong with all of you boys, no boy I've ever known has been happy with what he has, you run around out there, shouting and screaming, wanting what other people have, you forget to look back at what you already have, and when we try to remind you of what you do have, you look at us all like villains, like we can't be trusted, like we're trying to hold you back, but we've seen it all before, us, the ones who stay behind, the women, we know that nothing out there is going to give you what you want, and you try to get it in so many different ways, you leave, like Bilal did, go live somewhere else for years, and what did he do? He had his fill and then he came right back, or you do what your grandfather did, you go and you work and you work and you work and at the end of it all, you sit on the sofa and you watch old cowboy films and then you die, you miss everything, or you do what your uncle did, run around like you're the biggest man, think that if you shout loud enough, if you bite hard enough, people will be scared of you, but no matter how loud you are, no matter how hard you hit, there is always going to be someone who hits back harder, and your uncle, he learned that the hard way, but that's the thing with you boys, there is no stopping you, you have to learn this yourselves, you have to go and do what you're going to do, and when you're fallen, we'll still be here to invite you back in, to hold you, to rock you to sleep when you need us to, because that's our job, that's always going to be our job, and sometimes we don't mind it but, sometimes, we just want to take you by the ears and ask you, what did you think was going to happen when you went and you kicked at people? Did you not think they were going to kick back? Did you think you were something new, something better, something different? Because you're not, no one is, we've all been here before, and the people who come after us are going to do exactly what we did, there is no new, and this, this thing in you that you feel, this thing that is going to drive you out of that door into the world, make you do things you know you shouldn't be doing, no one can fix that for you, no woman, no baby, no house, no car, no TV, no money, nothing, only you can, just ask your uncle,' she said, picking up her vegetables, gesturing to Amir to get the ones that she'd left behind. 'You can stay here,' she said, 'for as long as you want, but know that I'm not your mother, I'm hers.'

Forty

Amir's uncle came back in the evening, the three of them sitting at the dining table, eating the food Amir's grandmother had made, chickpeas and pilchards, swimming together in a thick sauce, spiced and warm. His grandmother talked, mainly to his uncle, about a man who had died back in Pakistan, someone from the village, saying that she wanted to send money there, to help his family, build a well, donate to mosques in his name. 'He was a good man,' she said, 'he took care of the house and the land for us when we first came here, we should do something for his children,' and Amir's uncle said he would look into it.

Amir was given the spare room, his uncle pressing a bag of clothes that he had pulled from Amir's room into his hands, Amir's toothbrush in there too, phone charger, his uncle telling him that he didn't know what else he wanted but if there was anything, he could go back, told Amir to follow him to his room, to get a blanket and a pillow for the bed.

Years ago, before Amir's uncle was engaged, this room was used for storage, Amir's grandmother loading it with blankets and duvets and pillows and old suitcases she would never open or throw away, filled with clothes and dish sets from when she got married and all the other things she had hoarded over her life, but then Amir's uncle told her he wanted to get married, so she set about finding him a wife, rolled up her sleeves and found a far cousin from Sheffield, six years younger than Amir's uncle, who had been looking to get married but couldn't find anyone, Amir's grandmother telling his mother that it was because the girl had a PhD, that she had spent so long in education, she had forgotten how to be a wife, she needed teaching, how to cook, how to clean, how to be for someone, but she was a good fit for Amir's uncle, so the two of them met and they liked each other enough to get married, and suddenly, that back room was emptied, things were thrown away, other things found a new home, but that wasn't enough, Amir's uncle deciding to demolish the room and begin anew, putting in a bathroom, so that husband and wife didn't have to use the one downstairs, putting in shelves and a new bed and other furniture, and the family watched him spend every penny of his savings doing up this one room, and when he finally got married, when she finally moved in, they all thought this would be the beginning of his life.

She stayed for two years, and in those two years, she fought constantly with Amir's grandmother, who told her that she didn't need to work anymore because she was a wife and it was Amir's uncle's responsibility to take care of her, even though she, as a lecturer at the University of Birmingham, was earning around more than twice as much as he was, who was continuing her research there, research into the interaction between politics and the lived experience of Muslims in Britain, Bilal and her sitting and talking about her work whenever they got the chance, Bilal the only one in the family who seemed to care about what she did, Amir's mother smiling but not asking any follow-up questions, Amir barely interacting with her, and she told Amir's grandmother that she didn't want to give up her job, so she didn't, and she didn't want to cook all the time, so she didn't, and she didn't want to clean constantly, so she didn't, and Amir's grandmother made her life hell, broke her down, the critiques, the attacks, the want for more and more, and Amir's uncle said nothing, did nothing, so they started to fight too, she wanted him to defend her, he didn't want to go against his own mother, especially because Amir's grandfather had died by this point. He was all she had, his uncle said, over and over again.

So she left. Two years in, she disappeared, and now Amir's uncle stayed in this room, with its purple and white walls, with its floating shelves, with its king-sized bed and its complete bathroom. Amir stood there now, by the door, not going in, never going in, because it felt too sad to go in, knowing what his uncle once had and what he no longer had.

Amir thought about her sometimes, when he saw his uncle, what they might have been like together, if they might have had children by now, if they might have built a life for themselves. At the very beginning, just when she had moved in, Amir's uncle had never looked happier, years wiped off his face. They barely saw him those first few months, the two of them spending all of their time together, before all the holes appeared.

If only she had wanted less, Amir thought, if only she knew what being a wife meant, if only she hadn't been such a selfish bitch, maybe Amir's uncle wouldn't be alone now.

Forty-one

Amir's brother came at midday, knocking on the door to the spare room where Amir had spent the night, opening the door before Amir could say anything, but he'd been awake for a while, listening to the sounds of a different house, Amir's grandmother awake early, opening and closing cupboards, rattling dishes, dragging chairs on the floor, the sorts of noises that she didn't question making because this was her house. Amir's uncle was talking to her as he ate the breakfast that she made for him, though Amir couldn't make out the words, he wondered if they were talking about him, and then Amir's uncle came upstairs, the metal clink of a belt being buckled, and then, before he went downstairs, Amir heard him walk softly towards the door, the soft crunch of his shoes on the carpet, and then silence as he listened at the door for Amir before he left.

'Mum told me you were here,' Bilal said, walking over to the bed, sitting on the edge of it, Amir sitting up, pulling the duvet so that Bilal wasn't on top of it. 'What happened?' Bilal asked.

'Have you asked Dad?'

'I'm asking you.'

Amir clenched his jaw, hands curling into fists under his duvet, where Bilal couldn't see them. 'He told me I needed to pay for your wedding,' Amir said, looking away from his brother as he spoke.

Bilal laughed, then stopped, said, 'What?'

'That's what he said.'

'That's insane.'

'Is it?' Amir asked, looking back at his brother. 'He said that it's what good brothers do, what he did for his sister—'

'No,' Bilal said, 'it is insane, and I didn't ask him to do that, I don't know what he's talking about, Momina and I have already talked about this, we have enough money saved up to pay for the entire thing ourselves, and we're not doing something huge, and even if we were, why would we ask you? Why would we …?' Bilal said, letting the sentence hang there, unfinished. 'I don't know why he would say that.'

'Because he's a prick,' Amir said. He looked away from Bilal to the window next to the bed, out to the road, to the cars driving past, people walking, the same sight his grandparents had woken up to every day for the past five decades, Amir's grandmother had never known anything else here, but his grandfather had, the house before this one, the one he shared with seven other men, all of them working shifts in the factories, sending money back home, saving whatever was left, so that they could bring their wives over, and after a few years, that was what they did, one by one, women arriving, and they would stay at the house too, cooking for the men, cleaning the house, domesticating what hadn't been before, and one by one, each couple moved out once they had enough money, and Amir's grandparents were one of the very first ones, buying this house for practically nothing, no money to their name, their entire lives playing out here. Did they know, Amir wondered, when they moved in that one of them would die here?

'So he told you to pay for the wedding?' Bilal asked.

'I told him I wasn't going to,' Amir said, and then shame appeared, embarrassment, so he added, 'because I can't, I'm not working—'

'You don't have to explain yourself to me,' Bilal said, 'I get it.'

'He told me that it was his house, all the usual bullshit, so I told him I was leaving.'

'It's not just his house,' Bilal said, 'it's our house, and if he wants to get specific about it, Mum owns half of it, her name is on it too, so he can't just say shit like that.'

'Mum knew,' Amir said, and he knew that she knew, that his father had been planning to have that conversation with him that morning, why would she have left? Why wasn't she there? And he knew that if he asked her, she would say, *No, I had no idea what your dad was planning to say, this was his idea*, but Amir knew they'd spoken about it, that his mother hadn't fought for him, wouldn't have even considered telling Amir first, so he could prepare himself. No, she'd just given in, because it was what she always did. It was her husband before her sons, a wife before a mother, always.

'I don't know,' Bilal said, 'but you're not being kicked out of the house, I'm not letting that happen.'

'You think you can stop him?' Amir asked. 'If he wants me out, I'm out, and even if you stop him now, what happens when you leave?'

'Leave?' Bilal said.

'Yeah, leave,' Amir said, 'you're telling me that you're staying there after you get married?'

Bilal's face was a blend of confusion, hurt. 'I don't know,' he said slowly, 'but that's not happening yet.'

'Yeah,' Amir said, 'it's not happening yet.' He turned to look at his brother, said, 'You know, he put his hands on me.' His father's fingers, on his face again, digging into his cheeks, holding him still.

'He hit you?' Bilal said, and Amir said nothing, but the two of them knew what that silence meant, they'd been here before, Amir running to Bilal when he was younger, face red from a slap, sides pulsing with pain, skin bruised, crying into Bilal's arms, wanting to know why their father was so intent on harming him, *I didn't do anything*, he'd say, *I just asked a question, I just said something, I didn't say anything*, he couldn't ever get it right, what their father wanted from Amir switched at any moment, years passing like that until Amir learned not to expect anything from his father but violence, but anger, until he learned to stay quiet because speaking was never worth what came after.

'It's not like it's the first time,' Amir said.

'He shouldn't have done that,' Bilal said, 'he shouldn't have done any of it.' Amir said nothing. 'I'm going to talk to him,' Bilal said, 'today, I just wanted to see you first, hear your side first.' Amir nodded, looked away from Bilal, down at the duvet, hands itching underneath it. 'Will you come?' Bilal asked. 'Tonight?'

'No,' Amir said, 'I have something.'

'Oh,' Bilal said, 'friends?'

'Yeah,' Amir said.

'Okay,' Bilal said, standing up. 'I'll go and talk to him and then, I don't know, maybe we can find some time in the week that works for you, whatever.' Amir nodded, and Bilal walked over to the door, stopped for a moment, turned back to Amir, said, 'Just tell me if you need anything, money, clothes, food, whatever, just tell me,' and he looked at Amir with such worry in his face, it nearly made Amir stand up then, say, *I'll come back, it's fine, it's all fine*, but then Amir remembered the look in his father's face, his fingers in Amir's cheeks, and he just nodded, said, 'Yeah, of course,' and then Bilal was gone.

Forty-two

Amir's exams came and went. He sat in dusty halls with the others in his class, and when they were done, he and Mohsin went to Mohsin's to get high, Mohsin talking about his plans for the summer, now that he was free, about Europe, 'Let me go be a white boy with a backpack,' and he asked Amir if he wanted to come with him, not just to Amsterdam but to the whole thing.

Amir wanted to, wanted so desperately to follow him to France and Spain and Italy and Belgium and Germany, places that had only existed for him on TV screens. 'I'll pay for you,' Mohsin said, and it was that, his offer, that made Amir say no, even as he feared the summer stretching out ahead of him, nothing for him to do but watch the days pass. 'Paris is great,' Mohsin said, 'I went there before uni, just me and the boys from home, for like two weeks, French women are fucking great, you should come, think about it.'

Farrah was mentioned once, by Zain, a week or so after Amir had left her house that early morning, walking home, the whole hour and a half, over roundabouts and along dual carriageways, up Alum Rock Road, stopping at Greggs, soft blue and white, to buy a cheese-and-onion pasty, which took him back to when he was at secondary school, him and Adnan and the boys hopping the gates, walking down Alum Rock Road, grabbing burgers and chips and cans of Coke, but sometimes Amir wouldn't be in the mood for it, he wanted a pasty, so he made them walk further, risking coming back too late, just so he could feel its warmth. When he got home that morning, he ignored his mother when she asked where he had been all night, heard her sigh and ask herself why she even bothered with him, and he went to his room, closed the door, lay down on his bed.

'Did you?' Zain asked when he saw Amir, the two of them meeting by Birmingham Library again, and Amir knew exactly what he was talking about but wouldn't give it to him so easily, asked him, 'What? Did I what?' and Zain told him how Sana had told Zain, Sana, that was the name of the girl who had opened the door as he was leaving, Sana, the girl who had told Mohsin that Amir and Farrah were a thing, Sana, the girl who told Zain that Amir had hurt Farrah, and Amir knew there was a different word that he wanted to use but didn't, held himself back. 'I didn't do shit,' Amir said, 'When was the last time you saw her?' Zain asked, 'When we were all out,' Amir said, 'And you went home with her?' Zain asked, 'Yeah,' Amir said, 'And did something happen?' Zain asked, 'We fucked if that's what you're asking,' Amir said, 'And that's all?' Zain asked, 'Yeah,' Amir said, 'that's all.'

Zain wanted to ask more, it was on the edges of his tongue, and Amir wanted him to, wanted him to ask, *Did you fuck her when she didn't want to be? Did she say no? Did she tell you to stop?*

Amir wanted him to say, *Is that what people like you do? People who look like you? People from Alum Rock? Is that what you mans do, yeah? Is that how you treat women? Is that what you're all fucking like, fucking monsters, deranged, every single one of you?* Amir wanted him to say, *Is this what you were born to do? Is this who you were always going to fucking be, just a fucking beast tearing through the world?* But Zain didn't say anything and they both moved on.

Amir deleted Farrah's number from his phone after he saw Zain, because he knew then that there was no going back, and he told himself not to think about it, but when he lay his head down at night, just before he disappeared into sleep, he played back the memory of that night. After all, he wasn't the one who'd been drunk, he was barely high, he remembered everything, the way Farrah had pushed herself on him in the club, how they'd kissed in her house, how she had gone upstairs to get the condom, how she had given it to him, the fucking, the sleeping next to him. If she didn't want it, why didn't she say it then? She said she did, but Amir had been there, how could he not have heard her? Why didn't she say so? Why didn't she push him off? Because she wanted it, Amir told himself, she wanted to get fucked and then told herself a different story when she woke up. Maybe seeing him in the morning light changed her mind. Easier to say that the big scary guy from Alum Rock fucked her without asking than admit that she'd wanted it.

Forty-three

Amir spent the night at Mohsin's, hovering on the outside of conversations, every so often tilting his head, nodding, agreeing, laughing, and then moving on to the next, using the toilet as an excuse, 'Just gonna go get a drink, gonna go have a smoke,' and while everyone around him steadily got drunker, Amir stayed sober, not even smoking, finding everyone irritating.

When Mohsin announced that they were going to a club, Amir told him no, Mohsin grabbed Amir by the back of the neck, and though Amir pushed him off, Mohsin grabbed him again, Amir realising just how strong Mohsin was, and Mohsin said Amir was definitely coming, so he should stop fighting, 'It's the last party of the year, don't be such a fucking dickhead,' and for a moment, Amir was thinking of letting him have his way, but then he pushed Mohsin off, said no, and when Mohsin smiled at him, Amir said, 'Fuck off, I'm not coming,' and Mohsin's face flickered, his understanding of the moment slipping, and Amir turned away, walked out of the apartment, ignored Mohsin calling for him.

That was when he saw her, stepping out of Mohsin's building, stopping for a second, taking a moment for himself,

Farrah, walking towards him, head turned towards her friends, purple dress that snaked down her body, rip in one side so that he could see her leg flash with every stride, she didn't see him and something in Amir told him to run, and something in Amir told him to ask to speak to her, to apologise, and something in Amir told him to stop looking at her, but it was too late, her eyes falling on him, half-laugh drying on her lips, face turning to surprise and then fear, Amir saw it in her eyes, and she moved to the side of her friend, and the four of them walked past Amir without a word exchanged, and Amir watched them as they walked away, watched Farrah as she walked away, waiting for her to turn around so he could see her face again, but she didn't.

JUNE

Forty-four

Amir lay in bed, listening to the sounds of his grandmother praying, the muttered Arabic, the small sighs as she changed positions, standing then sitting, pressing her head against the floor.

When he was younger, he had done all of that too, gone to mosque, learned to read the Quran, though he had never learned how to understand Arabic so whatever he read on the page made no sense to him, had fasted, had prayed, both at home and in the mosque on Fridays, worn his jubbah and his topi, woken up before the sun rose and prayed long after it had set. Even when Bilal stopped, and Bilal stopped quite early, years before he went to university, Amir carried on, pressing his head against the floor. Then, when he was fifteen, he stopped, waited for the world to turn against him, and when it didn't, he never went back, prayer mat untouched, Quran unopened, his relationship with God disappeared.

Amir went downstairs, his uncle sitting at the dining table, looking up at Amir as he walked in. Amir glanced at the time, saw that it was nearly one in the afternoon.

'You busy today?' his uncle asked.

His exams finished for the year, no more classes until September, Amir shook his head, 'Nah,' he said, 'I've got nothing.'

'Your mum called.'

'Yeah?' Amir said, walking into the kitchen, running himself a glass of water.

His uncle said nothing until Amir walked back into the room, sat down at the table. 'She's worried about you,' he said.

'Yeah,' Amir said, 'I'm sure she is.'

'Don't be a prick,' his uncle said, 'she hasn't seen you in a while, she's worried about you.'

'Is that all she had to say?' Amir asked. 'Nothing about what he said to me?'

'She didn't mention your dad,' his uncle said, leaning across the table to Amir, who had chosen to sit opposite him. 'Look, I know I can't tell you what to do, if I did, you wouldn't be fucking around with Adnan.' Amir opened his mouth to defend himself, but his uncle put up his hands, 'I'm not saying shit to you about that boy, I've said what I've said, but I will say this, you should speak to her, even if it's just a phone call.'

'I have nothing to say to her.'

'I don't think that's true,' his uncle said. 'I'm not asking you to move back in, no one is saying that, but she deserves to hear from you, at least.'

Amir looked at his glass, both hands around it, fingers tapping on the surface. 'Today?' he asked.

'Any time you want,' his uncle said, 'just call her, she'll be there.'

Amir nodded, and his uncle stood up, walked around the

table, put his hand on Amir's head, like they were father and son, and then said, 'You wanna come get some more parts with me?' and Amir chuckled, said, 'Sure, fine.'

So he changed, went out with his uncle, to the same shop with the same man, who gave them more parts to take with them, and Amir picked them all up, putting them into his uncle's car, and they drove back to the house, taking them inside and setting them all up.

His uncle's plan had seemed bad to Amir at first, these TV parts that required so much time to look up and tag properly, to make sure that they weren't selling people the wrong thing, had seen the messages his uncle received on the websites he put them up on, people haggling over pennies, people asking him questions about the pieces, asking for videos and more photos, and Amir had told himself it couldn't possibly be worth the hassle. He thought about the money he made with Adnan, which required so little from him. No, he thought, it couldn't be worth it.

But over the last few weeks, his uncle had made eight grand from selling the parts. When he told Amir, Amir had refused to believe him, but his uncle showed him how it broke down. He'd paid five hundred for five hundred parts. Each part varied in how much they were worth, but the cheapest he'd put up was around thirty quid and the most expensive was two-fifty. He'd sold nearly three hundred of that first batch, and after he'd paid the websites, for postage, for the tape and the Sharpies and the envelopes, he was left with eight grand.

'In what?' his uncle said. 'Less than two months, and that's me doing this in my spare time, imagine if I was doing this all the time,' and then he'd given Amir a look, and Amir had said, 'Nah, nah, get your free labour somewhere else, I'm not doing this for you,' 'Not even for the money?' his uncle said, and Amir said, 'You haven't even paid me yet.'

But eight grand wasn't bad, Amir thought, not bad at all, and beyond that, it made his uncle happy, to sit there, organising the parts, wrapping them in bubble wrap, placing them in envelopes, addressing the envelopes, heading to the post office. He'd made friends with the four people who worked there, learned their names, their personalities, sometimes took in small treats for them because he was giving them so much work, and in turn, they'd told him the best ways to send all the parcels he was sending, and once, when Amir had gone to the post office for his uncle, holding two bags worth of parcels, around fifty of them, the woman at the till had asked him about his uncle, asking if he was ill or if something had happened, 'Normally, it's him,' she said, 'coming here,' and Amir had said, 'No, no, he's just busy, that's all,' and the woman had nodded, told Amir, 'Tell him we miss him,' and the man next to her had laughed, said, 'Yeah, tell him we miss him, he's a funny one, your uncle.'

Amir's grandmother came to sit with them, asked questions, told Amir's uncle that she didn't understand what he was doing, couldn't he take this outside and put it all in the shed? It was summer now, it wasn't going to rain, and besides, if it did, there was always that tarp that he could cover it all with. What would happen if people came? she asked, I have nowhere to put them, and Amir's uncle just laughed it all away, told her it was fine, he would move the parts soon, he just needed to get through these first, and he winked at Amir, who knew better than to get in between his grandmother and his uncle.

It was when she left, saying she was going to her sister's house, when his uncle picked up all the envelopes they had packed, told Amir he was going to the post office and then he'd go to work after, when Amir was alone in the house, that he reached for his phone and called his mother.

She picked up immediately. 'Hello, son,' she said.

'Hey.'

'Are you okay?'

'I'm fine,' Amir said, closing his eyes, 'how are you?' The stilted conversation reminded him of the phone calls his mother used to make to his brother, the generic questions she'd ask him, the generic answers Bilal would give.

'I'm fine, busy,' she said, 'the wedding.' She paused, then said, 'Are you coming home?'

'Have you spoken to Dad?' Amir asked.

'I have,' she said.

'And you know what he said?'

'I do.'

'Did you know what he was going to say to me before he said it?'

'No,' she said, and then, 'he told me that he was going to talk to you about being more involved in the wedding, I knew that much.'

'You knew that much,' Amir said.

'That's it,' his mother said, and it was as if their roles had been reversed, him asking the questions, her lying to appease him.

'So then why would I come back?' Amir asked. 'You know he told me I should leave? He said that to me, his son,' Amir said, and he closed his eyes, glad that she wasn't in front of him, 'is that what family does?'

'We can talk about it together,' his mother said, 'it doesn't make sense to fight like this.'

'I'm not fighting.'

'Okay,' his mother said, placating him, 'but I just mean that it doesn't make sense to be away like this, you should come home.'

'No,' Amir said, 'I don't think that I should.'

'Are you just going to stay there forever?' she asked.

'I don't know,' Amir said, 'I just know that I shouldn't be there right now.'

'You shouldn't be home right now, with your family?' she said. 'What a thing to say.'

'Maybe I shouldn't have been home at all.'

'What does that mean?' his mother asked.

'Maybe I should have left too, like Bilal, maybe I didn't need to stay there, for you, for Dad, maybe there was no point.'

'Amir—'

But he hung up, unable to take her voice anymore.

Forty-five

While Amir waited, he glanced at his phone. There were messages from Bilal, asking if they could talk, one from Zain, who wanted to see Amir before he went home, asking if he was free today or tomorrow, from Mohsin, asking the very same thing. Amir ignored them all, for now, putting his phone back into his pocket.

'Yo,' Adnan said a few minutes later, walking up to Amir, hand reached out. Amir took it, embraced him in a half-hug. 'What's up?'

'Not much, what's up with you?'

'Feeling fresh,' Adnan said, looking at himself in the window behind Amir. 'What do you think?' he asked, running a hand over his hair, the sides faded, skin lighter there, up to the top, where the hair was thick, slicked back.

'You look good,' Amir said, and Adnan laughed, punching Amir lightly in the arm.

'Yeah, I fucking do,' Adnan said, 'now all I need is a girl and I'm good.' Amir said nothing, a flash of Farrah's face. 'You hungry?' Adnan asked.

'I can eat,' Amir said.

Adnan laughed. 'You can always eat,' he said, and then started walking.

Amir had things he wanted to say, but he was waiting to sit down with Adnan to say them, and Adnan seemed content to be in silence, and as they walked through Sparkhill, Amir guided by Adnan, he was struck by how much it felt like Alum Rock, the way people had always talked about Sparkhill to him, it was like it was the most dangerous place in the world, as if simply breathing there would be enough to get him killed, and yet, there were mothers walking down the roads, pushing prams, scarves wrapped around their heads, talking to one another in languages he recognised, Urdu, Pashto, Punjabi, boys hanging around corners, walking together in tight groups, men in their cars, playing music too loud, the bass from their speakers reverberating around him. It was like both places were just folding into each other, like maybe the entire world was like this.

Adnan turned down a side road, walked up to a shawarma place, said hello to the three men behind the counter, each one of them pale and hairy, their arms darkened by all the hair, glimmers of white shining through. Adnan ordered for the two of them, asking Amir only what he would like to drink, and then he took Amir to the middle of the shop, to sit at a booth. 'This is a good place,' Adnan said, 'the kinda place most people don't come to, everyone's too busy walking up and down Stratford Road to notice it.'

'Yeah,' Amir said.

'Are you about to tell me you want out?' Adnan asked. Amir looked at him, eyebrows coming together in surprise. 'Oh,' Adnan said, 'you're not going to tell me that, this is about the time people like you want to get out, get a little taste of it, the money is good but not good enough, so you leave, go back to your little degree, your regular life.'

'I don't want out,' Amir said, and part of him was irritated, angry even, that Adnan would think that of him, that wasn't who he was, that wasn't why he was here.

'Okay,' Adnan said, leaning back, waiting.

'I wanted to talk to you,' Amir started, interrupted by one of the men behind the counter, who brought over two cans of Coke, two glasses half filled with ice and a plate of hummus with pitta, 'On the house,' the man said, smiling at Adnan, who nodded, reached for his can, opened it, the sound echoing. 'I wanted to talk to you,' Amir started again, 'about doing more.'

'Doing more?' Adnan asked, putting the can straight to his lips, taking a sip, before he poured the rest of it into the glass. 'Doing more of what?'

'More of what you do.'

'And what do I do?'

Amir swallowed his frustration. 'I mean, you don't just sit around and wait for someone to call you to go give them a bag of weed, so you must be doing something else.'

'Maybe I'm just sitting around waiting for you to come give me all that money you're making.'

'I don't think you'd just sit around and do nothing while everyone else made the money for you.'

'And why would I give you more? I barely know you.'

'You know me,' Amir said, scoffing.

'No, I don't,' Adnan said, and whatever humour there was in his face had dropped now. He leaned over the table to Amir. 'I don't know you,' he said, 'I haven't spoken to you in years, I don't know who you are and you don't know who the fuck I am.'

'I'm no different to who I was in school,' Amir said, but even to him, it sounded like a lie.

'I don't know you,' Adnan said again, 'and you've only been doing this for a few weeks, there are people who've been with me from the very beginning who are happy to be where you are, who don't ask questions, who don't want more, Tabby's been there for years, what makes you different? You too good for this part?'

'I'm not too good for this,' Amir said, he'd lost the conversation, it was gone, he'd been holding onto it but now only had the ends, trying to pull it back. 'I haven't complained once.'

'Oh, you haven't complained,' Adnan said, the same man coming again, this time sliding down plates in front of them, rice and chicken and lamb, left without saying anything.

'You know your uncle?' Adnan said. 'You know he was down in this shit?'

'Not anymore.'

'Not anymore,' Adnan said, nodding, 'because he saw God, right? Went to Umrah, decided to come back, decided to get married, because that's what good Muslim men do, right? They get married and they have families and they have wives and they become good men, so he gets married and he decides that this is his life, except now what? He ain't got shit, he left this world and the mad thing is, people respected it, people said, "Fine, you did all that you did, but you're out now and we're not going to bring you back in, we ain't going to collect on nothing," but what is he doing with his life? What does he do now,' he asked Amir, 'for money?'

'He's a delivery driver,' Amir said, looking down at his food.

'Do you want that,' Adnan asked, 'for yourself?'

'Fuck no.'

'Then you gotta fucking earn it,' Adnan said, 'you don't just come here and tell me you want to do more when you've spent a few weeks selling weed to a couple of kids and made a stack or two out of it.'

'How do I earn it?' Amir asked, looking back up at him. 'What do I do?'

Adnan took another bite, then another, then another, until his cheeks stretched, chewed slowly, closed his eyes for a second. 'I'll let you know,' he said.

Amir waited for more.

'You should eat,' Adnan said, pointing at Amir's plate, 'it'll be bad when it gets cold.'

Forty-six

Frosty was on the phone in the kitchen, door closed, but that didn't matter, Amir could hear every word, Frosty on the phone to his girl, who Amir understood was one of several that Frosty was currently seeing, telling her that he was busy tonight, he couldn't come over right now, she would just have to accept that, then there was silence, then he apologised, said he wasn't trying to be rude, just trying to be honest, then silence, then Frosty swore and came back into the kitchen, phone in his hand, tight.

'You good?' Amir asked.

'Yeah,' Frosty said, sitting on the sofa next to him, reaching for the remote, turning the TV on, even though the TV had nothing attached to it, forcing them to flick through the free channels. 'This is the shit that makes me money and she wants me to quit it, keeps telling me, "I know what you're doing", like, no fucking shit, you think I'm making this sort of money working in Tesco? That's not what I'm doing, of course I'm doing this shit, what the fuck else am I going to do? And this money, yeah, this money that I'm making, it doesn't just go to her, this money is for my mum, makes sure that she can buy the shit that she needs, that the rent is paid, that the bills are paid, for my sister, so that she can have the clothes she needs, shoes for school, whatever the fuck they need, this girl, fuck, she's out here telling me that she needs to be sure that I'm a good man before she does anything with me, nah, fuck that, I ain't fucking with no girl that's trying to tell me what I can do with my life.'

Amir said nothing, just listened, had sat with Frosty enough times now to know that he didn't want a response, didn't want advice, he just wanted to be able to sit and talk, so Amir let him.

One of his girls wanting something from him again that he couldn't give her, Frosty complaining about the audacity of them, and often, Amir wanted to ask him, *Why are you with three or four?* He wasn't sure what the exact number was, just knew there was more than two and less than seven. *Why can't you just pick one of them and be good with her? Why put the stress on yourself?* But Frosty was older than Bilal, he'd been at this shit for years, and it would take more than Amir to get him to change.

So Amir listened, and Frosty went on, and as he did, Amir thought about Adnan, the conversation they'd had just a week ago, and today, Amir had helped his uncle move all of the parts into the shed in the garden, and when he was done, his uncle had asked him, 'Are you still doing it?' and Amir had said nothing, and his uncle had just sighed, long, hard, and said, 'I wish you wouldn't,' and maybe that was what made Amir the angriest, that his uncle had the nerve to be disappointed in him, and when he'd left the house, his grandmother had asked him where he was going, and Amir had said he was going to spend some time with his friends, and his grandmother had said, 'Some friends you have, hanging out with them until the middle of the night,' and he had left irritated at her too, and he had forgotten about meeting Mohsin and Zain, had been fielding their messages for days now, saying he'd see them before they went back home, and that frustrated him too, because they'd get to leave, get to disappear, get to say goodbye to Birmingham for a few months, and Amir would have to stay here. All of this swirled around in his head as Frosty talked, and then his phone buzzed.

'Got something,' Amir said, an ask and a location, and he went back, confirmed the price, and then they stood up.

When the car came to a stop, Amir double-checked the bag he was holding, nodded at Frosty, who would leave the car running as Amir delivered. They'd agreed to meet by the bus stop, just at the end of the road, so Amir walked over, and he saw them, two of them, a man and a woman, the woman with her arms crossed over her chest, the man moving in front of her as he saw Amir approaching, which made Amir want to laugh, as if he was going to launch himself across the road at her.

'Yo,' Amir called out as he neared them, and the man lifted his head, and when their eyes met, Amir faltered, stopped.

Bilal stood there, looking at Amir, confused, eyebrows stitching themselves together, 'What are you—' he started saying, and then his eyes dropped to what was in Amir's hand, just some weed, that was all, and Amir's eyes moved from Bilal to the woman, to Momina, who recognised Amir too, who wasn't saying anything. 'What are you doing?' Bilal said.

'Fifteen,' Amir said, because he didn't know what else to say, 'it's fifteen,' and he put his hand out to Bilal.

'It's fifteen,' Bilal said, half a laugh dripping from his lips. He stepped towards Amir, took the bag from his hand, his fingers touching Amir's palm for a second, and with his other hand, he gave Amir the money, and Amir turned, immediately, his entire body hot, his breath short, shallow, half walking, half running back to the car, got in, told Frosty to go, and Frosty didn't question him, and Amir turned around, looked through the back window, saw Bilal and Momina standing by that bus stop, watching as Amir pulled away and vanished.

Forty-seven

Bilal called Amir and Amir ignored him each time, watching his phone light up and waiting for him to go away. Bilal sent a text after the fourth call, saying he just wanted to talk, that was all, could Amir call him back, please, and then Bilal called again, and when Amir didn't pick up, watched it fade away again, Frosty asked which one of his bitches was calling him so much, and Amir laughed with him.

As Amir and Frosty went from person to person, handing out bags, taking money, as the late evening slipped into night slipped into early morning, Amir realised he wasn't just feeling caught, as he had in the moment, he was also feeling surprised, shocked, betrayed that Bilal smoked weed. Bilal was the respectful one, the one who didn't fuck around.

But he smoked weed, and he knew where to get it from, and he was marrying someone who also smoked weed, what else was he doing? What else had he been hiding? Who was he when he wasn't at home?

Bilal hadn't looked angry when he'd seen Amir. He hadn't look shocked, either. It was disappointment that had reigned on his face.

Who was he to judge? Amir told himself. But it wasn't so

easy to forget that look in Bilal's eyes, to forget how Momina had looked at him too, as if this was exactly what she had expected from him.

When they were done for the night, just after four in the morning, the early sun breaking through the sky, the night disappearing to day, Amir went back to his grandmother's house, slipping in through the back door, because that was the quieter one, unlikely to wake anyone up, and he went up to the spare room, tiptoeing, closed the door softly, lay down on the bed and closed his eyes, it all playing on a loop in his mind.

Forty-eight

'How long?' Bilal asked.

'How long what?'

'Don't do that,' Bilal said, the two of them sitting in that same Nando's, Star City, Bilal suggesting it, no one would be there, not at this time of the day. Bilal wasn't at work, had told them he was taking the day, wanted to meet Amir without having to worry about running back. 'How long?' he asked again.

'A couple weeks, nothing big.'

'How did you get into this?'

Amir looked down at the menu, played with its bended corners, laminate peeling. 'You know where we live,' Amir said, 'it's not like it's hard, I know someone and he hooked me up.'

'Who?'

'You wouldn't know.'

'Try me.'

Amir laughed, 'Oh, because you know people now?'

'Just tell me.'

'You remember Ily, from school?' Bilal nodded. 'He has a younger brother, my age, we were at school together.'

'Adnan,' Bilal said.

'Yeah, Adnan.'

'That's who you're doing this with?'

'I saw him, in town, he's got bare money.'

'I know he's got money, I've seen the car he drives.'

'Then you get it.'

'Get what?' Bilal asked. 'Why you're doing it?'

'Yeah.'

'For money?'

'The money's good, I made a grand in a week.'

'That is good money,' Bilal said, but Amir couldn't read his tone, couldn't read his face.

'Don't be a dick.'

'I'm not being a dick, that's a lot of money.'

'Then what?'

'I just wanted to know why,' he said, 'and now I know why.'

Amir waited for more. 'That's it?' he asked. 'Nothing more?'

'What else can I say? Tell you not to do it when you literally sold me weed? I don't think I'm in any position to tell you what to do, and you're not stupid, anything I could say to you, about the violence, about Saqib, about being safe, you've already thought about,' Bilal said, 'so, yeah, I don't think there's anything else for me to say.'

A waiter arrived at the table, young, younger than Amir, Pakistani, Muslim, he thought, could tell just by looking at his face because his face was like Amir's like Bilal's like their father's like their uncle's like their grandfather's like Mohsin's like Zain's like Adnan's, pitta for Bilal, half-chicken for Amir, then left.

'I didn't know you smoked,' Amir said.

'Since uni,' Bilal said, biting into the pitta.

'Same,' Amir said, offering up an answer for a question that hadn't been asked, 'never really did it before but I started properly last year.'

'Feels good, right?'

'You drink too?'

'I did, at uni.' Bilal gave him a look. 'Don't you?' he asked.

Amir shook his head, 'No, I don't want to.'

'Not even once?'

'No,' Amir said, embarrassment trickling down his back, 'some of my friends do but I don't know, I just can't do it.'

'That's alright,' Bilal said, 'no one's telling you to.'

'Why did you?'

'I wanted to,' Bilal said, 'I got there, people were drinking, everyone drinks, especially that first year, no one pressured me to do it, there was this understanding, I guess, that some people might not want to, at Durham especially, everyone wants to act like they understand each other, so no one ever pushed a bottle into my hand and said that I had to drink, but I was curious, I wanted to know what it tasted like, and it's fine, I mean, it tastes awful, it's like smoking, you have to force yourself to like it because there's nothing good about it, sticks at the back of your throat, smells like chemicals, burns going down, but after a while, you start to learn what you like, I became a whisky person, double whisky and lemonade, that's what I used to get,' he said.

'Do you drink now?'

Bilal shook his head, 'Nah, I don't do it now, it was just at uni, didn't feel right to come home and keep doing it.'

'But you still smoke weed?'

'That feels different.'

'Yeah,' Amir said, looking down at his food.

'I can't believe we've never talked about this before,' Bilal said.

'Well,' Amir said, 'you left.'

'Left?'

'When you went to uni, you left, and then, I don't know, it felt like you didn't really want to talk to me about shit, and I get it, I guess, I was twelve, you were eighteen, we weren't the same anymore, you were grown up, but even when you got back, it felt like, I don't know, I wasn't someone you wanted to talk to.'

'I came back,' Bilal said, 'I came back all the time.'

'For a weekend here and there,' Amir said, Bilal turning up on a Friday evening, their mother returned, awaiting his arrival, already night by the time he got there, eating something and going to bed, leaving on Sunday, midday, because he needed to get back in time to prepare for the week ahead, he always said, the weekend compressed into a day and a morning, that was all they got, their mother leaving the second he was gone.

'I mean,' Bilal said, 'I guess you know what that feels like now, right?'

'What?'

'Not wanting to be home.'

'That's what you felt, you didn't want to be home?'

'Not back then,' Bilal said, 'you know all the shit that Mum gave me before I left, trying to emotionally blackmail me into staying, I didn't want to come home, it was a good life there, away from her, away from him, coming home whenever I wanted, not having to check with them whenever I left, not having her hound me all the time.'

'She doesn't do that to you anymore.'

Bilal laughed, 'Yeah, because I'm here and I'm getting married, but even then, it's not like she's completely stopped, I just give her what she wants now,' Bilal said, 'she wants to feel like she knows everything about me so I tell her a few things, she feels like she knows all of me, and it makes things easier.'

'That would never work for me.'

'It's different for you, you never left, I told you that you should have.'

'I didn't want to,' Amir said.

'I know,' Bilal said, 'but you should have, it was good to see what another part of the world looks like, I think sometimes, it feels like Birmingham is all that we have, people leave but they never go too far and they always come back here, for Eid or weddings or whatever, it was nice to get out of it, to go disappear somewhere else for a while, remind myself that the world is a lot bigger than we think it is.'

Amir had heard this before from Bilal, his speech about how good it was to explore the world, to find new things, to learn differences, how it all made for a better person, so Amir looked down at his chicken, cut at it, pulled the meat away from the bone.

'Although,' Bilal said, 'it wasn't all great, I had this girl at uni, this white girl.'

'A white girl?' Amir said, nearly choking on the chicken.

Bilal laughed, 'Yeah.'

'You were with a white girl?' Amir asked, looking at his

brother, a different person sitting in front of him now to the one he'd been living with all his life.

'Say it louder, why don't you?'

'A white girl,' Amir said again. It felt unreal to him, to think of Bilal that way, even though it was what their father had always said about him, that Bilal was going to marry a white girl one day, 'This one, this one, who doesn't even like his own kind, doesn't like his own people, he'll marry a white girl and move in with her and forget his own language, his own culture, his own people.'

'I know, it's a fucking cliché, brown boys goes to uni and dates a white girl, but there's not a lot of us at Durham, and she was nice and funny and smart, and we got on over the same things, and she was hot, and I don't know, maybe she had a thing for pakis, she'd make me talk to her in Urdu sometimes.'

'Fuck off.'

'Yeah,' Bilal said, laughing, 'she would make me tell her she was beautiful in Urdu, the way she would stare at me when I did, like I was some little boy she'd picked up from the side of the road, that she was saving, and she'd try to say it back but she never could, their tongues aren't made for that shit, and she'd get all embarrassed, all red in the face, like really, really red.'

'What happened to her?'

'It was never serious,' Bilal said, 'so we just fucked around for a while and when uni came to an end, so did we, she's married to her old boyfriend now, I'm pretty sure she was seeing him the entire time we were together.' Bilal laughed again, more to himself, 'I can't believe I'm telling you this shit,' he said.

'I had a girl too,' Amir said, 'Layla.'

'I know,' Bilal said, Amir looking at him, asking without asking. 'Everyone knew,' he said.

'Everyone?'

'Yeah, Mum and Dad knew too, I think they saw you with her somewhere, or maybe someone told them, I can't remember.'

'They never said anything.'

'They were convinced you were going to bring her home one day, tell them you were going to marry her,' Bilal said.

'Yeah,' Amir said, looking down at the table, 'but now you're the good one, getting married to the girl from down the road.'

'Yeah, the good one,' Bilal said, 'but never good enough.'

'What?' Amir said, looking back up at his brother. 'She thinks you're fucking perfect.'

'Yeah, only now, for a while, I was in her bad books,' Bilal said, 'you remember Shahid?'

'Shahid, our cousin, Shahid?'

'Yeah, that Shahid, you're too young to remember this but, you know, he was born like, what, a few months after I was? And the two of them, Mum and his mum, it was like you and Saqib, they were fighting through us, comparing our weights, dressing us in better clothes, shoving us in front of people, Mum always telling me I was better because I was thinner than he was or that I had lighter skin, fucked-up shit to say to kids, anyway, when I went to college and uni, he didn't, and everyone knew he was on weed, a lot of weed, and I'm pretty sure he was doing other shit too, you remember how he lost all that weight one year, just went crazy thin? He must have been on something, and then, what, three years ago, he just disappears, no one sees him for months, no one hears from him, Mum was always saying this fucked-up shit about him, about how he was probably in jail somewhere, made me look him up just to see if he was, or that he was maybe dead somewhere or on the run, she used to say all these awful things about him and when she met his mum, she was all smiles, I hate when she's like that, but anyway, I don't know how long it was, a year maybe, and he comes back, and he's wearing a topi and salwar kameez and praying five times a day and telling everyone that he's a good Muslim man now, and that he's married and he's got a kid, and he's married some white girl from Stechford, and everyone knows the truth, that he fucked around with her, got her pregnant, and for whatever reason, they decided they were going to keep it, everyone knows that's what happened, but now we're all meant to treat him like he's some great guy, like he never did all the things that we know he did, all the stealing and the fighting, and you know what's mad? When he reappeared, it was Mum who told me, that's how I found out, and she's telling me what a good thing it is, "Isn't it such a good thing that he's back now? He's living at home with his kid and his wife and he's got a job," security guard or something, and she's telling me that I need to learn from him, isn't that fucking mad?'

'She says some dumb shit sometimes,' Amir said.

'I know it's not nice to say this about your own mother, but she can be a dumb fucking bitch sometimes.'

Amir laughed, surprised, lifted his glass up to Bilal, who did the same, both clinking against one another. 'I never thought you'd say anything like that, ever,' Amir said.

'Don't get me wrong, if anyone else said that about her, it'd be lights out for them, but I think you and I can say shit like that, there's nothing wrong with that.'

'What about Dad?' Amir asked.

'Oh, that guy can absolutely get fucked,' Bilal said, grinning at Amir as he took another bite.

Forty-nine

'Back tomorrow,' Zain said. He and Amir were walking through the city centre, Zain melancholic as the summer arrived.

'Your mum coming to get you?' Amir asked.

'Yeah,' Zain said, 'my dad's already gone.'

'Pakistan?'

'Yeah, every year, he disappears on a plane for two months, but I can't even be mad about it, it's the best time of the year, don't have to deal with his shit, it's like he gets angrier over the summer, angry that his kids have the audacity to be in his house.'

'Mine isn't going this year,' Amir said, 'wants to save money for the wedding.'

'God, this wedding,' Zain said, 'I already can't wait for it to be over and it's not even my brother getting married.'

'Yeah,' Amir said. He hadn't told Zain about moving to his grandmother's house, about his refusal to see his parents, didn't know how to talk about it, and besides, Amir thought, was there any need to? Soon, Zain would be gone for the summer, surrounded by his own problems. What would Amir matter then?

'You good with Mohsin, about Amsterdam?' Zain asked. 'He said he'd booked everything.'

'Yeah,' Amir said, 'I gave him the money.'

'What, all of it?' Zain asked, looking at Amir.

'Yeah,' Amir said, 'I had some savings.'

'Oh,' Zain said, looking away from Amir.

Amir had gone to Mohsin three days ago, turned up at his flat, Mohsin opening the door in his boxers, 'Too fucking hot to wear anything,' he said, and though the sun was streaming in through the windows, though it did feel warm, warm enough that Amir's back was covered in a light sweat stepping through, Mohsin's flat had air conditioning that he could definitely turn on, but Amir said nothing. 'Here,' he'd said instead, handing Mohsin an envelope.

Mohsin had reached for it, surprised, hesitant smile, and when he'd opened it, when he'd seen the money inside, he'd looked at Amir, the envelope hovering in the space between them, Mohsin not quite taking it but not quite giving it back either. 'What is this?' he'd said, and Amir had said, 'Money for Amsterdam and the flat.'

He'd made the decision the day before, sitting before his stack, taking out a few thousand to put into his bank account, the most money his account had ever seen come in at one time. He could have just sent Mohsin the money from that account, told him it was from his savings, told him nothing, but he liked the idea of turning up with the envelope, so he'd taken the money for Amsterdam, had asked Zain exactly how much it was going to cost, because Mohsin wouldn't tell him, just three hundred for the flights and where they were going to stay, and then he'd added two grand to it, for the deposit on the flat and the first month's rent. He could have added more, but he thought that was enough.

'I don't understand,' Mohsin started, looking at the money in the envelope and then back at Amir, 'why do you have this?'

'Savings,' Amir said, 'just over the years, don't worry about it.'

'Don't worry about it?' Mohsin said. 'You've just given me,' he looked into the envelope again, 'what is this, like, two grand?'

'Twenty-three hundred,' Amir said, 'for Amsterdam and for the flat,' he repeated, and when Mohsin looked at him again, Amir's chest fizzed at the expression on his face. This was it, he thought, this was what money got you.

Mohsin had tried to give the envelope back to Amir, saying he didn't want the money, Amir could give it to him in September, when he moved in, he didn't need to give it to him now, but Amir refused, so then Mohsin said it would be weird for him to put this money into his account, his dad might ask him where the money had come from, so Amir said, 'Don't put it into your account then, use it however you want to use it, spend it in Europe,' and he'd put his hand over Mohsin's, squeezing it tight, 'it's your money,' Amir said, and Mohsin just stared at him, 'I don't understand,' he'd said, and Amir had laughed then, because what was there to understand? It was just money.

'Well, I'm glad,' Zain said, 'I'm glad you're coming, it'll be good.'

'Yeah, it will be,' Amir said, 'I've never been anywhere.'

'But Pakistan,' Zain said.

'But Pakistan,' Amir repeated, then laughed. 'Mad,' he said, 'mad that my dad came all the way over here when he was younger than me and never went anywhere else.'

'They're all the same,' Zain said, and Amir laughed, because it was true, every single one of these men, who came over to England when they were teenagers, pound signs in their eyes, married some cousin they'd hardly met before, fucked her enough to have a few children, worked as taxi drivers or in restaurants or some other bullshit manual job where they could get paid in cash and lie to the government about how much money they were earning to avoid paying tax, to get as many benefits as they could. These men, who lived in this space between here and there, always wanting to be in the other place, dreaming of Pakistan when they were here, dreaming of here when they were back there, they were split right down the middle, and they wouldn't admit it, wouldn't ever admit that the life they'd built for themselves here was a real life. They'd always be trapped in the past.

Fifty

As Amir walked back from Zain's, he thought of Mohsin's face when he'd handed him that envelope, the sound of Zain's hurt when Amir had told him.

This was who he was now.

He would buy the clothes, replace the phone, get the car. He would move in with Mohsin, join the gym, build the body. Slowly, he would become the person he had known he was all this time, buried underneath the shit that he'd been born with.

It was electric, this feeling, pulsing through him.

So Amir didn't hear them the first time, when they shouted his name, nor did he hear them the second time, but he did feel the pull on his shoulder, a hand gripping him, turning him around, two boys in front of him, staring at him, one of them asking, 'Are you Amir?' pronouncing his name wrong, and Amir tried to place their faces but couldn't.

'Yeah,' Amir said, shrugging the hand off him, moving back, 'who the fuck's asking?'

'Who's asking?' the smaller one said, though both of them were smaller than Amir. 'We're asking, you run with Adnan, yeah?'

But they didn't let him answer, the bigger one's hand, curled into a fist, driving itself into Amir's stomach, his body bending over it, folding itself over, the breath pushed out of him, the smaller one pushing him into the wall, Amir slammed into the brick, barely able to look up before a fist came for the side of his head, his ear ringing, and then a kick, aimed at his side.

Fear rolled through him as he held himself up against the wall. He thought of Saqib, gunshots, the boy with a screwdriver in his chest, blood on his shoe, his uncle with a bat.

Amir pushed himself up, hands on the bricks behind him, gritty under his palms, and he heard the two of them laughing, and then the fear was gone, replaced by anger.

'You run with Adnan, yeah?' the smaller one asked again, and Amir didn't answer, just pushed himself off the wall, head aimed right at the smaller one's nose, and when Amir felt it against his forehead, he heard the groan, felt the blood splatter on his face, the smaller one falling to the floor, but before Amir could even think, he turned to the other one, hand curled into a fist, and he swung as hard as he could, his fist connecting with the side of an eye, and then he hit him again, this time in the nose, felt skin and bone push back under him, and then he hit him once more, this time, the boy falling to the floor, Amir the only one standing now, the two of them on the ground.

It was the smaller one who stood first, who reached into his pocket, took out a knife, the bigger one who reached for his arm, touched him, said, 'He ain't fucking worth it,' and then spat at Amir, spit filled with blood, said, 'You tell Adnan he's fucked,' and then pulled at the smaller one, the two half running away, Amir watching them until they disappeared around a corner.

How long had that all taken? A minute? Maybe two? And yet, each second had stretched out to a crawl. He was aware of a pain in his stomach, on the side of his head, in his hands, but the thing that drew him was the pulsing of his blood in his ears, his throat tight, his breathing fast.

If anyone else had seen what had happened, they didn't seem to care, people passing Amir by as if he didn't exist.

He unclenched his fingers, ran a hand over his face, liquid under his fingers, blood, shiny, red, not his own, which he wiped on his shirt, then turned back in the direction he was headed and kept walking.

Fifty-one

Sparks was playing *Mario Kart* when Amir walked in, screen lit up with dizzying colours. Amir recognised the players from his childhood, his uncle buying him and Bilal their own console, a PlayStation 2, on the cheap, lying to their mother that it was legit, even though the manual was in Chinese, but it worked and that was all that mattered, two controllers, wires trailing from the box under the TV, their mother complaining about tripping over it, even though it was nowhere near the door.

Amir sat, watching Sparks play without watching. His mind was filled with those boys, the bruising on his hands, the small ache in the side of his head.

'You're quiet,' Sparks said, without looking at Amir, cigarette hanging from his lips, slowly smouldering.

'Just watching.'

'Yeah, but you're quiet.'

'Aren't I always quiet?'

'No,' Sparks said, 'well, yeah, but this time is different, the quiet is different.'

'The quiet is different,' Amir repeated.

Sparks looked at him, narrowed his eyes and then grinned. 'Don't fuck with me,' he said.

'I'm not fucking with you,' Amir said, though he was, just a little, 'I'm just thinking.'

'You don't want to be doing that,' Sparks said, turning back to the TV, 'it'll fuck with your mind.' Amir said nothing, watched the screen, all the characters racing over a bridge, flying through the air, spinning around, fists pumping the air. 'What are you thinking about?' Sparks asked.

'The summer,' Amir said, and it had started to feel like summer now, the days getting close to being too hot, his mother already starting her complaints about it despite spending the first half of the year complaining that it was too cold. Amir and Bilal had learned, quickly, that there were really only a few weeks where she found the balance was right for her.

'What about it?'

'Too long.'

'I forget,' Sparks said, 'you're still at school.'

'Uni.'

'Uni, college, school, all the same,' Sparks said, waving his hand at Amir.

'You go?' Amir asked, even though he knew the answer, he and Sparks the same age, maybe he was a little older then Amir, but Amir could tell, in the way he held himself, the way he talked, how he looked, that he didn't do well at school. It was how they all looked.

'Nah,' Sparks said, 'was never for me.'

'Yeah?'

'Yeah,' Sparks said, crossing the finish line, fifth, throwing the controller down on the sofa next to him and leaning back into the cushion. 'It was never really my thing,' he said, reaching for the lighter, lit his cigarette again, inhaling, orange end glowing. 'My dad wanted me to go, my mum never thought I would, guess I'm glad to have proven her right.'

'You live with them,' Amir asked, 'your mum and dad?'

Sparks scoffed. 'Nah, I don't live with them, you know what it's like, nah, I moved out a couple years ago, with the boys.'

'The boys?'

'Yeah, me and Tabby, we live together,' Sparks said. Amir couldn't imagine it, the two of them together, couldn't imagine what the house might look like, couldn't imagine what any of them did when they weren't in this house, sat on that worn-down sofa, controllers in hands, cigarettes in lips, waiting for a phone to go off. 'You still with yours?' Sparks asked.

'Yeah,' Amir said, 'but I'm moving out soon.'

'Oh, yeah?'

'Yeah, moving in with a friend when uni comes back around in September.'

'You get along with them?'

'My friend?' Amir asked. 'Yeah, of course.'

'Nah, your family, Adnan said he knew your brother, you only got one?'

'Yeah,' Amir said, 'older than me, he's at home too, we get along, but I can't be there no more, my parents can act mad sometimes.'

'Tell me about it, your dad from back home or your mum?'

'My dad.'

'It's the other way around for me,' Sparks said, 'married his cousin from back home, let me tell you, I don't know if it's just the women in my family, but the girls from back home, they're fucking crazy, they're mad manipulative, sly as fuck, you never know what game they're playing until you're right in the fucking middle of it.' He stopped speaking, the phone in his hand lit up, tiny rectangular screen glowing a dull yellow. 'Let's go,' Sparks said, standing up.

Amir got up, waited for Sparks to grab what the ask was, plastic bag, white, pressed into Amir's hands, and the two headed out to the car, Sparks in the driver's seat, Amir next to him, and they drove, their conversation already forgotten.

'Fuck,' Sparks said when he parked up. Up ahead there was a man watching them. 'Listen,' Sparks said, 'let me take this one,' his hand stretched out to Amir.

Amir dropped the bag into Sparks's open palm. 'Why?' he asked. 'What is it?' but Sparks was out of the car before Amir could even finish asking, so Amir got out too, followed him, slowly.

The man walked towards Sparks, older than Amir had first thought, maybe in his forties, hands shoved into his hoodie, which hung off him.

'You got the money?' Sparks asked, putting a hand up to the man to stop him from coming too close, Amir stood behind Sparks, watching, breath tight. The man smiled at Sparks, Amir surprised to find that his teeth were white, blazingly white against the dark of his skin, 'Yeah, man, of course I do, when don't I? You got what I asked for?' Sparks showing him his hand, bag of white, and the man took a step forward. 'Money first,' Sparks said. The man stopped, took one hand out of his pocket, crumpled notes inside of it, and Sparks stepped forward, took the money at the same time that the man reached for the plastic bag, two men with their hands wrapped around one another. Sparks pulled back, looked at the money, sighed, 'This isn't enough,' he said. The man looked at him, the two of them too close to one another, and he grinned. 'I'm good,' he said, 'I'm good, you know I'm good, I just don't have it today, but I'll have it tomorrow, I'll have it tomorrow.' Sparks shook his head, 'My guy, I can't do it again.' The man pulled at Sparks's hand, 'Tomorrow, I'll have it tomorrow.' Sparks pulled back, 'I can't do that, we all have people to answer to,' the man laughed, 'Yeah, we do, we do,' he said, and he pulled back, forcefully, hand slipping out of Sparks's, and he stumbled back, surprised that he was free, and for a second, the two of them were separated, Sparks's hand reaching out to him, to help or to hold or to harm, and then Sparks was on him, quick, fist to the mouth, the soft but hard sound of it, the man stumbling back, tripping over his own feet, landing on the floor, Sparks taking the bag from his hand.

'I told you, my guy, I can't do this again, if you've got the money tomorrow, you let me know, but you can't have this today.' Sparks let the money fall on the fallen man, turned around, and when his eyes landed on Amir, his face twisted with surprise, he said, 'I told you to let me take this one,' walking past Amir to the car, Amir's eyes landing on the man, who had one hand pressed to his face, his eyes on Amir, the desperation in them thick, sharp, painful to look at, but he didn't say anything, not as Amir turned around, walked back to the car, forced himself not to look behind, and when Amir got into the car, he saw that the man hadn't moved at all, still on the ground, looking right at the car, headlights casting him in light, and then Sparks drove and Amir didn't look back.

Fifty-two

Amir's grandmother had come to his room, knocking on the door before opening it and telling him to come downstairs. 'Enough of this waking up late,' she said, opening the curtains, letting in the dazzling sun and then pulling on the duvet too. Amir, who had come home at just past four in the morning, looked at the time, saw it was only just nine, and closed his eyes for a second, thought of going back to sleep, but then forced himself up.

'Good,' his grandmother said when she saw him, 'I'll make you some eggs,' and Amir told her she didn't have to, but when he came out of the bathroom the eggs were busy boiling, the kettle too, and mugs were on the counter, teabags and sugar already in them. She handed them to him, and then told him to put the bread in the toaster, so he did. Standing together like that, it reminded him of when he was younger, when he used to come and stay here, waking up even earlier than her sometimes, coming downstairs, waiting for his grandmother to wake up so they could eat together.

Once the food was made, the two of them sat at the dining table, and somehow, though he had made this very meal for himself countless times, it tasted completely different with her.

'So,' his grandmother said, 'tell me, what are you doing now?'

'Now?' Amir asked.

'Your exams are over,' she said, and how she knew that Amir didn't know, neither his mother nor his uncle had gone to university, and she hadn't asked him about his exams before. 'Will you get a job, go work somewhere? I know you're helping your uncle with these TV chips, but it would be good to have something for yourself.'

'I don't know,' Amir said, his stomach tightening. This was about money, he thought, she wanted him to pay his way, just like his father did.

'It's good to get out,' she said, 'and a job can keep you busy, you should think about it, and it's no bad thing to have some money too, to spend on yourself.'

'I have money,' Amir said.

'Oh, yeah?' his grandmother said, arching an eyebrow at him. 'And where did you get this money from?'

'I don't think you need to know that,' Amir said, grinning at her.

His grandmother gave him a look and then returned her gaze to the food. 'Just don't do anything stupid,' she said, 'I know you young people don't like to hear that from us old ones, but just think about us if you're about to do something stupid, think about how sad it would make me if something terrible happened to you,' she said, 'will you …' she asked, Amir meeting her eyes, seeing worry there, 'will you promise me that you'll think about me before you do anything stupid?'

Amir nodded, food stuck in his throat, hard to swallow. He reached for his tea to take a drink and then said, 'Yes, I will.'

'Okay,' his grandmother said, 'that's all I can ask.'

It was as his grandmother finished eating that the doorbell rang, her looking up, surprised, glancing at the clock, saying, 'Who could that be at this time?' Amir pushing himself up to go get the door, his grandmother reaching out to him, saying, 'No, eat, eat, I'll go,' and he listened to the sounds of her walking to the door, opening it, and then heard his brother's voice, asking if Amir was awake, Amir's grandmother saying, 'Yes, yes, inside,' and then she made a joke about how she hadn't seen Bilal in so long and now here he was, twice in as many weeks, what had she done to deserve such luck?

Their grandmother went straight to the kitchen, poured herself a glass of water, and then came back out, telling the two of them that she was going to pray and then read some Quran, put a hand on Amir's shoulder as she spoke, and when Amir looked at her there was softness in her eyes, and it shifted something inside of him, his chest hollow, so all he could do was nod, and then she was gone.

'I spoke to Dad,' Bilal said, 'about what he said.'

'Yeah?' Amir said, looking across the table at his brother, the urge to eat no longer there, the food unfinished in front of him. 'What did he say?'

'He gave me a lot of shit,' Bilal said, 'about family, about duty and loyalty, and he told me the same thing, that he paid for his sister's wedding so you should be helping me with mine, but I told him, it's not his wedding, I get to decide what happens in it, and I don't want you to pay for it, it makes no sense to ask you to do that, you're a student, where are you going to get the money to pay for anything?'

'Well,' Amir said, 'I mean, I don't not have—'

'No,' Bilal said quickly, 'I know what you're going to say and I don't want to hear it, that money, that's yours, and you can do whatever you want with it, but if you give some of it, even a little, it just opens a lot of conversations that we don't need,' he said, shaking his head at Amir, face still, cold.

'I just meant, if you—'

'I don't,' Bilal said, warmer now, 'Momina and I have been saving up for this for a while, and if I need anything, then our parents can pay for it, not you, that's not what a younger brother does.'

Not what a younger brother does, Amir thought. He looked away from Bilal for a second, to the sofa that was on the other side of the room, hardened with age, covered in pink and purple covers. *Not what a younger brother does*, he thought, but why not? He had money, he had means to make more, this wedding wasn't for another year, he could work harder, with Adnan, do more days, prove his loyalty, start making real money. But he knew that it didn't matter what he did, Bilal would never accept it. 'Because it's embarrassing,' Amir said, looking back at Bilal, 'for your younger brother to pay for something?'

Bilal laughed, surprised. 'No,' he said, 'no, I'm not embarrassed, I'm just saying, you don't have a job, you're a student, you can't pay for anything—'

'But what if I could,' Amir said, 'you know—'

'Where is this coming from?' Bilal asked. 'I'm here to tell you that you can come back home, I've spoken to Dad, he's not going to pull that shit with you anymore, I sorted it.'

'You sorted it,' Amir said, 'and what if I don't want to come home?'

'You don't want to come home,' Bilal said, small laugh, until he saw the look in Amir's eyes, 'you'd never come back?'

'I don't know,' Amir said, 'maybe not never, but I've been thinking about moving out.'

'Here?'

'Nah,' Amir said, shaking his head, 'maybe with a friend or something, from uni.'

'From uni,' Bilal repeated, 'not Adnan?'

'No, not Adnan,' Amir said. For a moment, he forgot that his uncle was out, already left, almost expected him to leap out from behind the door, listening this whole time. 'I wouldn't live with him.'

'So where would you live?'

'I have a friend,' Amir said, 'I can move in with him, nothing big, just a flat in the city centre, other people do it all the time.'

'And that's what you want?'

'Yeah,' Amir said, 'is that so hard to believe? You did the same thing.'

'Yeah, I know,' Bilal said, shifting in his chair, as though he wanted to reach across the table but had stopped himself, 'but it's different, you're not in a different city, you're here, I, I don't know how that'll go down.'

'She doesn't give a fuck,' Amir said.

'Who, Mum?'

'Yeah.'

'What are you talking about? She cares about whether you're at home or not, she wants you to be at home.'

'Yeah, but that's all she wants, she just wants me to be there like I'm a fucking kid, like if I leave the house, something will happen to me.'

'She's worried, she did the same thing to me at uni.'

'Yeah,' Amir said, 'and she moved in here too, because she was so fucking sad that her favourite son had left the house, and only came back when he came back, and now he's getting married, and it's a lot easier for her to pretend that her shit son doesn't exist.'

'That's not—' Bilal said, shaking his head, mouth slightly open, 'she doesn't pretend that you don't exist.'

'Doesn't she?' Amir said, pulling his hands back, holding them tight. 'Do you care that she did that, that she left for three years when you left, or do you just never think about it?'

'I didn't know—'

'You knew,' Amir said, 'I heard Dad telling you on the phone.'

Bilal's face twisted and he paused, closing his eyes for a second. 'Okay, I did know, but I didn't know it was that bad—'

'It was that bad, but you didn't care,' Amir said, and now he was getting angry, angry that his brother was sitting there, telling him that his money didn't matter, angry that Bilal thought he could fix everything with a single conversation, 'you left, you didn't care about anyone but yourself, and she begged you to stay, didn't speak to anyone for months, came to live here, and then you'd come back and it was like she was alive again, but then you'd disappear, run back there, and it was back to it, her not speaking, her not even at the house, just me and Dad, three years of that, that's what it was like being here when you weren't, but what do you care?'

'That's not fair,' Bilal said, 'you can't put that on me, I didn't tell her to do that, to act like that—'

'I can't put that on you, but me wanting to move out

because she doesn't give a fuck about me, that's entirely on me, yeah? Her either ignoring me or treating me like a kid, or Dad talking to me the way he does, telling me I ain't shit, telling me to get a job, that's fine with you?'

'I'm not saying that—'

'So what are you saying then? You left, you went out there, lived however you wanted, smoked, drank, fucked that white girl, came home and pretended everything was fine, came and spoke to my teachers like you were my fucking dad, telling me to do my homework, like that's fucking normal, came back after three years away, all high and fucking mighty with all these new opinions, the climate, workers' rights, racism, all this shit you say that no one can fucking stand, and I stayed, I stayed here, because she was so fucked when you left, I didn't know what she would do if I left too, but I guess it didn't matter really, because you're back, what the fuck do I matter? Maybe I thought a bit too much of myself because maybe the truth is, they shouldn't have even had me, why did they need another one when the first one was so perfect? It'll probably make everyone's life a lot fucking easier if I just left, so yeah, I'm not coming back, I'm not living with them again.'

Neither of them said anything, Amir looking away from Bilal, not wanting to see his brother's face.

'Fine, that's on me,' Bilal said, in a way that made Amir even angrier, 'but look, no one wants you not to be there, not even Dad, you should come back, talk to him, all he wants to do is explain himself.'

'Nah, man, fuck that, they know I'm here, if they want to talk to me, they know where to find me.' Amir leaned back in his chair, space between them, conversation over.

Bilal said nothing, then nodded, standing up. 'Fine,' he said, 'I'll let them know that's where you are right now, but if they do come over, will you at least promise me that you'll be here to listen to them?'

'Sure,' Amir said, not looking at Bilal, eyes across the table, at the wall. Bilal stayed standing by the door for a moment, waiting for more, and then he left.

Fifty-three

There was nothing else to do with the day, Mohsin, Zain, the others all gone home for the summer, and he hadn't wanted to sit in his grandmother's house, and he didn't want to go home, so he'd decided to take himself to Ward End Park, to walk along the big pond that he'd thought was a lake when he was younger, sitting on the edges of it, staring into the still, murky water, dreaming up monsters that lived underneath, up the hill, past the smaller park, around the football pitches, to sit in those memories of when he was a kid, coming here for joy, and then the call came.

'Yo,' Amir said, 'what's up?'

'I'm good man,' Mohsin said, 'I'm good, I'm good, just at home.'

'Yeah?' Amir said. 'How is it?'

'Home,' Mohsin said, 'home is the same, always the same, nothing changes here.'

'How's your dad?'

'My dad,' Mohsin said, and then he laughed, 'my dad has taken himself to Greece for a month.'

'Greece?'

'Yeah, he went last week, didn't tell anyone,' Mohsin said,

'well, that's what my mum says, but she could be lying, trying to get me on her side, but yeah, he's gone, says he won't be back for a few weeks.'

'Greece,' Amir said, and he thought about what it would take to impulsively decide to go to Greece, the money it would take, the time. 'Maybe you can go see him, after we go to Amsterdam.'

'Ha, yeah,' Mohsin said, 'maybe, just drop on him, remind everyone that he has a son.'

'Yeah,' Amir said, 'or we can run up on him if you wanted, me, Zain, Nadeem, we could do it, you just point him out to us, he won't know what hit him.'

'That Alum Rockie energy, yeah,' Mohsin said.

'Absolutely, ain't nothing like it in the world.'

Mohsin laughed, then said, 'What about you? How's home?'

Amir looked around him, groups of children all playing with one another, parents hovering around the edges. 'I'm fine,' he said.

'First summer without Layla,' Mohsin said, and Amir closed his eyes at Layla's name, had been trying not to think about her as the summer closed in around him.

'Yeah,' Amir said, 'it's fine.'

'You don't have to pretend—'

'Mohsin,' Amir said, 'it's fine.'

Mohsin took in a breath, said, 'Okay, but if you wanna call, talk to someone, just call me, I'm around.'

'Until Amsterdam.'

'I'm glad you're coming,' Mohsin said, 'I thought you weren't going to.'

'Nah, I told you I'd make it work, I made it work.'

'With your drug-dealer envelope of money,' Mohsin said, laughing.

'My drug-dealer envelope of money,' Amir said, and he laughed too.

Fifty-four

'You hear about Slick?' Frosty asked.

'Nah, what happened?' Amir said. They were sitting on the sagging sofa, Amir watching as Frosty played a game Amir had never heard of before, controlling a bald man, thick with muscle, blades attached to his arms, which he threw every so often to defeat mythical creatures that came from everywhere, the ground, the air.

'He got stabbed,' Frosty said, the bald man spinning around, blades glowing orange, on fire, slicing through creatures three times his size.

'Stabbed?' Amir said, cold dripping down his back, those two boys, the knife in his hand. 'When? By who?'

'Just yesterday,' Frosty said, 'he was walking around ends and these two lads, they jumped him, asked him if he was fucking with Ily, Slick said yeah, and they stabbed him three times.'

'Where is he now?'

'He's in hospital,' Frosty said, buttons clicking audibly, the only thing Amir could hear. 'Adnan took him, he'll be fine, they didn't hit nothing big, and you know Slick, he's fucking lethal, it'll take more than some little prick stabbing him to take him down.'

'Yeah,' Amir said, leaning back on the sofa, watching as the game played a cutscene, the bald man climbing up a giant, raising a sword, twisting it into its head, the giant falling down. Amir thought of Slick, the small guy, both in height and width, the guy who talked to him like Amir had been around forever, who hadn't asked why Amir was there, just accepted that he was, that he was one of them now, the guy who looked like no one could ever take him down, impossible to stop him from getting anything he wanted, the guy who had been stabbed three times, sharp knife sliding into flesh, his body just as vulnerable as Amir's. Amir almost ran his hands over his own body, to check if he'd been stabbed too.

'Don't worry about it,' Frosty said, 'Adnan is on it, he's been hearing some shit for a while now.'

'Some shit?'

'Yeah, some shit about some new boys, but this happens all the time, Adnan and Ily, they got links to guys in London, you know that, right?'

'Nah,' Amir said, and maybe now it was occurring to him how much there was to Adnan that he didn't know. 'What guys in London?'

'I don't know them personally, I've never met them, but Ily, he's tight with them, spent a year or so down there a while ago before coming back here, him and Adnan have it down tight, every time someone pops up, they beat them back down, so don't worry about it, we're good.'

'I'm not worried,' Amir said, even as his chest tensed, his heartbeat a little louder, a little quicker, his breath a touch shallower. He should have said something about those two boys, should have mentioned it.

'No one even knows you run with us,' Frosty said, glancing at Amir, grinning, 'the ones who should be worried are the rest of us, or, you know, maybe they'll try to make an example of you, anyone who fucks with us fucks with them.'

'Yeah,' Amir said, his mouth dry, his throat tight.

'I'm just fucking with you,' Frosty said, just as the phone in Amir's hand vibrated, a text coming through, some weed, a location, Amir replying, confirming the price, their text coming in seconds later. 'You got something?' Frosty asked, watching him.

'Yeah,' Amir said, standing up. Frosty put the controller down, the bald man coming to a stop, softly moving as he took a breath, waiting to be told what to do. 'Let's go.'

Fifty-five

Amir spent the rest of the night not acting like himself, Frosty said, when he decided to call it a night and head back to his grandmother's. Amir wanted to tell him it was because he was worried about Slick, but the truth was far more selfish, he wanted to know, desperately, if he was going to get stabbed, wanted to know if he should be carrying something with him, wanted to know if Frosty had something tucked away, if the others did. Would Amir be so lucky the next time?

But he wasn't just lucky, Amir thought, he had fought back.

As if he could hear Amir, just before he vanished into the night, Frosty put a hand on his shoulder, 'I know the Slick shit has you fucked up, I can tell, but don't worry, so long as you're with us, you'll be fine,' lifting up his shirt, taking out a knife that had been sitting inside his jeans the entire time, not big, but big enough. 'Anyone comes after you,' he said, grinning, 'I'll fuck them up, don't you worry.'

Fifty-six

Amir didn't sleep that night, lay awake as the sun crept across the sky, as his grandmother woke for Fajr, and then stayed awake, as she did, moving around downstairs, plates crashing into one another, doors opening and closing, his uncle waking up just before midday, heading downstairs, talking to her, voices muffled, his uncle in the shower, the thrum of the water vibrating through the floor underneath Amir, and Amir just lay there.

He reached for his phone, looked up the *Birmingham Mail* to see if there had been any news of the stabbing, but there was nothing, only something from a few weeks ago, two teenagers stabbed, one of them dying, the other in the hospital, around Handsworth, and underneath that one was the article about Saqib, which Amir scrolled past.

'You awake?' his uncle asked, coming into the room without knocking, Amir quickly putting his phone down. 'Come downstairs,' he said, 'we want to talk to you,' and before Amir could say anything, he was gone.

Amir dressed and headed downstairs, found his grandmother sitting at the table. He paused by her but she told him to wash his face, brush his teeth, so Amir went and did those things, thinking, if they kicked him out, if they told him to go home, where would he go? He could tell Adnan, that's what he would do, but Amir didn't want to do that, didn't want to go there, but Adnan would understand, wouldn't he? But what if he didn't? Amir thought, but he could figure that out if he got there, there were other people he could lean on, weren't there? People he could ask for help? But Amir couldn't imagine turning up at Zain's house, asking to stay there for the summer, Amir being who he was, looking how he did, coming from where he did, Zain's mother would never let it, she wouldn't let him step foot across the threshold, maybe Mohsin's, maybe, but how would he even get there?

'Sit,' his grandmother said to him, a plate of sliced apple in front of her, which she ate from slowly. Amir took the only other seat at the dining table, in between her and his uncle.

'Your parents are coming today,' his uncle said, 'to talk to you about what's going on between you and them, why you don't want to go home.'

'Okay,' Amir said, not looking at either of them. It was as if he'd suddenly gone back in time to when he was eight years old, when he wanted to go to the shop and didn't have any money, and instead of asking anyone, he stole money from the pot that his grandmother had always had, spare change in there, donating it during Ramadan, escaping the house to go to the shop real quick, buying himself an ice lolly in the dead heat of the summer, coming home to find everyone panicked, looking for him, and when Amir's mother found him, she had screamed at him, asking why he had left the house, and when Amir told her what he had done, crying, because he didn't understand why she was shouting, she'd hit him, a hard slap right on his face, and then she'd hugged him tightly, told him she was so scared that something had happened to him, to her boy, but all Amir could feel was the red spreading on his cheek.

'Where do you spend your nights?' his grandmother asked, 'When you go out and you don't come back, where are you?'

'Nowhere,' Amir said, and immediately he knew that was the wrong thing to say, her entire body rigid, 'with friends,' he said, 'from university,' he added, because that might make things better.

'With friends,' his grandmother said, looking over at his uncle, 'where have I heard that before?'

'We just hang out,' Amir said, 'nothing crazy.'

'Nothing crazy, but you come home at two, three, four in the morning, don't wake up until twelve, one, and then do nothing,' his grandmother said, and though her tone wasn't hard, her words were, 'don't you think you should get a job, earn some money, instead of just wasting this time?'

'I know you have this thing with your parents, and this is your home, Amir, this will always be your home, but it can't be some place where you just sleep in and do nothing else for, there are things that need doing,' Amir's uncle said, 'you can't spend every night somewhere else, come back here just to sleep and then do it all again the next day, this isn't a hotel.'

'It's not good,' his grandmother said, 'all this sleeping late and waking up late, it's not good for you, you should get a job somewhere, spend time with other people, work for something.'

'So I can pay,' Amir said, not looking at either of them, just staring right ahead, itching with anger. He thought of the money he had upstairs, the money Adnan pressed into his hands every night, thought of the envelope he'd given Mohsin, of Bilal's wedding, of his father, of his mother. 'Is that what you want?' he said. 'My money, that's all you guys ever fucking want.'

'Don't swear in this house,' his uncle said, voice tight.

'Nobody is asking you to pay,' Amir's grandmother said, 'nobody is asking for any money—'

'Money,' Amir said, standing up, 'that's all you want, all of you, you just want us to give you our money,' the chair teetered behind him, caught on the carpet, and then it fell, but no one seemed to notice, 'that's all it is with you, do this, do that, money here, money there, you talk all this shit about family but none of you actually give a fuck about family, it's all bullshit, everything, everything comes with a price tag.'

His uncle stood up, raised a hand to Amir. 'Don't,' he said, 'don't talk like that, not here,' he said, a warning in his words.

But it was enough, Amir'd had enough, so he went to the door, went upstairs, his uncle shouting after him, Amir catching a few words, his uncle asking him to come back, to have the conversation, Amir's grandmother saying something about a job, about money, about who had asked Amir to pay anything? And as Amir listened, his heart thudding in his chest, he thought how easy it would be to go back down there and fix things, how easy to just say he was sorry, to say that he would try to be better, to do better, but then he grabbed the thick wad of money he had shoved underneath the bed, slipped on his shoes, grabbed his phone and wallet, and was gone.

Fifty-seven

When Amir got to Adnan's, Adnan was outside the house, talking to his mother. He noticed Amir, gave him a look that stopped Amir before he reached the house, so he stood a few doors down, and when Adnan finished talking to his mother, gave her a brief hug, he waited for her to go inside before walking up to Amir.

'What are you doing here?' he asked.

'I needed to get out,' Amir said, 'I heard, about Slick.'

'You heard about Slick?' Adnan asked. 'Who told you that?'

'Frosty.'

'Frosty's got too big a mouth, one of these days …' Adnan said, more to himself than Amir, 'okay, so you heard about Slick.'

'I want to help,' Amir said, 'with whatever this is,' and then he added, 'two boys ran up on me the other day, nothing happened, I'm fine, but they asked me if I ran with you, so, yeah, I wanna help.'

'Help, how are you going to help?'

'I don't know,' Amir said, 'but whatever you need, I'm here for it, I told you, I'm in, I'm here.'

Adnan looked at him, 'Why are you here?' he asked again. 'Why aren't you at home or something?'

Amir looked away from him for a second, which was enough answer for Adnan, his face shifting, but he said nothing, waited. 'My parents,' Amir said, 'they're making it hard to be there.'

'You need a place to stay,' Adnan said, and from the way he said it, Amir understood that he wasn't the first one to come to Adnan asking for this. He wondered, who else had asked? Who else had stood here in front of Adnan like this? He wondered what house Tabby and Sparks lived at.

'Yeah,' Amir said.

'I've got you,' Adnan said, gesturing with his head for Amir to follow him back to the house, back to the car. Amir slipped into the passenger seat, and as he did, he saw Adnan's mother watching them from the window, her face so much like his own mother's.

Fifty-eight

Bilal called when Amir got there, Amir pulling the phone out, seeing Bilal's name flash on the screen, and he considered picking up, but Amir already knew what his brother was going to say, ask Amir where he was, ask him to come back, just sit with them for a moment, talk things through, but Amir didn't want to, he was so tired of being talked at, of having to explain himself, his parents were never going to give him a real chance to talk, all they wanted was to say what they thought. Amir silenced his phone, pocketed it.

They were at another warehouse, Ily and Adnan, a few men Amir didn't recognise, talking softly, the men listening, and when they were done, they left, Adnan coming back to Amir.

'Come with me,' Adnan said, and Amir followed him immediately, walking across the floor, past tables of bags of weed, pills, cocaine wrapped up tight, all the way to the other end, where an office sat, and he walked in, Amir behind, the door closed after him. 'We have this house,' Adnan said, 'you can stay there.'

'The house we hang at?' Amir asked, thinking of the cracks in the ceiling and the ugly kitchen and the sagging sofa.

'Nah, nah,' Adnan said, shaking his head, 'we have another house, some of the boys live there from time to time, it's nothing special, but you can stay there if you want.'

'Thanks,' Amir said.

'But, look, there's something I need from you first.'

'Anything.'

'Slick,' Adnan said, 'he's in the hospital right now, you know he got stabbed a few times, he'll be fine, they're just flesh wounds, nothing big, but it's an attack on us, you get that, right? The two boys that came for you, these boys on Slick, it ain't no joke.'

'Frosty said that it was just a couple of boys.'

'Forget what Frosty said, it's not just a couple of boys,' Adnan said, 'look, you've only been here for a month or two, you don't know anything yet, it's just the way shit is, we don't tell everyone everything, for a while now, we've seen some boys move in on our shit, started small, we heard that there were some boys selling weed that we didn't know so we put out some feelers, thought they were connected to nothing, now we're hearing that they're tied to some boys in Manchester, and now they've stabbed Slick, that's an attack on me, so whoever these boys are, they're down with some people we don't want thinking they can take us, you get me?'

'Yeah,' Amir said.

'Okay, good, so, Tabby found them.'

'The boys?'

'Yeah,' Adnan said, 'and we're going to go, me and Ily, and you're going to come with us.' Amir's body tensed. 'You ain't gotta do shit,' Adnan said, noticing, 'I just need the numbers, nothing mad.' He moved over to the desk, opened a drawer, pulled a knife out, handed it to Amir, it hung in the air between them for a moment and then Amir took it, cold, hard, not like the knives that his mother had in her kitchen, this, serrated edge, black handle, heavy, was the kind of knife that was made to end lives. 'You won't need to use it,' Adnan said, 'but it's good to have, just in case.'

'Just in case,' Amir said, holding it in his hand, his uncle, bat in hand, open wound on his head, Saqib, on the floor, knife in his chest, that boy, screwdriver inside him.

'Yeah,' Adnan said, coming around the desk to him, putting an arm around Amir's shoulders, 'just in case.'

Fifty-nine

It was Amir, Adnan, Ily, Sparks, Frosty, Tabby, spread over two cars. Sparks in front with Frosty and Tabby, Amir with Adnan and Ily, Amir sitting at the back while Adnan drove. No one talking, radio turned off.

They drove up, away from Sparkhill, to Aston, talked about in the same way Alum Rock and Sparkhill were talked about, Amir's mother telling him not to go there, there was danger, there are people there, she would tell him, who wouldn't think twice about robbing him, about beating him until not even she would recognise him, and Amir felt like telling her that these things happened here too, she just didn't know it, and those people she was talking about, they were all around her, her brother had been one of those people, maybe Amir was one of those people.

Alum Rock, Sparkhill, Aston, Washwood Heath, Small Heath, Handsworth. What made any of those different from each other? Mothers in each one pointing fingers at all the rest, standing in front of their sons and their brothers and their husbands, screaming, shouting, that the danger was all coming from over there, refusing to look at what lay at their own feet.

Amir's phone rang again, Amir taking it out of his pocket, missed calls from his brother, from his mother, from his uncle, and now his father was calling, Amir watching the screen until it went blank, call ended. Something like guilt clawed at him. Maybe he should pick up, maybe he should tell Adnan that he couldn't do this, maybe Amir should tell him that he wanted to go back to his parents, that all of this, this is not the way he wanted to live.

Then Amir remembered why, why he was here, what he wanted, and he put his phone away.

Sixty

Sparks pulled into a road of abandoned outlets, the shutters all pulled down. Amir thought of his uncle, he delivered pizzas from a place like this, shutters opening to reveal just a kitchen, men cooking pizzas, rolling the dough out, layering it with cheese and sauce and vegetables and fake meat, shoving the pizzas into ovens, Amir's uncle one of three men who delivered, putting boxes into their bags, driving off on their motorcycles to deliver to people who thought they were ordering from a real restaurant with booths and seats and a person behind the till to take an order.

Both cars stopped and they all slipped out, the knife in Amir's jeans, at the back, Amir tightening his belt to make sure that it didn't slip, the blade cold against his skin. Adnan and Ily took the lead, the four of them following as they walked towards one of the shutters, knocking on the flimsy metal, standing back, waiting, the shutter drawing up, the six of them entering.

Amir walked into what looked like a miniaturised version of Adnan and Ily's warehouse, smaller, but with all the same shit inside, and there was a group of men, young men, boys who'd just left school but not yet looking like men.

It was like looking into a reflection.

One

I call you again, phone to ear, listening to it ring out, and when you don't pick up I look back at how many times I've called you, the number twelve next to your name, bracketed, our mother asking me to call you again, she is convinced that I'll be the one to get through to you. 'He listens to you,' she says, even though I think we both know that's not true, so I try calling again, listening to it ring over and over again until it hits your voicemail, and I can't even hear your voice, you haven't recorded a message.

My phone rings as I reach to call you again, our uncle, and when I pick up, there is panic in the air, spilling through the phone. 'Come outside,' he says before I can say a single word, 'come outside now, I'll be there in a minute.'

'Why? What is it?' I ask, our mother looking at me, face creased with worry.

'Just come outside, I'll be there in a minute,' and then he's gone, silence.

I grab my shoes, slip them on, step outside, just in time to see him racing down the road, car pulling up just outside the house. He doesn't fully stop the car, doesn't roll down the window. I walk to him, half run, our mother asking him,

'What is it? What's wrong?' as I open the door, and when I sit in, he tells me to close it and then we're gone, engine roaring.

'What is it?' I ask him. 'What do you know?' but he says nothing, hands gripped tightly on the wheel.

'Did you know?' he asks.

'Know what?'

'Did you know what he was up to?'

'What?' I ask, but I know what he's talking about, the drug dealing, of course he would know, of course he would have found out, someone telling someone, telling him, 'Yo, is that Bulldog's nephew?'

'Did you know what he was up to?'

'I don't know anything,' I say, and I can see you looking at me, disdain on your face, for lying, for not being brave enough to answer the question, but this isn't about being brave, this is about being smart, and I don't know how telling him I know helps anything.

'He's been fucking dealing,' our uncle says, snarling the words, turning the car at the end of the road without slowing down, 'I told him not to, he's been hanging around with that Adnan guy, you know?' I nod. 'One of my boys saw them together. He's been dealing for weeks. I told him not to, but you know what he's like, he won't listen to anyone.'

'No,' I say, 'no, he won't.'

We stop at a traffic light, his fingers drumming on the wheel. 'He thinks he's too smart to get fucked up by all of this, and he is, he is smart, smarter than any one of us, but being smart doesn't help you here, it gets you fucked up more, because you think that you know better, that you don't need to worry, it removes your fear, you don't think I've seen plenty of people like him come and go?' he asks, lights turning green, car jolting forward.

'You think something has happened?' I ask, and suddenly, my mind is filled with images ripped from films, men lying in the street, bullet holes puncturing their bodies, blood spilling out into empty roads, concrete painted with their lives. I think of Saqib, his body lying alone, no one around to help him. I think of you like that, and then shake the image from my mind.

'I know something has happened,' he says, and then he hits the steering wheel with his hand, 'he's so fucking dumb, I swear to God, I told him not to.'

'What is it?'

'I don't know,' he says, 'I don't know, just, Mo, he told me that there was a fight happening, one of Adnan's guys got stabbed, and now they're going to fight back, and you don't get involved with a guy like Adnan without being pulled into shit like this,' he glances at me, eyes manic, 'you know what that means, right? Adnan wants to know if he's ready to die for him.'

Die. My stomach jolts, a wave of nausea passes through me.

'It's about loyalty, what are you willing to do for me? Are you willing to lay down your life for this shit? That's where he is, that's where your brother is at right now.'

I close my eyes for a moment, hands in fists, reach to open the window, hard to breathe, like there isn't enough air in the car. I can't help thinking about myself, I should have, I could have, I would have, but I know you, there was nothing I could have done, nothing I could have said, I'm already building my defence for when our parents ask me, did I know? I'm already thinking of you dead, lying on the ground, waiting for someone who might not come. My stomach twists, empty but still threatening to expel what's in there.

'Here,' our uncle says, and we turn into an empty car park, shutters down, ugly grey everywhere. He parks the car and we both step out, me following our uncle as he half walks, half runs down one side, looking for something. I look too, though I'm not sure what it is I'm meant to be seeing. The shutters all look old, all padlocked, covered with graffiti, black and blue and purple and red and white, I'm not sure what any of it means, postcodes with names and signs.

'Fuck,' our uncle says, putting his hands on his head.

'This is where it's meant to be?' I ask. 'This is where they're meant to be?'

'Yes,' he says, 'I don't know, that's what Mo said,' and he reaches for his phone to call Mo, and I turn around, panicking, it's eating me alive, and I race back down the other side, looking, looking, looking for something.

On this side, between two of the outlets, there is something else, a gate, leading somewhere, no padlock, I notice, as I walk up to it, and I pull at the handle when I see it, on the ground, something dark, liquid, reflecting the light at me, and as the gate creaks open, there you are.

There you fucking are, not even far from the gate, lying on your back, eyes closed, face turned to the sky, and I kneel by you, reaching out with a hand, I'm not even sure if you're real or something my mind has conjured up, and when my fingers touch you, the soft fabric of your hoodie, I shout your name, pull at you, 'Hey, hey,' I say, getting closer to you, shaking you, but you don't open your eyes, 'Hey, hey,' I keep saying, even as I look at the rest of your body, as I pull the hoodie back, see the wound there, your shirt ripped, put my hand over it, blood thick, slick, wet, so wet, 'Hey, hey,' I look back at your face, fuck, fuck, I don't know what to do, put both my hands over the wound, apply pressure, that's all I can think to do, 'Hey, hey,' I shout again, and now I can hear our uncle coming behind me, 'Fuck,' I hear him say, and then he's on the phone, calling for help, asking me, 'Is he breathing? Can you feel a heartbeat?' asking me, 'Is he alive?' but I don't know, why aren't you opening your eyes? Why aren't you telling me you're okay? 'Hey, hey,' I say, barely audible, because I don't know what else to say.

Acknowledgements

The publication of a book is the work of a team, despite the singular name on the cover. My thanks to: Juliet Pickering, for being the sort of agent I sorely need; to Kishani Widyaratna, for letting me change my mind so many times; to Ana Fletcher, for the push; to Matt Clacher, for the vision; to Eve Hutchings, for doing the work no one ever thinks needs doing; to Emma, Annabel and Kate at FMcM for their ears and their quick brains; to those I don't know working behind the scenes on contracts, sales, rights, production and more.

Personally, a life lived alone is no life at all. My thanks to: Shaikyla White, for listening, for reading, for the company; to Gaar Adams, for his quick brain, his great wit, his wonderful heart; to Shantel Edwards, for all the voice notes (and her son, Otis, for his pure and innocent soul); to Nicole Witmer, for the patience; to Sania Riaz, for the companionship (and her son, Esa, for the simple joy that comes from holding a baby); to Lucy Rose, for the conversations, big and small; to Courtney Milligan, for keeping Newcastle a home for me (and her sons, Ayaan and Zaiden, for the reminder that life doesn't have to be so insular).